munchausen by proxy for fun and profit

a novel
by Ken and Solomon Goudsward

ISBN: 978-1-989940-02-0
© 2021 Ken Goudsward
Dimensionfold Publishing
Prince George BC CAN

1

Eliminator

Shit! Luke sat up, suddenly awake. Somewhere in the back of his mind was the memory of having already disarmed the screeching hell that was his phone alarm. *How long ago was that?* he wondered to himself. Minutes? It seemed much longer. Months, perhaps? Since then, he had toured Europe with his rock band and had foiled an international plot to shut down the Jelly Belly Factory in Fairfield, California. He vaguely recalled having grown four long cybernetic arms out of his back. Their iridescent purples gleamed and shone in such an intriguing way that all the forest creatures had gathered around to investigate them.

But now the mundane clarity of reality fell around him like the tangled blanket tugging at his feet. He clawed at his phone, managing, through his bleary vision, to check the time. *Shit! Oh shit! Oh shit!* It was 11:32 — almost lunch time. *It's almost past breakfast,* Luke thought. Luke was hungry and late. He rolled off his mattress and onto the floor, crushing several empty cans of the cheapest beer the liquor store sold. Luke moaned something unintelligible in a low sleepy voice. He could not see. He was trapped in a tangle of three blankets now. Luke struggled to free himself, calling out for help to an empty apartment.

Minutes later, Luke, in his best dress shirt and favourite jeans, stood in front of the open refrigerator, waiting for a miracle. He couldn't show up to a job interview on an empty stomach. But his options were severely limited. A bottle of mustard. Half a pack of Kraft Singles. A tempting glob of jam smeared on the handle of the empty vegetable crisper. These were the only contents of the fridge of Luke and Luke's roommate, Jason. Jason had a grownup job in the heart of downtown, but Luke couldn't remember what kind of grownup job it was. He knew only that it involved computers and something called a Slack. The interview Luke was late for was for a job at a janitorial service company. Jason said that this job would not qualify as a grownup job. Luke said he didn't care but he also strongly disagreed with Jason's definition of adulthood. "You're like, not even in a position to make a statement about being grown up, like as a whole!" Luke had complained. "I mean, what about people in Africa? Like Sudan? Maybe over there being an adult is like, totally different. Like just having fun and getting high?" Jason hadn't responded to that.

Luke gave up on finding breakfast in the fridge after closing and reopening the door a couple times. He checked out the cupboard and saw nothing constituting an appealing or nutritious first meal of the day. He looked on the counter and saw an empty bread bag. Then he looked in the toaster and saw one slice of white bread sitting in the left-side slot. Luke had put this slice in the toaster who-knows-when and forgot about it. That mindless act was now his saving grace. Luke opened one of the cupboards above him and pulled out an almost-empty jar of no name peanut butter. Shoving the dried piece of bread deep inside the jar, he scraped as much peanut butter as he could from its dark recesses. He was out the door with breakfast in hand in time to catch the 12:10 bus.

"Running late again, Luke?" Hans was one of the bus drivers on Luke's route. He was a first-generation Austrian immigrant with a heart of gold that had not yet been hardened by the miscreants and ne'er-do-wells of the number 15 line.

"Yeah, but I think it'll be okay," Luke responded before walking to the back of the bus. Luke had developed a habit of instinctively moving to the back of whatever room or space he happened to enter. This habit had its roots in high school, that glorious era of minimal responsibilities and free seating. High school was when Luke had learned to play a G-chord on guitar, to fib to adults, and to do multiplication. High school was also when Luke had first met his sweetheart, Sylvia.

Luke sat down beside a large woman and finished eating his bread slice. The bus smelled like sweat and cigarette smoke, like always. It was a smell that, although not exactly fragrant, Luke had always secretly kind of liked. As he looked out the window, Luke thought about the opportunities awaiting him at his new job. Even after being rejected so many times by so many potential employers, Luke was not discouraged. He remained unflinchingly optimistic about his employability. And he had a very good feeling about this interview in particular. As he looked out at the world, Luke saw people walking briskly along the sidewalk, only to be overtaken by Hans and the number 15 bus. There were tall people and short people. People smiling and people frowning. People holding things in their hands: grocery bags, briefcases, purses, children and dogs on leashes. Luke thought the sidewalk was a lot like a zoo, but instead of smelly animals pooping on the floor it was just people holding stuff and walking around, and instead of being locked in cages they were all out in the open. For these two reasons, Luke considered that maybe the sidewalk was even better than the zoo.

"Look at that one," Luke said out loud, crumbs falling from his mouth. He was looking at a young couple holding hands. One of them, a blonde guy, was wearing two backpacks, one on his back and one on his front. Luke chuckled before realizing that he was among strangers. The woman next to him stood up without a word or a nod of acknowledgement and walked to the front of the bus.

At Luke's stop on 6th Avenue, he said farewell to Hans and hopped off the bus. He hopped off the bus in the literal sense, with both feet in the air at once, and he landed in a small puddle, the majority of which quickly absorbed into his jeans. He walked one block down the street and entered a small office with a small paper sign on the door that read: "Eliminator

Sanitation." When Luke had first seen the job posting for Eliminator Sanitation on Kijiji he had thought the name of the company was extremely cool. In fact, that was the primary reason he had responded to the ad. The owner of Eliminator Sanitation had quickly returned Luke's email and the two had decided on a time for an interview that would fit Luke's schedule. Now here Luke was, stepping into the office of Eliminator Sanitation to meet the boss — *his* potential boss. Luke swung open the door and stepped into the small office and was greeted by a thirty-something lady sitting at a cheap aluminum desk.

"Hi there," she said, smiling. "How can I help you?"

"Hey, I've got an interview," Luke said, re-tucking his dress shirt.

"Okay." She glanced at some papers on her desk. "Luke?"

"Yeah."

"Okay, I think you can go ahead and head into Scott's office."

"Is Scott the boss?" Luke asked.

"That's right," the secretary said.

Luke went ahead and headed into Scott's office, but when he stepped inside and closed the door behind him, he found himself all alone in the room. Luke couldn't help wondering where Scott was and why he wasn't here for his interview. Luke sat down in a chair in front of Scott's desk and waited patiently. The office was small and mostly empty. The floor was carpet with a big coffee stain underneath the desk, which was arranged perpendicular to the door. The walls were off-white and on two of them hung big empty bulletin boards. On Scott's desk there were two bobbleheads. One of them was a Mario Lemieux and the other was a Biggie Smalls. Luke sat for a few minutes looking at the bobbleheads and flicking their heads to make them wobble back and forth. Luke wondered whether it was considered proper bobblehead etiquette to face your bobbleheads toward your own chair or toward the chair of the person visiting your office. Then Luke realized that the chair he was sitting in was a lot nicer than the chair on the other side of the desk and he thought it was nice of his new boss to be so considerate to his employees and visitors.

In the 'Employees Only' bathroom at Eliminator Sanitation, Scott, the company's owner and sole manager, sat sweating and red-faced on the toilet. He was fighting a battle with the Thai green curry he had eaten the night before. Or maybe it was the leftover Thai green curry he had eaten for a late breakfast just before 10:30 am that morning, the time he had set aside to interview a young prospective employee named Luke. Scott was disappointed when Luke didn't show up, not because he felt Luke had wasted his time, but because Scott was in desperate need of workers. After his last employee, Jenn, had quit the week before, Scott had learned that it was difficult to run a janitorial business without any janitors. Now, in the bathroom, after another turn for the worse, it seemed his day was just not destined to be a good one. Scott had the runs. Bad.

After several idle minutes, Luke noticed something interesting about the drawers of Scott's desk: they opened on *his* side. Suddenly the office door swung open and a balding man in a polo shirt and cargo shorts walked in. The man looked surprised. In fact, he *was* surprised. Scott wondered who this person was, sitting at his desk, in his chair. Scott stopped in his tracks and stared at Luke. Luke looked up at Scott. They were caught in each other's eyes, unable to look away, each of them wondering who would speak first. Both of them sputtered out a meek, "Hi," at exactly the same instant. Then Scott said timidly, "Who are you?"

"I'm Luke," Luke said, surprised at having to explain himself. Scott was like a deer in the proverbial headlights. "Oh," he said. Scott was in pain. Scott didn't want to sit down. But as the owner and sole manager of Eliminator Sanitation, he had a responsibility to himself and to his company to conduct a proper interview, even if it was two hours late. Scott let Luke keep his chair, and without a word about it he sat down in the folding chair opposite from Luke.

"So," Scott said, "did you bring your résumé?"

Luke said, "No, I don't have one. But I remember all my work experience."

"Okay, good," Scott said. "So, where have you worked in the past?" Luke had been fidgeting with his chair and had finally discovered how to make it recline. He leaned back in the chair and folded his hands behind his head.

"Well," he began, "when I was in grade twelve I got a job at the Wendy's on Lonston. Then after that, I worked for my girlfriend Sylvia's uncle." Scott had pulled out a pocket-sized notepad and a Holiday Inn pen from his cargo shorts and was diligently copying down everything Luke told him.

"What sort of business does your girlfriend's uncle run?" Scott asked, looking up from his notes.

"Oh, it's a very good business," Luke said. "He ran a pretty tight ship. He told me that's why he had to let me go."

"Okay," Scott said, a little perplexed. "What kind of work did you do for him?"

"Pretty good work, I would say. I just couldn't move boxes and shit fast enough."

"Oh, I see. That shouldn't be a problem," Scott said. So far, he was impressed with Luke's confidence and disappointed with his own interviewing skills. Scott was not used to being a boss yet. "Can you clean?"

"Sure," Luke said enthusiastically. "I used to have to clean my room all the time when I was a kid."

"Me too," Scott said. "I always hated cleaning my room."

"Me too," Luke said.

In a matter of minutes the interview was over and Luke was shaking the hand of his new boss. *I can't wait to tell Sylvia about this,* Luke thought as he left the office and walked back out onto the sidewalk. The air was brisk but the sun was shining brightly. It was a lovely day to be alive. Luke strolled proudly down the sidewalk and pulled out his cell phone to call Sylvia. He called and held the phone to his ear, grinning widely at all the people and vehicles he passed.

"Hey, hon," Sylvia said.

"Hey, baby. Guess what? I got the job."

Sylvia made a sort of screeching noise and Luke pulled the phone a few inches from his ear. "Yay, Luke!" she said. "I'm proud of you, sweetie pie."

"Thanks, Syl. Hey, how about we meet for lunch and I treat you to a burger to celebrate?"

"Okay," Sylvia said. "I'll just let Charlie know I'm leaving early again."

"Okay, meet me at the Wendy's on Lonston. Love you."

"Love you." Sylvia swooned and slid her phone back into her jeans pocket. "Charlie!" she shouted from the front of the store. "I gotta leave early again." Charlie grunted from the back room and Sylvia grabbed her purse from under the counter and skipped out the door of the liquor store where she had worked for the past three years.

Sylvia strutted down the sidewalk of 15th Avenue with a spring in her step. Her boyfriend, Luke, was now a man of respectable employ, and to top it off, he was treating her to a Wendy's lunch. Sylvia was beaming. Her mom's car was parked on the street a block down. It was a red 2002 Pontiac Grand Am. Sylvia got into the driver's seat, turned the ignition and cranked up the volume on the radio, before putting it in drive and heading for her date with her man.

Luke had saved a booth inside the restaurant. He had ordered a regular fries to tide him over until Sylvia arrived. "Hey, baby," he said when she approached the booth.

"Hey, my working man," she replied. They shared a long tender kiss.

"How was work?" Luke asked after the long tender kiss.

Sylvia shrugged and scowled simultaneously. "Sucked," she said. "My boss is such a jerk."

"Well, don't worry about him now. What do you want, my sweetie?" Luke said. "You can have anything on the menu."

Sylvia, smiling and clinging to her man's arm, perused the Wendy's menu. Her eyes landed first on the value menu section, her usual range of options, and then ventured away toward the regular cheeseburgers, and even went so far as the fancy chicken burgers. She salivated. This was exciting new territory.

"Okay, I know what I want," Sylvia said after a moment of determination. The two of them stepped up to the counter to place their order. "I'll have the spicy Asia go chicken club," Sylvia said.

"And I'll have a double bacon cheeseburger, please," Luke said. And when asked by the young girl behind the counter whether they wanted combo meals, Luke grinned and declared confidently for the both of them, "Yes please."

As Luke pulled Sylvia toward him for a hug he saw a familiar face appear from out of the kitchen. The middle-aged woman smirked knowingly as she caught Luke's eyes. "Luke," she said. "Good to see you. How are you?"

"Hi, Patty," Luke said warmly. "It's going good. How 'bout you?"

"Wonderful," she replied. Sylvia looked from Luke to the woman behind the counter and then back again. And then back at the woman and then at Luke again. Patty had been Luke's manager when he worked at this Wendy's in high school. Luke had always been fond of Patty, and would sometimes even bring her dandelions that he found growing out of the sidewalk on his way to work. While she always appreciated the gifts and Luke's generally positive demeanour, Patty was well aware that Luke was without question the worst employee the Wendy's on Lonston had ever had. She had avoided firing him as long as she could, but in the end, she did what she had to do for the sake of the franchise. Luke never held it against her. In fact, he had always blamed the higher-ups at corporate for letting him go.

"Still working here?" Luke asked unironically. Patty glanced at the counter separating herself from Luke and Sylvia, the counter separating the customer area of the restaurant from the employee area.

"Yes," she said. "I am."

"Cool," Luke said. "Glad to hear that."

"What are you doing these days?" Patty asked, not merely from social obligation, but also from a genuine, if slight, interest in the life of her former employee.

"Well, actually," Luke said, "I just got myself a new job today."

"Oh, congratulations," Patty said. "Where at?"

Luke told Patty all about his new job with Eliminator Sanitation and the two of them caught up in the few minutes before Luke and Sylvia's food was passed over the counter to them. At that point Luke said a friendly farewell to his old manager and she replied with a smile and a goodbye of her own.

When Luke and Sylvia had filled up their drinks at the pop fountain and sat down with their tray at a table near the back of the restaurant, Sylvia was visibly upset. Luke didn't notice this until after he had taken a large bite out of his double bacon cheeseburger. When he saw that she was pouting and hadn't yet touched her food, Luke froze mid-chew. "What's wrong?" he asked with half-masticated food in his mouth.

"Nothing," Sylvia told him.

"Oh," Luke said. He swallowed hard and took another bite of his burger.

"You know," Sylvia said after a moment, looking down at her chicken club but still not touching it, "it's kind of funny to have the name Patty when you work at a Wendy's. Roundest one you're likely to find around here, at any rate."

Luke was confused. "Huh?" he asked, his mouth again full of food.

Sylvia looked up at him, her gaze penetrating his eyes. "You would never cheat on me, would you Luke?" Sylvia had not liked the friendly exchange between Luke and his old manager. In fact, despite the large age difference and the implausibility of any forbidden romantic interaction between them, Sylvia couldn't help feeling an amount of jealousy that was enough to put her off her special Wendy's lunch.

Luke was stunned by her question. "Of course not, baby," he assured her. "You know you're my world." Sylvia smiled, succumbing to the charming affection of her sweetheart, Luke. Now she felt ready to enjoy her special meal.

And they enjoyed it thoroughly. Sylvia and Luke sat together in the booth in the Wendy's on Lonston for almost twenty minutes, talking about the future, their hopes and dreams, and revelling in the warm, stupefying love they shared.

"What now? Wanna come over and watch TV?" Sylvia asked as she and Luke got up from their table, leaving on it their tray full of garbage.

"I gotta visit Nana," Luke said. "You can come with." This he said almost as if it were a question to which he did not expect a favourable answer. Sylvia pouted her lips.

"I wanna cuddle, Luke," she complained.

"After," Luke said. "I gotta visit Nana, Syl. You know she doesn't have any trustworthy friends in that place."

The place Luke was referring to was the care home where his Nana Esther lived. Luke resented the fact that his nana, who he admired so much, had to live in such a terrible place — he considered it well beneath her. Sylvia sighed and agreed to go with Luke to visit his nana.

<div style="text-align:center">~~~</div>

Sylvia double-parked her car in the visitor parking lot of Willow Lodge Seniors Care Home and she and Luke walked through the front door of the building.

"Oh, hi, Luke. Hi, Sylvia," said the receptionist immediately upon their entrance.

"Hey, Tracy," Luke said with a friendly wave.

"Hi," Sylvia said flatly before looking around the lobby and scowling.

"Is Nana at hymn-sing today?" Luke asked.

"Should be. I know she was out and about this morning. They all went on the bus to the Denny's this morning for breakfast and cards. They got back about an hour ago, though." Luke's Nana liked to take advantage of the bus service at Willow Lodge and frequently attended the planned outings and activities.

"Who all went?" Luke inquired quite seriously, his brows furrowing.

"Oh, Esther, Barb, Junie, George, Art-"

"Lester?" Luke questioned sternly, interrupting Tracy, who immediately went silent. "Lester went too, didn't he?" Luke scowled and grunted.

"Well, yes, I think so. You know how Lester is. He won't miss an opportunity to-"

"Yeah, yeah. I know. Thanks, Tracy," he said, now heading down the hall.

Sylvia followed Luke, folding her arms and looking around in discomfort. She had come with Luke to the care home before, but she always disliked being here. She didn't like Tracy. She didn't like the dark red carpet in the lobby. She didn't like the ugly paintings of trees, flowers, and ducks on the walls. As they walked, the relative silence of Willow Lodge was broken by the soft sound of singing, which grew louder and louder.

Luke opened the door to Activity Room C and the sound of twenty-six seniors singing "How Great Thou Art" with varying degrees of vocal talent became clear, if inharmonious. Immediately, Luke's Nana stopped singing, split off from the choir formation and walked as quickly as she could — which was, in fact, quite slowly — toward her grandson. Luke stepped forward to meet her halfway and embraced his Nana with a long, loving hug. Sylvia didn't watch, but remained fixed in place by the door with crossed arms, staring across the room at a spot where the wall met the ceiling.

"Hello, Lukie," Nana said warmly, before adding, "Good afternoon, Sylvia."

"Hi, Nana Esther," Sylvia responded flatly.

"How's your day, Nana?" Luke asked as the choir finished their hymn.

"Oh, just fine!" Nana assured him. "We went for cards and breakfast this morning. At…at…" she sighed, struggling for the name. "At Denny's."

"Yes, I heard. Did you have fun?" As the seniors' choir group dispersed, evidently at the end of their practice time, Luke's eye was caught by a familiar face which made him wince. It was the sallow, self-satisfied face of Lester Bauman. Luke's eyes instinctively narrowed and his fists clenched behind his dear Nana's back. Luke audibly growled as Lester approached.

"What's wrong, Lukie?" Nana asked.

"Well, Luke! Hul-lo, son! It's good to see you," said Lester patting Luke firmly on the back.

"Oh, Lester!" Nana exclaimed, blushing a little. "Luke, let go of your Nana now, please."

Luke, who had still been hugging Nana quite tightly, let her go. "Hi, Lester," Luke said with a scowl, his eyes drawn to the unnatural sheen of the old man's slicked-back hair.

"I had the pleasure of dining with your lovely grandmother this morning," Lester said, smiling. He grabbed

Nana's hand and kissed it, looking up at Luke all the while. Then he gestured toward Sylvia, who was still looking away, and said, "And who is this lovely lady?"

"My woman, Sylvia," Luke said quickly and defensively. "Me and her are in love…" There was an end to the sentence, which Luke decided to keep to himself. The rest of the sentence was …*something you wouldn't know about!* Luke considered that this would be an effective insult were it to be used out loud. Had his Nana not been standing there, Luke was sure he would have said it to Lester.

"Of course you are!" Lester said loudly — as loudly as he said everything else. Nana was still visibly blushing. When Lester had kissed her hand she had grown especially red and a smile had formed on her face.

"Well, I'll let you kids visit with your grandmother. But why don't the three of you come down later and we can all play a game of canasta?"

Why don't you eat your own shit and die and go play cards with Lucifer and keep your filthy paws off my Nana? Luke thought.

"Oh, that would be fun, wouldn't it, Luke?" Nana said excitedly. Luke just nodded and then shrugged dismissively to counteract the nodding. Sylvia was motionless. She was hoping to leave Willow Lodge as soon as possible and never return. Then Lester parted with the group, saying, "I'll see you all later, then," before whistling a lazy tune and exiting the room.

Luke led his Nana by the arm to the elevator. On the way up, Nana held her stomach and gripped the railings. "Oh, Lukie, this has been happening for a week now. I just feel so sick on the elevator."

"Are you okay, Nana?" Luke asked worriedly. The elevator stopped on the third floor and the doors opened.

"Oh, yes, yes. I'll be fine in a moment. I just need to sit down." Luke led his nana down the hall to her room and all the way there, through her queasiness, she told him about her week at Willow Lodge, much of which Luke had heard already when he had visited a few days before. Luke was listening attentively but was not in the best of spirits because he couldn't stop thinking about that no-good ne'er-do-well Lester.

Luke knew that Lester was interested in his Nana and he couldn't stand the thought of her being seduced or felt up by the worst of the perverted old men at the care home. Luke was positive that Lester and most of the other men at Willow Lodge were trying to "get into Nana's pants," as he put it. Luke was positive that his Nana was the most beautiful woman in the whole lodge and that without his protection she would succumb to one of these men and lose her virtue. This was unacceptable.

After the encounter with Lester at the hymn-sing, Luke had forgotten all about his new job, which, on the way to the Lodge, had been the only thing on his mind. He had been very much looking forward to telling his nana all about it. After Luke, Sylvia, and Nana sat down around the coffee table in room 305, and after Nana offered her grandson and his girlfriend a sugar cookie, Luke, with an exclamation muffled by half-chewed cookie bits, finally remembered his big news.

"Gabba!" he shouted with a full mouth.

"Luke…" his Nana said.

Luke finished chewing and swallowed his cookie. "Sorry, Nana," he said. Then, regaining his excited animation, he said, "Guess what?" and Nana Esther said, "What?" and Luke said, "I got a new job today!" and Nana beamed proudly.

"Oh, Lukie!" Nana shouted, embracing her grandson, "Good for you, honey!"

"Yeah, I know!" Luke said excitedly. "And guess what the name of the place is called?"

"Guess what is the name of the place," Nana said in a corrective tone, smiling dreamily.

"No, like, *you* guess what it's called," said Luke gently, who was now worrying slightly about his poor Nana's mind. Luke knew she was not getting any younger.

"I don't know," Nana said. "What's the place called?"

"Eliminator," Luke said. "Like Terminator."

"So you've become a hitman, Luke?" Nana smiled wryly.

"No, Nana." Luke's concern was growing. "I'm just a janitor."

"Oh, I see."

At this point in the conversation, Sylvia was occupying a very small slice of the end of the ugly floral couch, digging her fingers firmly into her thigh to pass the time.

"Well, I'll always be proud of you no matter what you do," Nana continued.

"That's why you're my Nana," Luke said, which wasn't strictly true.

2

Cantstanzya

"It's time for canasta," announced Nana sometime later. She rose from the couch with the ease of a woman half her age. Luke felt proud of how well Nana was aging, aside from his concerns about her diminishing mental state. He made a note to speak to his parents about that. He could tell that Nana was beginning to slip. All the more reason to protect her from Lester and the other horny old men at the care home. Luke's parents tended to Nana's official business — insurance and special medical appointments and the like. They were pretty organized, Luke would give them that much. They just weren't very fun to be around. And while they were busy worrying and bickering about matters of logistics and practicalities, Luke was the only one who cared enough to actually spend any quality time with Nana. So now here he was, about to begin an arduous game of canasta with Lester Bauman. Luke could not understand why his grandmother associated with someone like him. Luke was perplexed. Luke was exasperated. He supposed Nana's decision-making skills were just not what they used to be.

Luke, Sylvia, and Nana Esther took the elevator to the main floor and met Lester at a table in Activity Room A. He was waiting patiently, the cards laid out in front of him, his grey hair greased back to the top of his dome, a big smile on his face. Lester stood up to greet the party.

"Hello, you young thing," he crooned, grinning at Nana with his buttercream teeth. Then, turning to Luke, "Hullo there sport! Are you ready for some fun?"

"No," Luke wanted to say. He stared blankly, resisting the urge to choke Lester out with his bare hands. Sylvia also stared blankly, as though she were likely to die of boredom at any moment. They had been at the home all afternoon, the home which Sylvia despised so much it made her stomach churn and her eyes glaze over and narrow so that they bore an uncanny resemblance to the mancala stones on the next table over. (The hard tinkling of a small pile of colourful stones being dropped into place by another elderly resident momentarily roused Sylvia from her trance.) Luke appreciated Sylvia coming to visit Nana with him. It was one of the reasons he loved Sylvia so much — she was occasionally willing to do things she didn't want to to make him momentarily happy. But even having Sylvia by his side didn't make it any easier to be around Lester.

Wicked old Lester was shuffling. That is to say, he had already finished shuffling over to Nana, taking her tiny arm in his, shuffling back to the table with her, pulling out her chair and sitting down, and he was now shuffling the cards. Sort of. He was cheating, Luke thought. Luke unsubtly pointed his thumb toward Lester, casting a sidelong glance at no one in particular and smirking in disgust as if to say, "Get a load of this guy."

"What's that, Lukie?" Nana asked. *Oops.* He had actually said it out loud. Lester was using a battery-operated shuffling machine instead of shuffling the cards by hand. Luke decided this made him less of a man. He picked up the cards and dropped them into the bin, then flipped the little switch. The cards shot into the bottom tray with a flapping sound that Luke found quite humorous. In fact, he almost chuckled out loud at the sound but stopped himself. He could not let Lester think he was enjoying himself in any way. After the cards had run through the machine, Lester picked the deck up and ran it through the machine a second time, and then a third.

"Pretty cool, huh?" asked Lester with a toothy grin on his face.

"I've seen one of those before," Luke said faux-casually. "I already know how to use one, even." Lester nodded slowly, patronizingly. Finally satisfied with the randomization of the cards, Lester set aside the Shuffle-matic 250 and began tapping the deck against the table. It was a large deck composed of no less than seven regulation poker decks, for the game was "Four-Handed Ascending and Descending Hand And Foot Canasta," and this was, in fact, the minimum-sized deck for this particular and most refined of all canasta variations. Lester looked into the eyes of each of his companions: Nana, who was seated in the chair to Lester's right, and Luke and Sylvia, both of whom were still standing, and who had in fact been blocking the path of an elderly woman with a hunchback and a walker. Neither Luke nor Sylvia wanted to take the other seat next to Lester but neither wanted to force the other to take that seat either.

"Well, what's it gonna be?" bellowed Lester, "Guys against gals? Or seniors vs kids?" Everyone looked at each other for a response. "Or shirts and skins?" Lester added slyly.

"Seniors vs kids!" said everyone, all at once.

"But we're not kids," added Luke, under his breath.

"Well, siddown, stay a while," Lester boomed. Lester stood up to take the seat across from Nana, his partner. "We'll go first," he said.

"Age before beauty," muttered Sylvia with contempt, under her breath but loud enough that it was heard by Luke — and also by the elderly woman with the walker, who was still patiently waiting to pass, her bowed head hovering a mere three feet above the wheels. Luke shot a dirty look Sylvia's way. He didn't appreciate his Nana being insulted, even if the insult was aimed mostly at Lester.

"Age before beauty," Lester said. He seemed to be hungrily staring at Sylvia as at a ripe Christmas ham. Luke was sure he even saw him lick his lips. He seethed with doubled jealousy. With Lester in his new spot, both Luke and Sylvia had to sit adjacent to him. The table wasn't terribly small, but the way Lester leaned over it like a gargoyle meant that Luke and Sylvia could smell his coffee breath and his dandruff. *At least I get to sit beside Nana,* Luke thought.

Lester dealt out the hand and foot piles for each player, placing the remaining cards in four stockpiles in the centre of the table. He looked at Luke, seated to his right, as if waiting for him to do something.

"What?" said Luke.

"Start the discards," said Lester.

"Huh?"

"Just take one off the top," said Lester.

Luke begrudgingly obeyed and stared at the card.

"Now put it face down right here."

"Umm, okay." Luke placed the card where Lester said to. "Why couldn't you just do that yourself?" complained Luke.

"That's not how it works, my boy!"

I'm not your boy. Luke just barely managed to keep this retort to himself. Sylvia stifled a laugh, seeing the frustration in Luke's face, which had suddenly turned a shade redder. Though she sympathized, she sometimes liked to see Luke get embarrassed and flustered. She thought it made him look cute. So did Nana. "Okay, now what happens?" she asked. Sylvia was perhaps the world's greatest expert at balancing sincerely sweet and totally sarcastic. This skill, which she had honed to a fine point, sometimes perplexed Luke. But at most times he seemed completely oblivious to her use of it. It was a subtle art form.

"Ah, I'm glad you asked," continued Lester without hesitation. "Now, everyone, look at your hands!" He sounded as though he believed doing so would bring some kind of amazing revelation. Both he and Nana picked up one of their piles, and after a moment's hesitation, so did Sylvia. Noticing that they had both chosen the pile on their left, she did likewise.

Luke meanwhile stared at his right hand. He noticed a small smudge of some kind of black gunk on his palm, and scratched it off with his left index finger.

"Luke, pick up your cards," prompted Sylvia.

"Why?" said Luke, confused. But he obeyed his girlfriend and started picking up both of his piles.

"Just these ones," said Sylvia, reaching across the table to block his other pile.

"That other pile is your foot," explained Nana. This comment did nothing to alleviate Luke's impression that his Nana may not be playing with a full deck. He shot Sylvia a weird look. She shrugged slightly, scrunching up her left cheek in that cute way she did sometimes.

"Now put all your red threes on the table," Lester instructed. Luke felt embarrassed again because he didn't have any red threes. Had he done something wrong already?

"The aim is to get rid of all the cards from your hand, see. And then once you've done that, you have to get rid of all the cards from your foot. To get rid of your cards you've gotta *meld* them. Like this." He laid down three aces on the table in front of him.

"Oh, what a good start!" Nana exclaimed. Sylvia rolled her eyes. Lester explained about clean melds and dirty melds, wild cards and threes. Luke didn't understand any of it. A couple of times Sylvia had to explain all the rules over again to Luke. After the second time, he pretended to get it and tried to make all his moves when no one was looking.

As the game continued, the teams seemed to be keeping fairly even. The players joked around and teased each other, and for a while Luke almost forgot that Lester, his kinda-smart and almost-funny-at-times canasta competitor, was actually the devious and dastardly Lester Bauman. But just when everyone was finally having a good time, their friendly game was interrupted.

BLAM! The door to the activity room slammed shut. It always did that. The hinge spring needed adjusting. It had for months. Nevertheless, the loud noise shocked all those who heard it. Luke, Sylvia, Esther, and Lester all turned quickly toward the source of the sound. An old man at the next table flinched and sent blue and green mancala stones flying across the room.

"Dammit!" whispered Lester, sure that no one would hear. He was not fond of cussing. But in drastic circumstances such as this, he occasionally let his tongue slip. For there, in front of the dark stained oak door with the maladjusted spring, stood Horse-face. Horse-face was always causing trouble for Lester and his friends here at Willow Lodge, and today would be no exception.

"Well, look who's here," said Horse-face to Lester, coldly.

"Hello, Horace," replied Lester, begrudgingly. Despite his feelings, Lester always tried to maintain a facade of civility. It was the Christian thing to do, after all. Horace was Horse-face's real name, of course, although most of the Willow Lodge residents called him Horse-face behind his back. He really did have a sort of horse-ish look to him: the long bridge of his nose pointing down to a long chin, his bangs hanging down his long forehead nearly to his eyes like a shabby mane. It made Lester want to strap a pair of saddlebags onto him and use him as a pack animal. He often imagined Horace ambling through the lodge, bringing supplies to the other residents. These thoughts brought Lester a deep sense of satisfaction.

"Hogging the good table again, I see. Couldn't wait 'til Wednesday night, eh?" continued Horse-face.

Wednesday night was cards night at Willow Lodge. It always had been, and it always would be. It was the lodge's greatest social institution, and its greatest cause of social division. Not all the residents took it as seriously as they ought to. Many were content to sit at the casual tables, playing crazy eights or go fish, but the real movers and shakers of Willow Lodge knew that to be taken seriously, you had to side with one of the major factions. It all came down to bridge versus pinochle versus canasta. Willow Lodge politics revolved around this three-sided dance of power.

Laverne Sanderson and her "Bridge Hens" controlled the literary guild, and had a corner on afternoon tea in the sunroom. Lester's group played canasta on Wednesdays and held Thursday afternoon Bible studies led by Lester himself. These studies consisted of Lester leading a quick prayer and reading several devotionals from "Our Daily Bread" in reverent succession, followed by a more in-depth scripture study.

Then there was Horse-face's pinochle crew. They controlled the black market flow of cigarettes into Willow Lodge. Not that cigarettes were actually banned from the care home. But they didn't carry them in the official Willow Lodge corner store, so unless you had family that would bring them to you, or were willing to walk three blocks to the 7-Eleven, you'd have to go through one of Horse-face's boys to get smokes.

Horse-face sauntered up closer to the table where Luke, Sylvia, and Nana sheepishly watched Lester's ire continue to rise. Horse-face really knew how to get Lester's goat. "I suppose I shouldn't be surprised, hey Lester? You always get whatever you want, don't you? Like the biggest table with the best view out the activity room window."

"You *know* we need the big table," Lester countered. "Canasta takes room! You gotta spread out all these cards!"

"As if you even need all those cards! Look at the size of this deck, for crying out loud. It's like ten packs! Is that even a real game?!"

"It's SEVEN!" cried Lester. "SEVEN!"

Nana looked uncomfortable. She didn't like conflict. Luke reached out to pat her hand, a gesture which she offered to him fairly regularly. Sylvia slipped her phone from her pocket and checked for texts. There were none. Lester was irritated, and had had about as much as he could take from Horse-face. His facade was crumbling. He lashed out. "Why don't you go take a long walk off a short pier, Horse-face?!" He slammed his palm on the table, muddling up the cards. Lester immediately regretted his loss of control. He couldn't believe he could be pushed so far as to insult a man's face, right to his face. It was not easy being a leader. Sometimes there was too much pressure. He tried to be a good Christian and to humbly serve his followers. So why was he so often met with disrespect and verbal abuse? And it wasn't just Horse-face. The Bridge Hens talked derisively about Lester too. He had seen their furtive glances as they whispered behind their teacups. He had heard the term "bible-thumper" used in passing.

Suddenly, Lester didn't feel much like playing cards. He had broken down in front of Esther. He had humiliated her in front of her guests. "Excuse me," he said flatly, leaving the table and the activity room with downcast eyes.

"Oh dear," muttered Nana, as Sylvia and Luke exchanged an awkward look.

"Umm, we better get going anyway, don't you think?" Sylvia asked Luke.

"Uh yeah, I guess we better," replied Luke. "Let's walk Nana back to her room."

On the way to her room, Nana insisted that they stop by the pharmacy counter. Of course, the counter was not open at this time of the evening, a fact Luke only remembered upon reaching the darkened counter.

"Oh well," said Nana. "Lukie dear, I wonder if you could pick these up for me tomorrow?" She handed Luke the sheet of paper bearing her prescription information. Luke couldn't say no to his grandmother. She was far too precious. And besides, this gave him an excuse to come back to Willow Lodge tomorrow. Sylvia rolled her eyes. She hated the way Nana took advantage of Luke's innocent devotion.

Back at Nana's room, they all said goodnight and Sylvia and Luke left, heaving a collective sigh. "Wow," said Luke, as they crossed the parking lot. "That got kinda intense."

"Holy shit, Luke. Don't ever make me play cards with that freak again! My God!"

"I won't, baby." They walked in silence for a minute, then Luke said, "You know what, though? Horse-face is right; Lester is trouble for sure. He acts like the freaking high priest of the holy canasta. He almost tricked me into liking him. He thinks he can just take whatever he wants, and now he wants Nana. It makes my skin crawl!"

"That whole place makes my skin crawl," replied Sylvia.

3

Denecorp

"You know, I'm a little worried about Nana," Luke said after a long silence on the drive to Sylvia's house.

"I hadn't noticed," Sylvia responded coolly.

"Yeah. It's just… I think she might be starting to slip."

"Like in the shower?"

"No, like… in here." Luke pointed to his head.

"In your memory?" She was teasing him.

"No, Syl. I mean I think she's starting to go penile."

"Well, maybe that's what the little blue pills are for." Sylvia didn't really expect Luke to laugh, but she couldn't resist a good viagra joke, even if she was the only one who got it. Luke often missed her jokes, just like he often misused words. In a way, the two idiosyncrasies balanced each other out. Luke inadvertently made just as many jokes as went over his head.

Luke frowned and looked out the window. He was hoping it would start raining. He thought it would make the moment more dramatic — like a movie.

"You'll come with me tomorrow, right? To get Nana's medicine?"

Sylvia groaned as she turned a corner, failing to avoid a large pothole in the road. "You know how much I hate that place."

"Please? I know Nana wants to spend more time with you."

Sylvia scowled to herself. She didn't believe that Nana wanted to spend any time with her. She thought Nana wanted her out of the picture — wanted Luke all to herself.

"Fine, I'll come," she grunted.

Luke said, "Yippee!" Then, returning to gaze out the window, and now leaning his head on the glass, he quickly became sombre once again. "I just hope she doesn't get demension," he sighed.

Sylvia glanced at Luke and her heart filled with affection. "Baby, everything's going to be fine. Nana seemed fine to me. And besides, you've got me. What else do you need?"

"I love you, baby."

"I love you, baby."

As they kissed, the car swerved, narrowly missing a frightened house cat.

They pulled into Sylvia's driveway. The house was old and worn and in need of renovations. But renovations were expensive and Sylvia's mom needed money for smokes and the casino. The yellowed vinyl siding, once a pristine eggshell white, was drooping in spots and the front steps, which creaked when you stepped on them, were festooned with loose nails. As they walked toward the house, Sylvia turned to Luke. "What does that prescription say, anyway? What's it for?"

"For the pharmacy at the lodge," Luke explained.

"No, I mean what kind of meds?"

"Oh. Hmm." Luke pulled out the prescription from his pocket and analyzed it, trying to make sense of all the words and numbers and symbols. There was an R with an extra line in it that he didn't understand.

"Let me see." Sylvia grabbed the slip of paper from Luke's hand. "Dramamine/Dimenhydrinate. Whatever that is. Oh, and there's one more — donepez-"

Just then, Luke's phone rang. "Hullo?" Luke answered. It was Scott, Luke's new boss from Eliminator Sanitation.

"Luke?" he said, sounding timid and uncertain, as if he had never had to make a telephone call before.

"Yes, it's Luke."

"Hi, Luke..." Scott hesitated, unsure how to proceed. "Uh — how are you?"

"I'm okay. How about you?"

"Pretty good," he said, with a slant in his voice that revealed that his answer was perhaps not entirely honest. "Uh — hey, Luke. Look, I - we just got a new contract and they need us to... I was wondering if, umm. Do you think you could — it's okay if you can't — are you able to start work right away?"

Luke considered this for a moment. He had no plans for tomorrow other than visiting Nana and filling her prescription.

"For how long?" Luke asked.

"Oh, we shouldn't be much later than four. It'll be just you and me. I'll show you all the ropes."

"Okay, sure," Luke said. He was excited about starting his new job.

"Perfect. Thank you, Luke. Meet me at uh…" Luke could hear the rustling of paper on the other end of the phone. 'Denecorp Systems.' It's on… 8th."

"Okay, boss. See you in the morning."

"Oh. No."

"Huh?"

"I meant, like… right now."

"Right now?"

"Yeah."

"Oh."

"Oh."

At the exact same time, after a three second pause, they both said, "Sorry." Luke held the phone to his chest while he asked Sylvia for a ride to work. Meanwhile, across town at the Eliminator Sanitation office, Scott was profusely apologizing into his flip phone for making such an audacious request. Luke, having heard none of this, brought his phone back to his ear.

"Okay," Luke said. "I'll meet you there."

Sylvia silently, moodily drove back in the direction from which she had just come. Luke had thought her response to his question was "yeah." What she had actually said when Luke asked her to drive him to work was "uehh." But Luke had hung up the phone before she could rectify this misunderstanding, so she had conceded. But she was decidedly not happy about it. Sylvia had been looking forward to cuddling with her man all day long. This new job was turning out to be less wonderful than it had first seemed. Sure, Luke would have money to buy her lunches and gifts, but would she even get to spend time with him anymore?

"Luke, I don't like how your job is interrupting our alone time," Sylvia said after several minutes of silent driving.

"Aw, come on, Syl. We'll spend all day together tomorrow."

Sylvia scowled. "Yeah, together at the stupid old folks home."

"It's not stupid, babe," Luke pleaded. "It's where Nana lives."

Sylvia glowered for the rest of the drive.

As they turned onto 8th avenue and neared Denecorp Systems, Luke was buzzing with anticipation. Sylvia stopped the car by the curb in front of the brick building.

"Well, this is it, baby. I'm a working man now. Wish me luck." He leaned in for a kiss. At first, Sylvia resolved not to kiss him. She stared straight forward down the row of streetlights. But she couldn't resist a kiss from her working man. She turned and leaned in and felt her heart flutter when his lips met hers.

Luke tried the front door of Denecorp Systems and found it locked. He turned around to see the taillights of Sylvia's mom's car disappearing down the street. Luke tried the door again, just to be sure. Then he knocked on the door and waited. Then he searched the dark brick wall with his hand for a doorbell, but found none. Perhaps he had beaten the boss to the job. That was a sign of a good work ethic, right? Luke's career as a sanitation specialist was off to a great start. Luke waited for several minutes in front of Denecorp Systems, occasionally peering through the glass door to see if he could detect any movement inside. *Eliminator Sanitation,* Luke repeated over

and over in his head as he stood in the darkness. *Eliminator.
Like Terminator. Eliminator. Eliminator.* Wasn't that the name of
a ZZ Top album? Yes, it was. Luke remembered the old car on
the album cover, its headlights streaming brightly into the top
corners.

Just then, another set of headlights appeared, streaming
brightly into the top corners of Luke's vision, practically
blinding him. An old white Dodge panel van pulled up onto the
curb before reversing slowly, clumsily dropping a sudden seven
inches. The engine groaned, wheezed, coughed and spit.
Exhaust spilled out from below the rusty fenders of the
passenger side. The entire vehicle seemed to rattle and tremble
as if it were about to collapse or combust at any second. Scott
shut off the engine and stepped out of the van.

"Hi, Luke," he said.

"Hi, boss."

"Thanks for coming so quick."

"No problémo."

Scott opened the sliding door of the van and he and
Luke began hauling sanitation equipment onto the sidewalk,
including a canvas toolbox full of sponges and spray bottles, a
broom wrapped in duct tape, and a mop in a big yellow bucket.
It was one of those buckets with built-in wheels, and a handle
on top for squeezing the water out of the mop.

Whoa, awesome, thought Luke to himself. He hoped
that someday he would get to use this mop bucket. Instead he
selected for himself a ragged stained cloth, and the broom with
the duct-taped handle.

Scott then crossed the sidewalk to open the door to
Denecorp Systems.

"Oh shit," he said, when the door didn't budge. "It's
locked."

"Yeah," Luke said, sympathetically.

"Oh. Hang on," Scott said, remembering the meeting he
had had with the manager of Denecorp Systems the week before

— the meeting after which he had been entrusted with a key to the building's front door. He opened the passenger door of the van and rummaged around in the cupholders, the glovebox, and the center console.

"Here we go," he said finally. He emerged, holding up a silver key which glimmered in the streetlights as Luke watched it. After watching Scott unlock the glass door, Luke put down his broom and helped Scott pile all the equipment into a large armful, and brought it inside. Luke was impressed by how organized Scott was. He had all his supplies in order and he even had his own key to this fancy downtown commercial building. What was this place anyway?

Inside Denecorp Systems, Luke stood perplexed before a glass door which opened to a room full of computers. *It's like Skynet,* Luke thought. But he caught his mistake: *No, it's like Cyberdyne Systems.*

"We'll start in the conference room, I guess," Scott called from down the hall, looking around the place and scratching his head.

Luke turned from the shiny computer room and started down the hall, carrying the broom and cloth. "Whatever you say, boss."

Scott peered into the room and looked around. It looked pretty clean to him. He shrugged his shoulders. "Actually, we can probably skip this one."

Luke, reaching the door, stuck his head through the doorframe beside Scott. He spotted something small and white on the carpet under the table. Squeezing between his boss and the doorframe, he entered the room and bent over to pick up the gum wrapper.

"Good eye, Luke!" Scott praised. "See anything else?"

Luke gave a cursory glance around the room and saw no more garbage on the floor. The table looked pretty clean, too. "Nope," he reported. "This place is spotless." Seeing a small garbage can, he walked over and dropped the wrapper into it.

"Hey!" he suddenly exclaimed with wonder, reaching into the trash. "There's almost an entire Oh Henry in here!"

"Take it," Scott said.

"Really?"

"Perks of the job." His boss smiled. "Oh, and maybe put a fresh bag in the can while you're at it. We want to make sure we're thorough. Can't be missing any details."

"You got it, boss." Luke pulled the chocolate bar from the trash, folded the wrapper over the exposed peanut, caramel and fudge, and put it in the pocket of his jeans for later. Then he tied up the bag and replaced it with a new one from the toolbox in the lobby.

Luke and Scott continued to clean Denecorp Systems up and down until it seemed to sparkle. By the time they had finished dusting, sweeping and mopping, it was only ten o'clock.

"This place barely even needed cleaning," Luke remarked as they loaded the gear back in the van.

"Yeah. Some people are just clean freaks, I guess. Good job tonight, Luke. I'll call you tomorrow when I figure out our schedule. Goodnight."

"Hasta la vista, baby," Luke said as he watched Scott's van sputter off into the dark streets of downtown.

Luke called Sylvia and asked her to pick him up, expecting her to be happy that he was finished work so soon. She was, relatively speaking; and when she picked him up, Luke slid the Oh Henry! chocolate bar out of his pocket, tore it in half, and offered the unchewed half to her. Sylvia was radiant with appreciation.

So the two young lovers did get their cuddle time after all — though it was brief — and just before midnight Sylvia dropped Luke off at home, where he slept soundly, proud of all the hard work he had done during his first shift as a sanitation professional.

4

Cookies

The next day, Sylvia stood outside Willow Lodge, sneering at the stone and cedar pillars holding up the canopy over its entrance. She had never noticed it before, but the place was incredibly pretentious. *Look at all these fancy white window sills,* she thought with disdain. *Look at this perfect little stupid flower garden. Look at these smug old zombies sitting on their shiny wooden bench.* An elderly woman, clearly a resident, wearing gigantic black sunglasses noticed Sylvia looking at her, smiled wide and waved. *What a bunch of hags,* Sylvia thought, scowling.

Sylvia was waiting for Luke to arrive on the bus; she dared not enter the lodge without him. She had been standing on the sidewalk in front of the building for twelve minutes. She would have picked Luke up in her mom's car, but to Sylvia's irritation, her mom needed it today to run some errands. So she had also bussed to the lodge. Soon Luke's bus pulled up to the bus stop and Luke hopped off. Looking around him, he spied his girlfriend and gleefully walked up to meet her.

"Hey, Syl." Luke kissed her on the nose. Then he grabbed her hand and they walked inside.

"Let's get this over with," Sylvia spat.

The lobby was swarming with geriatrics. They pressed in on Sylvia and Luke like an undead horde. Sylvia clutched her stomach, convinced that the place was making her sick.

"I don't feel good, Luke," she whimpered.

Luke was sympathetic. "We better get you to Nana's room."

Sylvia forced a cough and then an exaggerated agitated moan for good measure. "Maybe we should just go home."

"We can't, Syl," Luke said gently. "We have to get Nana's medicine from the pharmacy."

Sylvia groaned, and held her stomach with her other hand.

"Why don't you go up to Nana's room and I'll go get the medicine and meet you there? Nana has ginger ale in her fridge."

"No!…I don't want ginger ale. I'll just come with you."

Luke led Sylvia through the lobby and down the hall to the pharmacy. All the way there, residents of the lodge smiled at them. Their smiles seemed to Sylvia to be omens of death. Although she knew she had made up her sickness, she was actually starting to feel queasy at the sight of all these shambling residents and their wrinkled grins, as if her body were playing along with the ruse. Luke felt good that so many people were smiling at him and his girl. He loved the people of Willow Lodge.

Luke stepped up to the pharmacy counter where a middle-aged woman with a greying ponytail was sitting, swivelling back and forth on a high stool.

"Hello," she said dreamily.

"Hello," Luke said. "I need some medicine for my nana."

"Oh, who's your nana?" the woman asked.

When Luke told her Nana's name the woman's face lit up.

"Oh, Esther! She is such a sweetheart."

Luke beamed. "Yes, she is! Nana's the best!"

"She *is!*" She sighed, smiling, looking from Luke to Sylvia. "And what are your names?"

"I'm Luke, and this is Sylvia," he said proudly.

"I'm his girlfriend," Sylvia cut in, now forgetting to clutch her aching stomach.

"Well, I'm Patti. It's nice to meet you."

"My old boss was named that too! She was the best!"

"Oh, really? That's funny."

Sylvia, stewing in contempt, thought to herself that in fact, it was not funny at all. That, actually, there was nothing funny about it and that probably there were millions of women in the world named Patti, or Patty for that matter, and all of them were probably nothing but snakes in the grass.

"Yeah," Luke said enthusiastically. "I got a new job now, though." And as Sylvia rolled her eyes, Luke began telling Patti all about his new job at Eliminator Sanitation and his new boss, Scott, and about Nana, until he finally remembered why he had come to the pharmacy counter in the first place.

"Oh yeah!" he continued. "I need some medicine for Nana, please. He rummaged in his jean pockets for the prescription for a few seconds. Luckily he was wearing the same pants he wore the day before. He pulled it out, smoothed out the creases on his stomach and attempted to read from it, but had some difficulty understanding.

"Here, honey, let me see." Patti grabbed the piece of paper from Luke's hands and read it. "Mhmm. I'll just be a second." She left the counter and went into a back room, leaving the prescription on the counter. Seeing that she was finished with it, Luke grabbed the slip of paper and shoved it back in his pocket.

In a minute, Patti returned with two translucent orange pill bottles, which she placed on the counter in front of Luke with a sunny smile. Luke thanked her, turning away and attempting to shove the bottles into his pocket. He managed to fit them in, just barely, but while he and Sylvia walked toward the lobby elevator, he kept fidgeting with his crotch.

"What are you doing?" Sylvia asked him.

"Now my pants don't fit right," he whined.

"Oh geez. Give them to me. There's lots of room in my purse."

"Aww, thanks baby!" Luke fished the bottles out of his pocket with two fingers.

"You're ridiculous. Is that better?"

"Yes, that's much better! Now let's go visit Nana!"

Sylvia resigned herself to it. Maybe she would have cookies. She usually had cookies. "Luke?"

"Yes?" he stopped mid-stride to listen intently.

"Can you do something for me?"

"Anything for you, my sweetie."

"Can you make sure she puts out the good cookies? Not the ones with the raisins?" Luke didn't like the sound of this. He wouldn't want to question Nana's judgement or refuse her hospitality. On the other hand, he wouldn't want Sylvia to have to eat a raisin cookie. What would he do? How could he tell Nana that her cookies were no good? Even if Sylvia was right — *raisin cookies are no good. Everyone knows that, don't they? So why does Nana make raisin cookies? Wait,* does *Nana make raisin cookies?* Luke tried hard to recall what kinds of cookies he had eaten at Nana's in the past. He had known her for a very long time — most of his life, it seemed. Had she ever given him a raisin cookie? Surely not! But then, maybe. He tried to recall. Was it possible that she had, and that Luke had eaten them without even realizing they were total crap?

Luke panicked more and more about the impending raisin cookie situation as the elevator slowly ascended. *How do we even know what kind of cookies she'll have this time?* he reasoned. *Maybe she'll have chocolate chip, or sugar cookies, or the ones with that red jelly in the middle.* He forced the worries out of his mind and hoped with desperation that it wouldn't be an issue. "Of course, baby," he finally responded.

They soon arrived at Nana's door, and Luke knocked "the secret knock," as he called it. The knock that Nana had always used when she came to look after him as a kid, the knock that, at nine years old, he had begged her to show him how to do. And the knock that, now that he was all grown up, he always used when he came to visit her. Luke blocked the door with his body so Sylvia wouldn't see his technique. He shared almost everything with her, but a man had to have a secret or two.

Sylvia scoffed, "Shave and a haircut."

"Huh?"

"Nothing."

Nana eventually opened the door, beaming to see her guests. They all settled on the couch, and Luke told her all about his first day of work at Eliminator. Nana interrupted his story when he got to the part about the Oh Henry!

"Lukie, dear. Bring us the cookies, won't you? They're on the dish there on the counter."

Luke jumped quickly to his feet, but approached the counter slowly, with great trepidation. Closer, closer, *YES!* Luke had never been so glad at the sight of shortbread in all his life. Shortbread wasn't great — it was certainly no sugar cookie or chocolate chip, or red jelly, but at least it didn't have raisins! Luke happily picked up the cookie dish and carried it over, setting it on the coffee table.

"Thank you, dear." Nana took a piece of the shortbread and Luke offered the dish to Sylvia, who took two, mouthing silently to Luke, "I'm starving!"

"Me too," said Luke. Thankfully, he still had six cookies on the dish. He thought about how he might get away with eating all of them without drawing too much attention to himself. How throughout their conversation he would say such agreeable things as "yes," and "mmhmm," while casually reaching for cookie after cookie, and chewing slowly so as not to make too many crunching noises.

"Now would you fetch me a dish, dear?" Nana held her cookie in her fingers, clearly pained at the impropriety of having no place to set it down.

Luke walked back to the tiny kitchen, still holding the cookie dish, to get two more dishes from the cupboard, which he set in front of Nana and Sylvia. Nana placed her cookie on her dish where it would stay for the remainder of the visit.

Sylvia ignored her dish, but not her cookies. Luke set the original dish down on the corner of the coffee table which he was claiming as his spot, and pulled up the pink wing chair from the other side of the small living area.

Some small talk ensued, and after a couple minutes Luke and Sylvia were both nearing the last bite of their respective second cookies. Luke watched warily. Would Sylvia make a move for another? He made up his mind. *It's okay if she does. In fact, I WANT to give her another one. Yes. Yes I do.*

"Would anyone like another?" Luke pushed his dish slightly toward the centre of the coffee table.

"No thank you, Luke" replied Nana.

Obviously. She had barely touched her first one yet.

"I'm good.," came Sylvia's reply. Luke smiled happily.

"...Lukie?" Nana was asking him something, but he had only heard his name. He looked to Sylvia, but she was already starting to zone out, her glassy eyes now staring at something above Luke's head.

"Umm..." Luke began, acting as though he were thinking about an answer. He trailed off and a couple seconds passed in silence.

"I asked how your job was going."

"Oh yeah! It's good — really good! They have this sweet yellow mop bucket!"

"I see."

"Yeah, but for now I'm using a broom."

"Oh, well that's good."

"Yeah — and I get free chocolate bars!"

"Oh my!"

And yesterday we cleaned up this really awesome place called Denecorp Systems. It's exactly like Cyberdyne!"

"Sounds exciting, Lukie."

"Yeah, except there were hardly any killer robots there."

"Well, maybe next time."

Sylvia was rousing back from her daydream state, having subconsciously heard mention of killer robots. "Are they here now?" she joked half-heartedly. "We better get out of here!" She hoped it might plant a subliminal message in Luke's mind. She was so bored. It felt like they had been sitting here for hours. She reached for another cookie, simply to give herself something to do.

Luke frowned, then reminded himself, *It's okay. I want her to have another cookie. I like sharing with her.* He actually really did. He quickly tried to prove it by pushing the dish toward her, and saying, "Have another one, Syl."

Instead of taking another cookie, Sylvia picked up her phone. "Oh! The bus!" she exclaimed and made a show of quickly standing and gathering her things. Her things consisted of her phone, which she shoved back into her purse, and her purse itself, which was literally right beside her, leaning against her leg. "Oops, almost forgot!" She noisily thumped one bottle of Nana's medication onto the coffee table.

"We got your medicine for you, Nana!" Luke beamed.

"Oh, thank you dear. Thank you both." She made as if to take Sylvia's hand, but Sylvia quickly pulled it away in order to fake cough into it, then immediately began inching toward the door and giving Luke the sideways head nod gesture which is the universal signal for, "can we please for the love of God get the hell out of here?"

Luke said goodbye to Nana and the two hurried to the bus stop, where they proceeded to wait for twenty minutes until the next bus arrived, just on time.

5
Bad News

In the evening, Luke's father picked up Luke in his 2007 Ford Focus station wagon in Brierwood Beige. "You'll be pleased to know your mother is making spaghetti for dinner," he told Luke after a minute of silent driving. This silent drive was a weekly tradition of father-son bonding.

"With garlic bread?"

"I imagine so."

"Me too." Luke proceeded to imagine the garlic bread — a nice thick slice of french bread, lathered in melted butter, herbs, and a generous sprinkling of garlic salt. After imagining this for a while, Luke told his father about his new job, while his father grunted in recognition at the appropriate key points of the description. His father had become quite adept at grunting at key points of conversation, even while remaining completely oblivious to their actual content.

They pulled into the pale paved driveway where Luke's father parked four feet from the garage door. He had long ago determined that four feet was the optimum distance, leaving enough room to walk comfortably in front of the car, and still enough room for another vehicle to park behind it. Parking inside the garage was of course out of the question. Luke could remember the inside of the garage vividly. It was packed full of tools and barely used sporting goods: three bicycles, a couple skateboards, a portable basketball hoop, a ratty old golf bag, and a pile of hockey sticks and tennis rackets with broken strings. The latter were piled on top of an air hockey table that, as far as Luke knew, had never been plugged in. Also contained within the garage was a lawnmower, an old fridge that made a strange gurgling noise, a half-empty freezer, two neat stacks of winter tires on rims, and a shiny blue tool chest on wheels.

Entering the house, the garlic bread scent immediately arrested Luke's attention, drawing him in and down the hall. He headed straight for the kitchen, forgetting to remove his shoes until reminded by his father, who was now sliding his feet into a pair of heelless fleece-lined sheepskin slippers — the pair he had received for Christmas from his wife, the same kind he received from her every year, whether last year's pair was worn out or not.

"Luke?" Luke's mom called from the kitchen, where she was straining the spaghetti in an aluminum colander in the sink. Her timing was impeccable, as always. Somehow she was always able to coordinate her supper presentation within a minute of her husband's return home from work, or the arrival of guests.

"Hi Mom!" Luke called back, while hopping on one foot, and wrestling with a stubborn knot in the lace of his red Converse sneakers. By the time he made his way to sit down at the dining room table, his plate of spaghetti was waiting, ready for him to scoop his own sauce, which he had always preferred to do.

After everyone was settled at the table Luke's mom spoke. "Luke, did your father tell you our news already?"

"No," Luke responded. He didn't think so anyway. What had they talked about in the car?

"Well…" His mother looked expectantly at his father.

"Luke," his father began, while reaching for the plate of garlic bread, "you know we've been considering this for quite some time, so I'm sure this won't be much of a surprise, but it seems the time is right. I've finally arranged it with the company, and it took a bit of arm-twisting but they're going to allow me to work remotely. So we are officially moving to Peachland."

Luke did not in fact know that his parents had been considering moving, and it did in fact come as a surprise to him. He knew his father liked peaches, but to actually move to

Peachland seemed a little extreme. He wasn't sure what to say. He tried to decide whether their moving would really make much of a difference. It would free up his Wednesday evenings, but he'd have one more dinner a week he would have to buy himself.

"Now, don't worry," continued his father, "We're still going to take care of Nana's bills and other arrangements, but we may have to rely on you to keep an eye on her."

As if I don't already! Luke thought. *When was the last time you visited her, anyway?*

His mother was speaking now. "We know you've been so good with visiting her, and it isn't always easy with her health issues. She really appreciates the time you spend with her."

"I know. We have great visits. Oh and look!" Luke pulled Nana's prescription from his pocket. "She even lets me pick up her medicine now."

Luke's parents exchanged a worried look. "Can I see that, Luke?" asked his father. Luke slid the paper across the table to him. His father examined the prescription, and showed it to his wife.

"When did she give this to you?" asked his mother.

"I dunno. Maybe like... Monday? or Friday?"

"Luke, listen to me," his mother scolded. "It's important that you don't put this off. If Nana is going to trust you with this job, you need to make sure that you go to the pharmacy right away, okay?"

"Yeah, I know, but..."

"Luke. It's important."

"I know." He hung his head, his bangs reaching dangerously close to the tomato sauce piled atop his plate of spaghetti.

His father handed the prescription back to Luke, "Just make sure that you go there first thing tomorrow morning," he said.

"I will." Luke set the prescription on the table and pushed it down with the side of his fist to smooth out the wrinkle his father had carelessly given its corner. Again his parents exchanged a silent look. His mother picked up a jug of water from the table and disappeared into the kitchen, calling for her husband's help a few seconds later.

Luke paid no attention to their whispers. He was now solely focused on fighting with a particularly hard-crusted chunk of garlic bread. He forced his teeth through its tough rind like a bear gnawing on a deer, a low primal growl audibly betraying this inner vision. Victorious, he swallowed the bread and moved on to his next task, that of forming a huge spiralling mound of swirled spaghetti. It hung onto his fork like a giant bees' nest. The bees buzzed loudly in his mind in an attempt to ward off the bear, who was now transfixed upon the honey-filled hive. The bees swarmed at the bear, stinging him on the snout. *Oh no you don't!* roared the bear, swatting at the angry swarm and sending a great red glob of spaghetti sauce sailing through the air. The sauce landed right on Nana's prescription.

"Shit, shit shit!" muttered Luke. He listened for a moment to ascertain whether his parents had heard. They were still speaking softly in the kitchen, and if they had heard him, they didn't let on. Or perhaps that was what they were speaking softly about. Luke glanced around for something to clean up the mess. He had a cloth napkin in his lap, and was about to apply it to the sauce, when he remembered from previous spills that these cloth napkins were not very good at cleaning up messes. They could barely handle soaking up a bit of water, or juice, or milk. It would be useless for this job. He almost panicked. *Think man, think!* he told himself. He was a sanitation professional now and he'd be damned if he couldn't find a way to eliminate this mess. Then it hit him. He grabbed the prescription and lifted it slowly into the air, careful not to let the sauce drip down and further mar its surface. Then he stuck out his tongue and licked it. He inspected his handiwork. Most of the sauce was gone, replaced by a nominal saliva splotch that he knew any napkin should be able to handle. He wiped the saliva with his napkin, lifting it only to find this had caused the ink, saliva and remaining sauce to smear across the paper. The prescription was now a wet, black and red mess. No amount of licking or napkin rubbing would undo the ink-smear.

Luke's mother and father were entering the dining room, returning from their top-secret kitchen work. Luke quickly shoved the prescription into his pocket. Some of the smear transferred itself from the prescription to his pants and seeped to the outside. He pawed at the stain frantically yet ineffectually, and tried to form his facial expression into what he hoped was a pleasant and innocuous smile.

"Good grief, Luke," said his mother, eyeing the soiled napkin.

"Sorry mom," Luke apologized.

The rest of the meal was spent in a slightly awkward silence that was fairly typical of the Clark household. Luke tried to focus on finishing the rest of his meal as neatly and quietly as possible. His mother and father tried to focus on pretending they were not also focusing on Luke trying to focus on eating neatly and quietly.

After dinner, Luke's father set up the chess board, as he did every Wednesday, and proceeded to soundly trounce Luke three games in a row while his mother tidied up the dining room and washed the dishes. Luke excused himself immediately after game three, explaining that he had to work in the morning, which, as far as Luke knew, may or may not have been true.

After Luke's father drove him home without so much as a word, and had arrived back home to settle on the couch with the TV remote to watch CNN, his wife questioned him.

"Did Luke say he has to work in the morning?"

"Yes, I think so."

"Hmm. I didn't know he had a job."

"Neither did I."

~~~

Luke stared out the window of his apartment's living room at the darkening sky, sipping a Coke and waiting for a phone call. Luke's boss Scott had not phoned him that day like he said he would. Luke was starting to wonder whether he would call after all, or whether Scott was avoiding him for some reason, whether maybe Scott had been lying about what a great worker he thought Luke was and he secretly wanted to fire Luke but was afraid to bring it up, or whether perhaps Scott's van had broken down on the outskirts of town and Scott had been forced to hitch-hike back into town, taking his own life in his hands with whatever psychos happened to be driving around.

Suddenly, the phone in Luke's hand simultaneously rang and vibrated, startling him so much that he dropped his Coke out the window.

"Oh hey, uh, hi, Scott?" Luke spoke into the phone as he watched his Coke fall to the ground.

"No, it's me," said Sylvia.

"Hey, baby! Good to hear you!"

"You too, hon. Whatcha doing?"

"Nothing much, but… actually, I better go. I can't talk right now."

"You're doing nothing but you can't talk?"

"Yeah. On the phone, I mean."

"What are you talking about, babe?" Sometimes he was hard to figure out, this man of hers.

"Well, I'm waiting for a phone call… And he might call while I'm already on the phone and I'll miss it."

"Oh, right. Okay. Well… who's gonna be calling, anyway?" *It better not be that bitch from Wendy's.*
~~~

"My new boss, Scott. He needs to tell me about work tomorrow. I don't know where I'm supposed to go."

Sylvia breathed an audible sigh of relief. "Don't worry, hon. You won't miss it."

"You think so?"

"Yeah."

"Well, okay," he said, but something in his voice caused Sylvia to doubt that everything was really okay.

"Is something else wrong, hon?"

"Uh, maybe yeah, I guess."

"Well, what is it?"

"Well you know that paper we got from Patti?"

"Which Patty?" Suspicion now crept into Sylvia's voice. "From Wendy's?"

"No, the other one, from the pill counter."

"Oh good." Her relief was discernible even to Luke. "Well, what about her?"

"You know that paper she gave us?"

"The paper she... You mean Nana's prescription? But we already got her pills."

"Yeah, but my mom said I have to go back."

"Oh. Okay, well, what were you saying about the prescription?"

"Um… I wrecked it. Like, I can't even read it anymore. And my mom said that I need to go get more pills for Nana right away, like tomorrow, and it's no good if you can't read it, right?"

"You have to get her more pills? Your mom said that?"

"Yeah, at dinner. But how can I if it's wrecked?"

Once in a while Luke would get like this, and it was usually his mother's fault. She would turn something small into a big deal, or at least Luke would fear that she would do so. He would work himself up and stress out about it.

"Okay hon, don't worry. I'll fix it. Show it to me tomorrow and I'll see what I can do."

"Aww babe, you're the best."

The door to Jason's bedroom opened suddenly and out stumbled a bleary eyed Jason. "Hey, Luke. What's up?" He continued mumbling something which Luke didn't hear because Sylvia was also saying something. He didn't hear what Sylvia was saying either. He hated having two people talking to him at once.

"Listen babe, I gotta go, okay?"

"Alright baby, I'll see you tomorrow."

"Okay, honey. You're the best"

"You said that alrea-"

Oops, shit. He hadn't meant to hang up on her like that.

"Sup, man?" Jason asked as Luke put his phone in his pocket.

"Hi, Jason," Luke replied.

"Maybe just a little," laughed Jason. "But now that you mention it, I do have a killer case of the munchies. What's there to eat around here?" He began opening and closing cupboard doors in the kitchen, but had to admit defeat after thirty seconds of fruitless searching. "What are you up to, bro?"

"Just waiting. Scott is supposed to call about working tomorrow."

"Oh yeah, right! Hey! Remember that job I applied for in Van?"

"Uh… sure?"

"I got it man! Can you believe that?!"

"Yeah." Luke could believe it. Easily, in fact. Jason was super smart, and he went to college and he had some kind of fancy adult job that you needed college for, and Luke imagined he was really great at whatever it was that he had to do. "That's really awesome, Jason."

"I know, right? And they're paying me like an extra twenty grand a year."

"Wow! So more money for pizza, huh?" Luke envisioned Jason in his new life of luxury, ordering in pizza every night. He already did it at least a couple times a week, a fact for which Luke was always very grateful. Luke had even offered to pitch in a few bucks the first few times after they moved in together. Jason always declined his offers, so soon Luke stopped offering. They both knew he could barely cover his share of rent.

"No doubt, bro!" replied Jason. "Except that really it's not 'cause I'll end up spending most of it on rent; it's insane down there, man. But at least I'll save on gas and insurance and all that shit when I sell my car. I'm gonna get a place right downtown, walking distance to the office. That'll make life a lot simpler."

The job is in Vancouver, Luke suddenly realized. Which meant that Jason was moving to Vancouver. Which meant that Jason wouldn't be around anymore. Which meant that Jason wouldn't be Luke's roommate anymore. Which meant that Jason, who had up until now paid the lion's share of the rent, since the apartment was technically his and Luke had really only been renting a room off him, would no longer be paying any of the rent. And not only that, he'd no longer be here to pay for pizza. All these thoughts whirled in Luke's mind. He felt a little lightheaded, and sat down on Jason's couch, in Jason's living room, in Jason's apartment, knocking over a presumed empty, but actually only half-empty, can of Jason's Coke, which proceeded to spill all over Jason's coffee table and drip onto Jason's living room carpet. *Shit, man. This really sucks.* Luke might have to find a new apartment. At the very least, he would have to find a way to pay all the rent on his own. How much would that be, exactly? He didn't know. He'd have to work extra hard, and maybe ask Scott about getting a raise.

His phone vibrated in his pocket and played the bridge from "All The Small Things" by Blink 182. It was just the part with the "na-na na-na" lyrics. Definitely the best part of the song, in Luke's opinion. Maybe, he thought, the best part of any song. It was the reason he had taught himself how to make ringtones. Looking up as he pulled the phone from his pocket, he noticed that Jason had disappeared. He hadn't heard him leave.

"Hello?" he asked his phone.

"Oh hey Luke, it's Scott. From Eliminator Sanitation."

"Oh, hi Scott."

"Um hey, listen, sorry for calling so late. I've been trying to figure something out all day, but it looks like there's no work tomorrow after all, okay bud?"

6

Glimmer of Hope

Luke shuffled along the sidewalk of Pine Street, dragging his feet in that way that always caused the soles of his shoes to eventually wear through on the inner heel. It was 11:02 and he was almost at the bus stop. He would have to wait about seven or eight minutes for Hans to arrive with the number 15 bus. He sighed as he neared the crooked aluminum post which passed as a bus stop in this neighborhood. There was no bench to sit on, and no covered glass booth to wait in. He was glad it wasn't winter at least. The frigid winter wind could really suck if you didn't have a glass booth to wait in. This morning wasn't that bad, as far as weather went. It had been drizzling lightly as he left his apartment, but the rain seemed to have stopped at some point during his walk. It wasn't the rain that had bothered him, though. Rain never really bothered him; as far as Luke was concerned, rain was just water falling from the sky. What really bothered him was that a guy just can't catch a fucking break in life. It really sucked. You always had to keep looking for a new job just to scrape by. Your roommates and your parents were always moving away, leaving you to fend for yourself. Sometimes you just felt like a piece of discarded trash. Like that old newspaper lying on the sidewalk beside the bus stop, or that soggy Canadian 2-for-1 Pizza coupon beside it. Or that small, rectangular, purple… *Holy shit! Is that…?* Luke stooped down to pick up a scrap from a shallow puddle. "YES!" he shouted. It was a ten dollar bill.

He held the bill up to the sky to check if it was real. The transparent section of the bill revealed grey clouds above him, and as the sunlight broke through a crack in the leaden sky, it glinted off the bill's shiny metallic strip. It was legit for sure.

He was still standing there holding the bill against the sky when Hans shouted down to him from the bus.

"Luke! Come on, buddy!"

Luke bounced up the steps into the bus with a new-found energy, feeling as if perhaps everything was going to work out alright after all.

"Hi Hans," he greeted the friendly driver. "Check it out — I found this in a puddle just now!" He brandished the still-damp ten, waving it back and forth with excitement, sending droplets of puddle water soaring in all directions.

"Very nice," responded Hans, nodding. He didn't bother asking Luke to show his bus pass. Luke, like many of the riders, was well known by Hans.

Luke practically skipped down the aisle of the bus toward the back seat, which was empty, as if the universe had saved a spot just for him. As he sat and gazed happily out the side window, he noticed a young girl running behind a large dog on a leash. The dog practically dragged the small girl, but she ran and giggled as though being dragged along like that was the best thing in all the world. Luke laughed too — and it wasn't even at the girl with her silly dog; it was just a laugh. A joyful laugh, not a mocking one. A laugh that said, "I'm alive in the world and I'm laughing. And that's pretty good, right?" It sure felt good. The girl was happy. The dog was happy. Luke was happy. The dog and the girl ran into the park as the number 15 zoomed by. It was a park full of happy grass and happy trees. There were happy couples holding hands and sitting on happy park benches.

At the far end of the park was a shadowy area with a thick grove of black spruce trees, where the high school kids hung out to smoke cigarettes when they skipped class. As the bus passed by, Luke saw two kids he vaguely knew. They were a couple years younger than him. A man in a dark hoodie rolled up to the two boys on a red BMX. Luke saw one of the boys and the hoodied man both reach into their pockets and exchange their contents with each other. A happy drug dealer selling pot to a couple of happy teenagers. *But drug dealers are bad,* thought Luke. They weren't supposed to be happy. They were bad people, mean people, terrible people. That's how it was on TV. That's how he remembered it from high school too. Certain shady characters from his school were the pushers. They were best avoided altogether. But Luke had smoked pot in high school a few times, when someone would spot him a few tokes. That pot must have come from somewhere. Luke turned away from the window and examined an advertisement near the ceiling of the bus. Two happy men, enjoying a cup of coffee in the cafe of a nearby resort.

The bus turned onto Lonston and before long Luke could see Wendy's in the distance. He imagined himself and Sylvia sitting at the table by the window, eating Junior Bacon Cheeseburgers and staring out through the glass at the number 15 bus; the bus he was on right now. Would they be able to see him from there? It was a long way across the parking lot. Would they be able to recognize him? He decided he would test the theory later on. He'd pick up Sylvia and they'd walk back the way he had come, back down Lonston to the Wendy's. Then, with the soggy ten dollar bill, Luke would buy them each a JBC. and maybe some fries to share, and they would stare out the window until the next 15 bus went by. Of course, Luke wouldn't really be on that bus, because he'd be in the Wendy's. But he would pick one of the riders out and pretend it was him. He would see if his features were recognizable.

The bus rolled to a stop and the rear door opened, but none of the passengers stood up to exit. After a few seconds, Luke heard Hans calling his name.

"Luke, it's your stop, buddy!"

"Oh! Sorry Hans. I was zoning." He jumped up from his seat and waved as he scooted down the step.

"See you later," waved Hans.

At Sylvia's place, Luke told her about the ten dollar bill and the happy people he'd seen on his way over, and announced his intention to buy JBCs.

"Good, I'm starving," said Sylvia. "But before we go, let me see that prescription you were so worried about."

"Oh yeah, I have it right here." Luke had forgotten all about his spaghetti incident. He pulled the prescription and the ten dollar bill from his pocket. Both were slightly more crumpled than they had been, and the prescription had now soaked up some of the sogginess from the cash. Sylvia examined the ruined prescription and determined that it didn't look that bad after all. Or at least, that although it looked bad enough to be embarrassing to take to the pharmacy, it was still legible enough that she could mostly make out what it said. She told Luke as much, but he wasn't convinced. He complained that Patti would think he was a loser for spilling sauce on it in the first place, and he thought that somehow this would shed a negative light on Nana, having a loser for a grandson, and Luke couldn't live with making Nana look bad.

"Alright fine," said Sylvia, annoyed that Luke cared so much what Patti thought of him. She woke up her laptop. "Look, I'll make a nice fresh new one, okay?"

"Wow, you can do that?" asked Luke, unsure.

"I mean, it's not that hard. Look, it's basically just a simple document. Check it out. I can type this up in like five minutes." Sylvia began typing and clicking in a calculated frenzy. "And just put some underlines in these spots here, and here. There, see?"

"Yeah but what about this smudgy part?"

"Sure, but I can read enough of the letters, look. It starts with 'Dram,' then 'something, something', then 'N-E' at the end, so just google it, and voila! See? Look at this: 'Did you mean: dramamine?' Yes, that's what I meant. I guess." She clicked her mouse. "Let's see, dimenhydrinate, also known as Dramamine or Gravol." She laughed. "Isn't Gravol for like, car-sick kids?"

"Oh yeah, remember? Nana was dizzy on the elevator."

"Hmm… Yeah, I guess." She continued reading the search results. "Blah, blah, blah… Oh, okay. 'Used to treat nausea, vertigo, and various conditions caused by chemotherapy…' Nana isn't on chemo, is she?"

"What?"

"Chemotherapy. For cancer. Nana doesn't have cancer, does she?"

"What?! No. No way."

"Okay, that's good."

"Yeah. Geez, Syl."

"Alright, well let's go get those burgers. I'm starving."

"What about the thing? You said you're gonna make a new one."

"Yeah, I can make it when we get back, or tomorrow, or something."

"But Syl, I need it. Can't you just do it now? How long is it gonna take, anyway?"

"I'm hungry, Luke."

Luke just stood there wearing a baleful look.

"Oh fine. Whatever."

It only took a few minutes for Sylvia to finish the document, and another minute to print it on her mom's ancient printer. The age and overall crappiness of the printer actually worked in her favour for once, giving the printout a half-faded quality that looked remarkably similar to the original.

As Sylvia printed the prescription, Luke sat on the couch, scrolling through 'For Rent' ads on his phone, becoming more and more dejected with each one he read. The gravity of the situation was beginning to sink in again. There was no way he could afford to rent a place on his own. Even the tiniest, dumpiest one bedroom apartments were priced significantly higher per month than any paycheque he had ever received, or probably could ever hope to. He barely looked at the prescription as Sylvia handed it to him, shoving it into his pocket almost subconsciously.

"Okay, happy? Let's go," Sylvia said, pulling on her jacket. Luke stood without a word, shoved his phone into his other pocket, and shuffled toward the door, whose knob shocked him painfully with an audible spark of static electricity. He yowled loudly, "Damn! Your carpet gets me every time!" Sylvia laughed. It did get him every time, and each time was just as funny as the last. He never saw it coming.

Luke was sullen as they walked to the Wendy's on Lonston. Sylvia thought he was making kind of a big deal about her laughing at him, but she figured he'd forget about it and be happy again once they got their JBC.s. She sat at a table by the window while Luke stood in line to place their order. She tapped her fingers on the table. All the way here she had had a song stuck in her head, which was perhaps one reason she didn't mind Luke's moody silence. But now the song was making its way out into the world, through her fingertips, and she soon couldn't help but start humming the tune. As Luke approached with their food tray, she locked his eyes and began dancing in her chair, and singing playfully:

Are you comin' with me?
Come let me take you on a party ride
And I'll teach you, teach you, teach you
I'll teach you the electric slide

"Ha ha, very funny," Luke responded, trying to hide a smile, but he couldn't help himself, and chimed in with, "You can't resist it — Boogie woogie woogie," before they both broke out laughing. Luke's happiness was short-lived though, as halfway through his JBC. his worries crept back into his consciousness. He put down his burger and spoke with his mouth half full. "Jason's moving out."

"Jason? Your roommate Jason?"

He nodded.

"Wow! So you'll have the place all to yourself? That's so cool!"

He swallowed and shook his head. "No. I could never afford that place." Suddenly an idea occurred to him. He spoke coyly. "Unless maybe if I got a new roommate. Like maybe a certain lovely lady that I happen to know."

"You better be referring to me, buddy," she threatened jokingly, but couldn't help looking back at the kitchen in case Patty was working.

"Of course, babe. You're the only girl I'd ever want to live with."

"Yeah, well don't get too excited, cuz it ain't gonna happen, baby. Even if I had the money, you know I couldn't. My mom would shit her pants." Sylvia's mom was a devout Catholic, which is to say she showed up at Holy Mass every Christmas and Easter. But she would never stand for her daughter shacking up with her boyfriend. Sylvia and her mom were not exactly what you would call close, but Sylvia's living with her mom was still advantageous for both of them. They had figured out a stable, effective relationship and there were some things that just wouldn't bend.

"Yeah, I know," Luke sighed.

Sylvia thought about Luke's predicament while taking another bite of her JBC. "You could always move back in with your folks, I guess. That would really suck though."

"Nuh-uh."

"It wouldn't?"

"No, I mean I can't."

"I know, but like, it may be your only choice." She knew perhaps better than Luke the limits of his earning potential.

"No. I can't 'cause they're moving away too."

"What? When did this happen?"

"They told me at dinner last night."

"Man, that's brutal."

"I know right?" His face was a curious mix of dejection and incredulity.

"So, what, are they going to Vancouver or something?"

"No. Peachland."

"Peachland? What the fuck is in Peachland?"

"Peaches, I guess."

"Damn. Well. So are they taking your nana with them?"

"No. At least Nana will still be around." The thought gave Luke some consolation.

"Seriously? So like, you're gonna have to take care of her all by yourself? This is ridiculous!"

"I already do anyway."

"Well… Yeah. I guess." Sylvia had certainly never seen Luke's parents at Willow Lodge, and had never heard Nana talk about them either. For that matter, when was the last time she had even seen them at all? Luke's father had dropped him off at her place a couple times, but what was that, like a year ago? It seemed like they really lived under a rock, those two.

The couple finished their burgers, pondering the great questions in life: How the hell do you scrape by on minimum wage and a couple shifts a week? What must it be like to grow old and have to rely on family members? And why the fuck would anyone want to live in Peachland? In the midst of all this pondering, Luke forgot to look out the window at himself on the number 15 bus.

7

Back to the Lodge

Neither Luke nor Sylvia slept well that night. In their respective homes and beds, each had tossed and turned for hours. Sylvia had dreamt of a strange cartoon-like land inhabited by huge animated peaches. They towered over her threateningly and she retched at their overpowering peach aroma. Why the fuck would anyone want to live in Peachland? Luke had stared at the ceiling as he worried about rent, and about how his job wouldn't be enough to pay for rent, and about how he wasn't even hardly getting any shifts, so he might have to quit the job he loved and find work somewhere else.

In the morning, he phoned Scott on his cell, but there was no answer. He tried the office number. Maybe the secretary would know something, or he could at least ask her to ask Scott to call him back; but again there was no answer. He then tried to call Sylvia, but she didn't answer either, due to the fact that she had just put on a Nelly Furtado CD and stepped into the shower.

"Ugh. Where is everybody?" Luke wondered. He was hungry. He should have bought a loaf of bread or something instead of those JBC.s — those delicious JBC.s. He decided to go visit Nana. He had the new prescription in his pocket still, didn't he? Yes, there it was. Shit, he was supposed to do that yesterday. *Better late than never,* he thought. *And hey, Nana has cookies!* He threw on his jacket and shoes, and rushed out toward the bus stop, not noticing until he was halfway there that he had left his cell phone sitting on the kitchen counter, or maybe the couch. Or maybe on the bathroom floor? At any rate, he didn't have it now, and if he turned back, he would probably miss the bus.

Arriving at Willow Lodge, Luke felt naked. Even though it happened to him fairly regularly, it always felt strange when he forgot his phone, like a part of him was missing. Like an arm or something. Yes. His left arm. Missing your phone was just like missing your left arm. You didn't really *need* it exactly, but it was very strange to not have it. He then realized that he had also forgotten his wallet. That didn't matter as much, as it was empty anyway, and he didn't need money today. The pharmacy automatically charged everything to Nana's account, which his parents paid for, he supposed. Hans had him covered for transportation. He'd scrounge some cookies from Nana. *Yeah, it's all good*, he thought.

Patti at the pharmacy was friendly as she had been before. She asked Luke if he had watched the game last night, and Luke had no idea which game she was talking about but had accidentally told her that yes, he had. So he pretended as though he had watched it, and made general remarks of agreement about how good the game was. Patti took his prescription, actually taking it this time instead of leaving it on the counter, and handed him two bottles of little white pills. As he waited for the elevator, he opened the bottle and shook one pill out into his hand. It was smooth and circular. He turned it over. The other side was inscribed with a secret code. It had a line in the middle, underneath which was a funny V-like symbol. It looked almost like one of those math signs for… what was it… square root, or dividing — one of those, anyway. Above the line, it said '0111'. Luke thought maybe it was a computer language or something. Computers couldn't use drugs, though. Maybe robots could; he wasn't sure. What would happen if a robot took drugs? That could be dangerous. It might go crazy and decide to launch its world domination plans prematurely. Then what? If a robot launched a plan it wasn't ready for, would it get confused? Would it make mistakes and cause its own evil empire to crumble out from beneath it. That could be good, he supposed. After all, it was an *evil* empire, right? But would the robot even care? Or would he be too high to notice?

The elevator door opened, startling Luke and causing him to drop the pill. It fell, bounced off the carpet, and rolled right into the crack between the elevator floor and the real floor, where it became lodged. It looked like a robot was holding the pill between clenched teeth. Was it having second thoughts? Was it considering the choice — to spit out the pill and avert disaster, or to fall prey to the temptation of ultimate robotic glory at the expense of temporary insanity and passing pleasure. *Wait, pleasure wouldn't be considered an expense, though. What's the opposite of an expense? There must be a word for that...*

The elevator doors closed in front of Luke's face. He almost stuck his hand in between the doors to stop them, but chickened out at the last millisecond. Instead he pushed the elevator call button again, and the door opened a second time. But now the pill was gone. The robot had made its choice. The drug would infect its brain and the world as we know it would come to an end. "Oh shit," said Luke, even as his own legs carried him forward half-consciously into the inevitability of the small metal capsule that would carry him to a higher level.

"Hold that elevator, son!" It was Horse-face.

"Hi Horse- ...Uh, hi." That was a close one.

"You're Esther's grandson, aren't you?"

Luke nodded, and grunted confirmation.

Horace paused a moment before continuing. "You're not half bad. I see you around a lot." He fumbled with a pack of Player's cigarettes in his shirt pocket, and then offered one to Luke, who waved him off. Luke wasn't sure if he was supposed to like this guy or not. He seemed to be some kind of arch-enemy to Lester, which in some fashion would seem to make him an automatic ally to Luke. *The enemy of my enemy is my friend,* Luke remembered from somewhere. On the other hand, he was almost as creepy as Lester, and as likely as not also had designs on Nana. Luke remained undecided.

"Not a smoker, eh?" said Horace. "Too bad. Don't know whatyer missin."

Luke disagreed. What he was missing was bad breath, lung cancer, and pneumonia. He wasn't an idiot. "Yeah," he said. The elevator stopped at Nana's floor. Luke wondered how it knew. He didn't recall having pushed the button. He gestured for Horse-face to exit first, with a sweeping arm movement.

"Not my stop, son. I'm going all the way to the top!" He flicked his Bic and lit a cigarette as Luke exited, leaning with his back against the elevator wall, right beside the huge red 'No Smoking' sign.

A few doors down the hall, Luke knocked on Nana's door, and was met with a booming male voice calling, "Yello?" *Shit*. It was Lester. Things were going from bad to worse. Luke toyed with the idea of turning away, pretending he had never been here. His stomach growled in argument. The door swung in.

"Oh! Hey there, Slim!" Lester's voice reverberated through the hall. "Come on in! I was just about to make Esther a cup of tea. You want one? Of course you'll have one, why not? Let's see here, mint? Tangerine? ah, here we are, Earl Grey." He barged around the tiny kitchen, intent on forcing hot liquid down Luke's throat.

"Lukie!" beamed Nana, struggling to rise from the comfy couch upon which she rested.

Luke ran over to give her a hand getting up, and then a hug.

"No Sylvia today?" asked Nana.

"Naw, she couldn't make it this time."

"Well, you tell her we missed her. She's such a dear."

"I will, Nana. I promise." This reminded him of his promise to his mother, to bring Nana her pills right away, and he reached into his pocket to retrieve the bottles. "Here's your medication, Nana."

"Take these, won't you dear?" Nana was passing him a stack of photo albums.

"What are these for?"

"Those are photo albums, Lukie. They're full of pictures from when your Nana was younger. How time flies..."

"Still as stunning as ever, though!" interrupted Lester.

"Oh, stop it!" Nana giggled. Luke groaned. Listening to Lester's bullshit compliments was like hearing fingernails scraping on a chalkboard. Why was he here? This wasn't right. The man was acting like he owned the place, answering doors, making tea — it wasn't right. Luke grabbed the photo albums and tucked them under his arm. "Here's your medication, Nana," he repeated.

"What are these for?"

Boy, her memory really is starting to fade, Luke thought with concern. "These are for your nausea, remember? My mom told me to give them to you."

"Oh, but Luke, you already gave them to me, remember?"

"Oh yeah. That's weird." *Why did mom tell me to give these to Nana?*

"Take these back down to Patti, would you dear? I think these must be extra."

"Take them back? Uh, okay..." Luke wasn't sure how to go about returning pills. Did he need an unprescription? How would he get one? The prospect was making him anxious.

"Crack open one of them albums, son," Lester crowed from the kitchen. Luke fumbled with the two bottles of pills and three photo albums tucked under his arm. He stuffed the bottles back in his jeans pocket and sat down on the couch, placing the photo albums on the coffee table. Luke opened the book to see several pictures of a gorgeous young woman in a swimsuit. *Woah!* This woman looked like a supermodel. Lester walked over and placed a cup of tea in front of Luke. "What a bombshell, huh?" Lester nudged Luke with his elbow. Luke had to admit, Lester was right. This chick was hot. Who was she?

"Where was this?" Lester asked.

"Oh, let me think," Nana said. "This must have been up at Vivian Lake. We used to have such a great time fishing in the summer. Goodness, it was so long ago now."

"Well, you're still as ravishing as ever, my dear. Still got those beautiful, er… eyes. Eh, Luke?" Lester winked in his direction. Luke nodded for a moment, before realization began to dawn on him. *Oh God! It's Nana!*

I'm gonna be sick, thought Luke. *This is bad,* Luke thought. *This is very bad. Nana's hot?!* Luke felt deeply unsettled. Here was this creep, trying to put the moves on her. *Oh God, he didn't spend the night, did he? Please, no.* He had to stop him. He had to run away. He had to return the pills. Would Sylvia even know how to make an unprescription? It was all too much.

"I gotta go," said Luke.

"To the bathroom, Lukie? Of course dear, you know where it is."

"No. Not… No, no," Luke muttered. He was walking sideways toward the door, as if sideways walking was somehow less noticeable. He was freaking out. He couldn't deal with this right now. He ran out into the hallway, carelessly slamming Nana's door behind him. As he reached the elevator, he heard Lester bellow down the hallway behind him, "What about yer tea?"

He ran right past the elevator, opting for the stairs. Down he ran. Down, down, down. The stairway seemed to stretch into eternity, like in some epic action movie where someone is being chased by a man with a gun, except that this was more like a horror movie, and the someone being chased was his Nana, not him, and the man doing the chasing wasn't holding a gun, but… *Oh God!*

At the bottom of the stairs Luke collapsed against the wall and struggled to breathe. His heart was racing. He was sweating intensely. He felt increasingly nauseous. He remembered this feeling. It was a panic attack. He used to get them when he was young sometimes when he took his ADHD medication. Or was it when he forgot to take it? He wished he had his old medicine now. He might still have some, actually. But if he did it was back at his apartment. Back at Jason's apartment. Yes, his old pills were there, along with the rest of his earthly possessions. His wallet. His phone. "Shit."

He felt one of the pill bottles in his pocket now, and took it out. *No, these aren't them. These are for Patti.* But Luke remembered what Sylvia had said — these pills were for nausea, weren't they? He tapped two pills into his palm and stared at them. He needed to bring these back to Patti. But did he? He didn't have an unprescription anyways, and besides, he was feeling very sick. *They're for nausea,* he reminded himself. *No, they're for Patti.* He felt bad, but he needed these pills right now. He popped them into his mouth and tried to swallow, wishing he had a glass of water. It took him a few tries, but eventually he managed to get the pills down.

Sitting down on the cold cement floor, he tried to compose himself. He closed his eyes, made two tight fists and breathed in deeply, counting to four. Then he breathed out, counting to eight and relaxing his fists. The bottle of Nana's pills dropped from his relaxed fist, rattled on the concrete, and rolled away in a great arc beneath the stairs. The breathing exercise worked well. He was starting to feel very relaxed.

Luke opened his eyes, startled by the pain of pins and needles in both legs. "Oww, oww!" He rolled around on the ground, punching his thighs to wake them up. *What the hell? Did I pass out?* Still feeling disoriented, Luke scanned the floor for the pill bottle. It was nowhere to be seen. "What the…?" He spun around, thinking the bottle must be behind him. Nope. Then he patted his pockets. "Aha!" He must have put it back in his pocket before he fell asleep. He pulled out the bottle and examined the little pills inside.

He was still holding the bottle when, after a few more minutes, he psyched himself up, or down, enough to stand and leave. He finally left the stairway, slowly opening the steel door that led to the lobby. No one was around. Good. He made it halfway to the front doors, the main exit, before he ran into any further trouble. Now, through the large glass panes of those very front doors, he saw a figure approaching. He really didn't want to talk to anyone right now, even if it was just to say 'Good morning' back to some nice old lady. But really, it wasn't worth running from, was it? He would be okay. It would be alright. Besides, there was nowhere to hide. He was too far away from the staircase door now. Too far from the huge ornamental fake fireplace, too. There was a couch near enough. He would have time to dive behind it, but his legs would stick out, and that would just serve to draw even more attention to himself as the person approached. They would surely start asking questions — 'Are you alright? What happened? What the hell are you doing on the floor?' That was no good.

He was too slow. The door was sliding open now as Horace approached it from the outside, making eye contact with Luke even as he butted out his cigarette in the ashtray beside the door. They nodded at each other from twenty feet away. Horace was pretty fast for a man of his age, and had reached speaking distance in seconds.

"What you got there?" he asked Luke.

"Huh?" *Oh, right.* Luke was still holding the bottle of pills. Horace nodded toward it. "Um, nothing."

"Let's see 'em. You gotta watch yourself around these pill pushers, you know. Trying to convince us we're sick so they can force more poison down our throats and make us dependent on their jacked up prices."

"No, they're just for my panic attacks."

"Panic attacks, eh? So these must be some kind of downer then?"

"Yeah, it psychs you down."

"Hmm… Lemme see one."

Not really knowing why, Luke complied to Horace's strange request, and shook one pill into his outstretched hand. Horace examined the pill's strange markings.

"It's some kinda computer code," explained Luke. "For robots."

Horace squinted at Luke, "No kidding?"

Luke nodded vigorously, "Yeah, like the elevator."

"Hmm… Modern technology…" He thought for a moment, then asked, "Mind if I try one?"

Luke shrugged. He couldn't return them to Patti now with two missing. It wouldn't be right. Horace popped the pill into his mouth and swallowed with ease, without so much as a sip of water. Luke was impressed.

"Oh, but also, you gotta breathe right with it, you know? Like this." Luke showed him the correct breathing technique with the fist-clenching and counting and everything. It was a technique he had learned from an anime years ago. Once again, Luke dropped the pill bottle when he relaxed his fists, but at least this time it hit the carpet and didn't bounce too far.

Horace breathed once. Then again. Then a third time. "Damn, sport. That actually works!"

Luke wasn't sure what to say. He just watched Horace breathe a couple more times.

"Tell you what," said Horace. "Would you take twenty for the bottle?"

"Huh?"

Horace dug into his wallet and pulled out a crisp twenty dollar bill. If the purple of the ten was beautiful, then the green of the twenty was immaculate. Luke's stomach growled. He had forgotten about the day's earlier problems. He had literally nothing on him. He had missed out on the cookie opportunity at Nana's. He had no cash, no wallet, no phone. And it had been a long day already. *What time is it?* he wondered. He could have been in the staircase for hours or minutes, he had no idea. No wonder his poor stomach was making a fuss. But still… He had to consider this carefully. He was no drug dealer. He couldn't be a bad person. These pills seemed to help Horace, though. And Luke didn't really need them. He probably wouldn't have another panic attack. After all, it had been years since the last one. He would just have to stay away from stupid Lester, and make sure he ate, and he'd be fine. Lester was the problem. Lester was a big problem. Luke felt his face flush. His pulse was rising, he just knew it. *Friggin' Lester*. No. No way. He would not let Lester win this game. He needed to psych himself down. He did the breathing thing again. When the pill bottle fell, he ignored it and kept breathing.

"You okay there, son?" asked Horace.

Luke held up his index finger, as if to say 'just one second.'

Luke managed to control himself, without panicking, or falling asleep. This was proving to be quite the effective technique, even without the pills. *Ha, I got you now, Lester!* he thought. "Okay, Horace, let's turn this thing around!" Picking up the bottle, he handed it to Horace, and took the beautiful green bill. "Don't forget to breathe," he told Horace.

"Back atcha, son. Back atcha."

8

The Bachelor

This time Luke played it smart. He spent part of the twenty dollars on groceries — bread, peanut butter, the essentials — and promised himself to be responsible with the rest of it, too. He was going to have to be careful from now on. No more extravagant spending, at least not until work picked up and he figured out this whole job thing. Luke decided to phone Scott.

"Hello? I mean... uh, Elimination — er, Eliminator Sanitation speaking."

"Hi Scott."

"Luke?"

"Yeah."

"Oh hey Luke, thanks for calling. Hey listen, I think I got something here. Back at Denecorp downtown. Tonight. Say six?"

"Yeah, great."

"Cool, I'll pick you up."

"Oh, sweet!"

"Okay see you then."

"K."

Awesome. Luke was taking care of business. Just like in that one song on the cassette tape his dad used to play during his Saturday afternoon beers in the garage. Luke hoped that this shift tonight would be as fun as last time. And as easy. He remembered his first shift as a Sanitation Eliminator with warm feelings of pride and fondness. Denecorp. Cyberdyne. Skynet. Maybe tonight he would find the room where they keep the robots. He should have kept those robot pills to feed them, he thought amusedly. *Would you care to cyber-dine with me tonight?* Luke laughed in the empty kitchen.

67

Continuing to take care of business, Luke made himself a PB&J Sandwich. Except without the J. He was never a big fan of jam. Or jelly, for that matter. It was too sticky and messy. He'd have to wash his hands way too many times. He noticed a note on the counter from Jason. 'When you're up call me — important.' This gave Luke a funny idea. He laughed again. Dialing his phone, he was doubly thankful for the lack of jam.

"Hello?"

"Hey, Jason. You're important." Luke stifled a giggle.

"Huh? You been watching Dr. Phil or something?"

"What?"

"Nevermind."

"No, *you* never mind"

"Fine, I will!"

"You mean you won't!"

They both laughed. This was a fun game they sometimes played.

"Anyway, what's up man?" said Jason.

"You told me to call you."

"Right, right. Hey listen, you know Cindy?"

Luke had no idea who Cindy was. "Umm…"

"From the building?"

Still, no clue.

"She takes the rent cheques?"

"Oh, THAT Cindy." Luke had never met her.

"Yeah, so I gave her the notice, right?"

Luke dreaded what might come next. No doubt he'd be thrown out on the street. He'd have to set up a tarp under the bushes in that shady place in the park where the happy drug dealer lives. He'd be fighting off meth-heads with his toothbrush, sharpened to a gleaming point.

Jason continued, "She said they have a one-bedroom you could have. Oh, and a bachelor too I think."

"A bachelor?"

"Yeah, I mean, that would be cheaper for sure."

"Like… as a roommate?"

"What? No. You remember I'm leaving town, right?"

"Yeah. So who's this bachelor dude?"

"Ha ha," Jason deadpanned.

"No, really. I don't think I would feel comfortable moving in with a guy I've never even met. What if he's some kind of meth-head, or a drug dealer or something?"

"Meth-heads are people too, man."

Luke was silent.

"Oh, you're serious?"

"Yeah, man. I mean, think about it. How would you feel?"

"Dude. It's a bachelor PAD. Not like, 'The Bachelor.' It means a place, man. It's a type of apartment. Like smaller than a one-bedroom."

"Huh? What's smaller than one?"

"Zero, dude. It's a zero-bedroom apartment. It's just like a kitchen and a living room."

"No bathroom? Shitty."

"Of course it has a bathroom, man."

"Okay, so it's a kitchen and a bathroom, and a living room, but no bedroom?"

"Exactly."

"Woah, cool!"

"And it's cheap too. You gotta give Cindy a call, man. But do it today, before they rent it to somebody else."

"I will, Jason. I'll do it right now. Bye!"

After hanging up, Luke immediately called Jason back to get Cindy's number, which he wrote on his arm because there was never any scrap paper around. Then he called Cindy.

"Hollyhaven Properties, Cindy speaking, how may I help you?"

"Hi Cindy, it's Luke."

"Luke?"

"Yeah, from the building."

"Umm…"

"Jason's roommate. He told me to call you right away." *Shoot, I probably could have made that into a joke. Hi, Right Away.*

"Oh, of course. Hi Luke. Thank you for calling. Jason mentioned that you may be interested in one of our single bedroom suites?"

"Or bachelors," added Luke.

"Yes, right."

"Not that I'm into that kind of thing."

"Sorry?"

"No, it's okay. It's just not how I roll, you know? But that's cool."

"So you're interested in the one-bedroom?"

"Or the bachelor."

"Uh… okay."

"But like, how much is it?"

Cindy told Luke the price for the one-bedroom and for the bachelor. Luke cringed at the numbers.

"Is there anything smaller?" *Smaller than zero bedrooms? As if, stupid!*

"I'm afraid that is our smallest suite. It's the most economical option."

Luke began to feel the panic rise in his chest once again, and he took a deep breath. He imagined himself taking a robot pill to psych himself down. His exhalation rustled loudly through the phone, sounding like dead leaves blowing along the curb the week before Halloween. It helped. The Halloween leaves danced comfortingly around the legs of the chill robot, their little jack O'lantern faces smiling up at him.

"Is everything alright?" came Cindy's voice over the crackling leaves.

"Yeah," Luke lied. "Yeah, I'm good, I just… uh… saw something…" *Lame excuse, dude!*

"Alright. Do you need some time to think about it?"

"Yeah. Good idea."

"Okay. Well, take your time. But just so you know, these vacancies typically don't last long."

Shit! "Okay. Well, thanks."

"Thank you for calling."

"Oh — I almost forgot. Hey Cindy?"

"Yes?"

"You're important!"

"Umm… Thanks."

Luke hung up. It was the perfect way to end the call. He played a video game on Jason's PS2 before work. It was nice to get his mind off his worries. He replaced his mundane real-life troubles with those of the gun-toting, drug-dealing, car-jacking hero of the game. Now *that* guy had trouble. Everybody was always trying to kill him, and the cops tried to chase him down every time he got in a car. He stole a white van that was parked in the alley where a drug deal was taking place. Then he crashed through a fence and raced along the beachfront road. The cops had not yet traced his location, and he knew he might have a chance at completing the mission. He had to go really fast though, or one of the competitor gang's thugs would beat him back to the hideout and shoot the place up. This van sucked. It was slow and unwieldy. He should have grabbed a better car, like a Corvette or something. The van was not responding well to his fast-paced analog stick maneuvers. He was on the beach now and the sand slowed him down even more. He tried to veer back up onto the highway. He hit a steep embankment and launched into the air. As it flew, the van slowly turned nose-down into a long front flip. It smashed into a billboard and crashed upside-down on top of two parked cars. One was a Corvette. But time was up. The scene cut away to the thugs pulling up to the safe house and cutting it up with machine guns. *Safe house, my ass.*

The intercom for the front door buzzed. Scott was here to pick him up for work. As Luke climbed into Scott's van, he noticed how eerily similar it was to the van from the game. Luke spent the ride over to Denecorp looking out the window trying to spot a Corvette.

Denecorp was about the same as the first time. They picked up some garbage, swept a few floors. Scott left Luke by himself while he worked in another area of the office. "Divide and conquer," he had said, mop in hand. Just as Luke was finishing his work, Scott poked his head in the doorway of the room Luke was sweeping. Luke quickly looked away from the screensaver that was bouncing around on one of the computer monitors.

"How's it going?"

"Good, good. Just finishing up here."

"Right on. So I figure we better wash all the floors this time. Trade me." Scott reached for the broom with the duct-taped handle, then disappeared with it back out into the hallway. Luke followed him out and there it was. The yellow mop bucket with the squeezy thing. Luke stared for a moment, unsure of Scott's intention.

"Well, go on," Scott encouraged.

"For real?"

"Sure."

"Woah!" Luke exclaimed. He dunked the mop and swished it around joyously like a duck in a muddy old pond, then lifted the mop gently, water rushing back down, and set it firmly into the wringer. He took a big breath then, beaming with joy, bent down to grasp the handle, which he pushed down to a gush of slightly sudsy water.

"Don't squeeze it out too much, now," Scott instructed. "It's gotta be pretty wet to wash the floor."

"Right, right." He tried again, dipping and sloshing, then squeezing — gentler this time.

"Now you've got it! Great job!" said Scott, as Luke began dragging the wet mop around the floor. "You're a natural,

Luke. I'll leave you to it." He disappeared around a corner toward the reception area.

Luke spent the next half-hour playing games with his mop. He spelled out words with wetness. He created watery pictures. His mop became a Corvette in a high speed street chase, crashing and bouncing off walls, skidding around corners, and narrowly avoiding the shots of rival gangs. Soon the floor was clean, and Scott returned.

"Alright, I guess that's it. Looks good, bud."

On the way home, Scott told Luke he was impressed by his work ethic and that he deserved a raise. He confessed that he always started employees out lower than his normal rate, "just in case." The raise would be effective next shift, so the envelope he now handed Luke was based on the old rate.

Luke took the envelope and quickly peeked inside just to confirm. Yes, it was full of cash.

"That's with no deductions — on the D.L. You good with that?" Scott asked.

"Uh. Yeah, cool," replied Luke. He remembered deductions from his previous job at the Wendy's on Lonston. He remembered how each paycheque's numbers had seemed to wither away in front of his eyes — Taxes, CPP, EI. He had only a vague idea of what it all meant: the feds were after his money. "Deductions suck!"

9

The Party

Sylvia counted the money a second time. "You're sure this is all of it?" The small stack of five dollar bills sat on her mom's dining room table. "Why is he paying you in fives anyway?"

"Yes!" Luke ignored the second question. He was almost sure it was rhetorical.

"You didn't drop some bills?"

"No, I told you I kept the envelope closed tight all the way here."

"Well, was this for just your first shift? Or is it for tonight too?"

"I dunno." It didn't happen very often, but once in a while Sylvia would start asking Luke a bunch of questions, and would get agitated when he didn't know the answers. It bothered Luke. It irritated him. It made him feel overwhelmed. But it wasn't so much that he was annoyed at Sylvia. It was more that he was annoyed that he was agitating her. It was love that was the root of the problem, really.

"Well, didn't you ask him?"

"I didn't think about it, okay?" This evening was not ending as well as it had started. He hated it when things took a turn like this. They both sat in silence for a moment.

Sylvia was frustrated at Luke's typical lack of concern. He didn't take much seriously. If she was being honest, she would have admitted that it was this very quality that had most attracted her to him. Everyone else was too uptight. Or too opinionated. Or just an asshole. But not Luke. Because he didn't care. He didn't worry about things. Things like ensuring he was being compensated fairly for his labour, for example. But it was this same quality that so often drove her to frustration.

Sylvia's phone buzzed on the table beside the cash. She usually ignored it if she was with Luke — nobody important ever texted her anyway — but she needed the distraction now. There was a Snapchat notification: "Danika sent you a snap!" *Who cares?* She swiped it open anyway. Yep, there was Danika, and a few of her friends, holding cans of beer.

"What's that?" Luke asked, hoping to change the subject.

"Just some stupid party."

"Oh." Then, a moment later, "Do you want to go?"

"Huh?"

"To the party?"

Did she want to go to a party? Not really. Why would she? Parties are so lame. She'd much rather stay home with her man any time. Well maybe not any time. Maybe not this time. Maybe it *would* be good for them to get out for a while. Maybe it would be fun. *But I doubt it,* she thought. "Do you want to go?"

"Umm… Maybe?"

"Really?" Luke hated parties even more than she did.

"I dunno. Why not?"

Why not indeed? "Why not indeed."

"Why not indeed."

~~~

The party was across town, so Sylvia borrowed her mom's car. Her mom didn't have anything to say about them going out so late, which meant she must have been really enjoying Steel Magnolias. Or had gotten far enough into her Merlot. Or both. On the way there, Luke remembered to tell Sylvia about his day — about how he had lost his phone and wallet, about Lester and Nana and his breakdown in the stairway, and about the deal with Horace and the robot pills.
~~~

"No fucking way!" exclaimed Sylvia. "You sold the pills? To Horse-face?"

"I know, right?" agreed Luke.

"No but I mean, you sold the pills? You sold Nana's pills?"

"No, it's okay, they were just extras."

"Oh, yeah! Before I forget again," started Sylvia, interrupting his thoughts, "the other bottle is still in my purse. Can you grab them, baby?"

"In your purse?" He hated digging around in there, but since she was driving, he reluctantly agreed to it. After all, they were for Nana, right? Anything for Nana.

Sylvia shook her head, still chuckling.

"Well, I wouldn't have done it, but… you know. I didn't get any breakfast. Or lunch. I really needed some money."

"You still do…"

"Exactly!"

~~~

Luke and Sylvia arrived at the party after stopping at the liquor store where Sylvia worked to buy a couple tallboys of Budweiser at a minorly discounted price. They walked onto the shabby little wooden porch and Luke knocked at the door — not his special knock, of course; he saved that for visits to Nana. They waited for a minute but no one answered.

"Just open it," Sylvia told him.

"I can't. It's impolite."

"It's a party. You just go in. No one will hear the knocks anyway." There was, in fact, very loud music coming from inside the house. The bass thumped through the front door as if knocking back from the inside. Luke tried knocking once more, a little louder this time, but Sylvia pushed past him and turned the knob, letting herself into the house.
~~~

Yes, this was a house party all right. There were strangers everywhere, standing around talking, drinking, lounging on couches, and the Spice Girls blared on the stereo like it was 1999:

Slam your body down and wind it all around
Slam your body down and wind it all around
(Huh! Huh! Huh! Huh!)

What does that even mean? Luke asked himself, for what seemed like the millionth time in his short life. Luke immediately wondered why he had wanted to come to this party in the first place. He guessed he just wanted a distraction from his woes. In the spirit of drowning sorrows, he cracked open his beer and started drinking, then noticed out of the corner of his eye a grey cat playing with a cardboard box on the carpet. It was adorable the way the cat climbed in and out of the box, clumsily flipping it over again and again as it did so. *Silly kitty,* Luke thought.

"Luke!"

He snapped out of his reverie and lowered the beer from his mouth. His can was now half empty. *Oops.*

"I said, this is my friend Laura. We used to play tee-ball together in grade seven."

"There's tee-ball in grade seven?" Luke responded.

"Yes, Luke." Sylvia was scowling a little.

"Oh."

"Nice to meet you," Laura said, reaching out to shake Luke's hand.

Luke was holding his beer in his right hand and reached out with his left. Laura, seeing this, switched hands. Luke, seeing that she was switching hands, passed his beer from his right to his left hand and offered his right to Laura. Their hands briefly floated in the air, almost touching, and seemed to flounder, Laura's finger's recoiling in cold confusion. Then

Luke clasped his right hand around her left in an awkward grip that made her very uncomfortable.

"Nice to meet you too," he said. "I played tee-ball too — in Grade three," he told her, releasing her hand.

"Oh, really?"

Sylvia was blushing from embarrassment at having witnessed this horrendous introduction. She was already wishing they had stayed home.

"Yup," Luke said proudly. "Coach said I was a tee-ball all-star. Wish I coulda made it up to Grade seven, but my parents pulled me out."

"Why's that?

Luke shrugged coolly. "'Guess they couldn't see my potential."

"Hey, have you seen Danika?" Sylvia interjected, cutting in between Laura and Luke, hoping to save herself from further embarrassment. She loved Luke, but sometimes he just didn't know how to handle himself in social settings.

Laura led Sylvia through the living room and onto the back porch, and Luke turned back to where the cat had been. *What the damned hell?* he thought. Not only had the cat disappeared, the box was nowhere in sight. Evidently, this was one industrious feline. Luke was determined to find the creature and give it a good petting. He set off into the kitchen, the closest room to where the cat had been. He scanned the linoleum floor, but saw no trace of the cat or the box. *Damn,* he thought. He crossed the kitchen, passing a group of people who smelled like body butter and marijuana, and turned down a hallway.

"Here, kitty," he whispered, tiptoeing down the hall. At the end of the hall there was a door to the outside with a cat-flap at the bottom. Luke opened the door and stepped outside.

"A-ha. There you are," he said, at last finding the cat perched among some tall grass near the side fence. "But where's your box, little guy?"

The cat meowed at just that instant, prompting Luke to consider that perhaps the cat could understand what he was saying. Maybe the cat would listen to his troubles too.

"How's life treating *you*, little guy?"

"Mrrrow."

"Yeah, same." Luke sat down on the concrete step outside the door and the cat walked up and rubbed its face against his leg.

"Thanks, man. Yeah, things are tough right now. My roommate's moving to the city, my parents are moving to Peachland-"

"Meoow."

"I *know!* And I can't afford to pay rent because Scott's not giving me enough work." He took a gulp of his beer and buried his face in his hands. "At least I'm getting a raise soon...

I don't know what I'm gonna do, cat."

The cat climbed into Luke's lap and started purring.

"Hey, you're pretty cool," Luke said to the cat as it looked up at him. He started petting the cat and the two of them sat there for several minutes while Luke finished his beer.

"Maybe things'll be alright," Luke said, staring at the night sky across the neighbor's yard. Somehow his problems seemed so insignificant as he stared at the stars in the sky. *There must be almost a million of them up there,* Luke thought.

"Who are you talking to?" a voice said, from where Luke did not know.

He lowered his gaze and looked around from side to side, then behind him. Seeing no one, his eyes widened. He looked at the cat and paused for a moment in disbelief.

"To...you," he said to the cat incredulously.

The voice laughed a young, mirthful, but mocking laugh. The cat got up and ran into the house. Then Luke noticed the face peering through the fence at him. It was a young girl, maybe eight or nine years old.

"Why are you talking to a cat?" the kid asked him.

"None of your business," Luke scowled, feeling embarrassed.

"Why aren't you talking to friends instead?"

"Why aren't you in bed?" Luke rebutted.

"I don't have a bedtime anymore," the girl responded in a proud, matter-of-fact tone.

"Well, you should."

"Why?"

Luke pondered this for a moment, taken aback by the simple question, a question for which he did not have an answer.

"I don't know," Luke admitted. "Well, where are your parents? You shouldn't be outside at night by yourself."

"My mom's asleep and my dad's in jail."

Luke nodded understandingly and gave a deep sigh. "My parents are moving to Peachland."

The girl nodded. They shared a moment of silent recognition.

"Well, I guess I should go find my girlfriend."

"I'm gonna watch TV and eat Eggos," said the girl, and she skipped away with a rustle of overgrown grass.

Luke envied this little girl. She had no responsibilities, no bedtime, no rent to pay, and a freezer full of Eggos. At least she probably did. Luke wished he had Eggos at home. Maybe with the leftovers from Horse-face's twenty he could buy some. Wait, he had a whole wad of fives to spend on Eggos! *No!* he thought suddenly. *I need to save my money to rent a bachelor.*

As he headed inside he realized he had to pee, so he found the bathroom down the hall. Returning to the hall after the completion of his business, Luke was struck by a suspicion. He suspected that the cat had entered one of the rooms off this hallway. Sure, the bedroom doors were closed, but cats were tricky like that. "Here, kitty," he whispered, pausing outside each door. He thought about opening the doors and peeking his head in, but he knew from stories of previous parties that if he did, he might be in for more than he bargained for. There might be a good reason that those doors were closed. He better find Sylvia, he determined. After all, that was why he had come inside. He walked slowly back through the kitchen, and began scanning the crowds for Sylvia. Luke thought it was weird how so many people looked the same when all you could see was the back of their heads. Everyone, it seemed, had the exact same brown hair as Sylvia.

As he walked he instinctively double-checked his fly. It was a post-bathroom habit he had acquired long ago, and it had saved him more than a few times. He hadn't forgotten to zip up in years but he still had to check. This procedure brought his attention to the bottle of pills in his pocket, which he then began to fidget with. As he passed them, the body-butter-smelling crowd were dancing in a somewhat aggressive manner, pushing each other around good-naturedly, like some kind of rave mosh-pit. A dude in a green t-shirt and a Detroit Red Wings cap came flying out the mosh-pit and slammed into Luke, nearly knocking him down. Luke grabbed the kitchen counter to catch himself, and in the process, the pill bottle clattered to the linoleum.

"Hey!" said the dude in the Red Wings cap, "What are those? Is that Molly?"

Luke ignored the dude in the Red Wings cap, but he persisted.

"Yo! Dude! Is that Molly, man?"

"No man, it's nothing." *Just some robot pills.*

"Dude! Yo, yo! I got you!" He started waving over one of his buddies.

"Fuck off! Leave me alone!" Luke jogged into the crowded living room, toward where he had last seen Sylvia.

"Yeah, there she is," he muttered to himself, and began to try to squeeze between two writhing girls and a flailing guy. For a brief moment he became lodged between the two girls as they gyrated maniacally. He felt like he was stuck against his will on one of those stupid massage chairs with the weird balls that dig into your back. *Why do they even have those?* Breaking free, he made it a few more meters toward Sylvia, before being blocked again by a veritable brick wall that was the back of an enormous football-player type. His dancing motion was extremely erratic. It seemed impossible to gauge which direction to duck to avoid the massive elbows that were already invading Luke's personal space. He called out to Sylvia. Maybe it would be easier for her to come to him. There was no response from Sylvia, so he called again, and as he did so, the girl who he had thought to be Sylvia tossed her average-length brown hair to reveal a decidedly non-Sylvia face.

"Dammit!" exclaimed Luke.

"Luke!" the real Sylvia shouted from behind him, "What the fuck are you doing? Where have you been?"

Luke whirled around to face her. "Oh, there you are!" He then remembered she had just asked him a question. Two actually. He hated it when that happened. *Which one am I supposed to answer first?* "Nothing; nowhere. Or nowhere; nothing." He sounded silly either way.

"I looked all over for you!"

Not out in the backyard. He wasn't stupid enough to say it out loud. "There was a cat."

"Jesus, Luke!"

You mean Jesus Christ. *Christ, what is wrong with me?*

"Never mind, let's go get a drink."

Luke took Sylvia's hand and followed her over toward where a couple girls were standing and chatting. He vaguely recognized them, but didn't know their names. It didn't matter. They handed Sylvia two cans of Blue Ribbon, and she passed one on to Luke. Luke nodded thanks to the one girl who barely noticed his presence, and soon became lost in thought as he swilled his beer. It wasn't that he was ignoring the girls and their conversation — although that would have been justifiable, given their near-complete disregard of him — but that he had no idea what it was they were talking about. The party was loud and overwhelming — all the voices and the music blurred into a messy and incomprehensible hum. As if that were not bad enough, the girls happened to have chosen the worst possible spot to have a conversation: right in front of a large, obviously rented, PA speaker, which was currently blasting Ke$ha, who was adamantly proclaiming that this place was about to blow. "She might be right," said Luke out loud to nobody.

He was beginning to feel the effects of the beer, and was either getting bored or feeling okay about all the noise and chaos around him — he wasn't entirely sure which. He tugged on Sylvia's sleeve in a gesture that he knew was sure to annoy her a little; but he was past caring about such minor consequences. He was tired of being alone amidst the crowd. If he was going to feel okay, he wanted to do it with Sylvia. He tugged her sleeve again.

Sylvia turned toward him, rolling her eyes. Actually, she crossed them more than she rolled them — Sylvia's ocular dexterity had always been lacking, a fact for which she had often been teased as a child — but either way the communication was clear enough. Additionally, her mouth moved in a way that looked vaguely like she was saying "What?"

Luke pointed at the speaker booming behind him, then to his ears, and then shook his head before nodding toward the kitchen.

"Fine," Sylvia's mouth appeared to say.

They walked across the living room and through the kitchen, and just far enough into the hallway so that it was almost quiet enough to hear each other.

"I think I want to go," said Luke.

"We've only been here for like a half hour!" Sylvia whined.

"I know, but... Like. It's really loud. And the cat got away. And that dude over there knocked into me, and I coulda been seriously hurt, cuz like, look at how sharp the corner of that counter is, and he wanted to buy my pills, and I thought he might try to steal them, and then that other big guy back there nearly took my head off with his crazy elbows, and then..." Luke had reached the end of his list of bullshit excuses. *And then no one talked to me,* he almost added, but it would have seemed way too whiny. He wasn't a baby.

"How much was he gonna give you for the pills?"

"What? I don't know. That's not the point!"

"What did he say exactly?"

"He asked me if I had molly."

"He thought your pills were molly?"

"I guess, maybe."

"Geez. Let me see that bottle."

Luke handed her the bottle and she poured a couple pills out into her hand to inspect them.

"But look, they're robot pills, see?" Luke pointed out the binary code imprinted into the tablets.

"Hmm," Sylvia grunted. "Which guy was it?"

"Over there, with the Red Wings hat."

"Those shitheads? Oh, yeah. This could work." Suddenly, she was off to talk to the smelly dude in the Red Wings cap. She returned after a brief exchange, by which it should be understood that Sylvia and the dude in the Red Wings cap exchanged a few words, and also exchanged goods and payment.

Sylvia chuckled. "Those suckers are so drunk, they'll never know they got duped!"

"What happened, Syl?"

"I just sold those idiots your 'robot pills' for five bucks a pop!" She waved five shiny blue bills at Luke, who grabbed at them. "Yeah, go ahead and add those to your envelope. You need 'em more than I do at this point."

"Hey! Cool!"

"You know what? I probably coulda got more than that, too. The guy was acting like it was a great deal. I shoulda gone for ten each."

"Next time…" said Luke.

"Yeah, next time," agreed Sylvia. "Hey, maybe if we hang around longer, we could sell a few more."

"You think so, Syl?"

"Sure, why not?"

Sure enough, they stayed at the party another hour, and had another beer that another group of acquaintances of Sylvia's offered them. And they only sold three more pills, but they got ten bucks each for them, so all in all, they considered the night a success.

10

That was Easy

Luke heard a knock at the apartment door the next morning and, groaning and stretching on his floor mattress like a jungle cat, he prepared himself to rise. "Hang on," he shouted in the direction of the door. He stood up and pulled on a pair of faded jeans. The knock repeated. *Who could it be?* Luke wondered. *The Landlord? No, Jason paid the rent. Scott? The police? Shit! Did they find out about the drugs?* Luke started panicking as he rifled through his clean clothes pile for a collared shirt. He figured if it *was* the cops, he should look as presentable as possible. *But wait,* he thought. *There were no drugs. Just ADHD pills. We never broke the law.* Relieved but still hesitant, he left his bedroom and walked to the door to peer through the peephole. It was Sylvia. *Thank God!*

"Hey, Syl," he chimed, opening the door. "What are you doing here?"

"I've been thinking," she said with a determined air.

Luke's face dropped. *Is this 'The Talk?'* he wondered with horror. He had heard rumours about this back in elementary school. "What about?" he asked timidly.

"About last night. And our money problems."

"What about 'em?" Luke sat down on the couch and Sylvia stood across the coffee table from him.

"That was the easiest forty bucks I ever made, Luke. And I can do it again. I mean, *we* can do it again."

Luke squirmed in his seat. "I don't know, Syl. It seems wrong lying to people like that."

"Luke, only bad people do drugs, right?"

"Right. Well, hard drugs."

"Of course."

"Bob Marley's not a bad person," Luke said defensively.

"Of course not," Sylvia complied. "But a lot of these people aren't like Bob Marley."

Luke nodded.

"A lot of these people are like Rob Ford."

Luke nodded more fervently, as if understanding completely.

"So it's not a bad thing to lie to them. In fact, we're actually helping them by keeping them off the real drugs."

This was starting to make some sense to Luke. "Okay, but I only have a few left."

"So we get more." She pulled a piece of paper from her pocket and handed it to Luke.

It was a prescription just like Nana's, but instead of Nana's name it read "Gallagher, Francine." That was Sylvia's mom's name.

"Looks legit, right?"

"Whaddya mean?"

"I made this. I typed it up and printed it and copied the signature. It's for my mom's antifungal medication."

"Gross." Luke dropped it on the coffee table.

"But here's the thing," Sylvia said. These pills don't look like party drugs. They're too big and they say 'Lamisil' on them. No one's gonna buy them. So…"

"So what?"

"We should go visit Nana today."

~~~

Back at Willow Lodge, Luke and Sylvia walked down the hallway's red carpet toward Nana's apartment. He had never noticed it before, but now Luke saw that the carpet had a perplexing pattern in a slightly darker red. To Luke, it looked like a bunch of snakes all slithering around and through each other. Or maybe like a big plate of spaghetti noodles. Or like some kind of drunken spider web. *A web of lies,* Luke thought,
~~~

sighing. He was having his doubts about this plan, but he had to trust Sylvia's judgement. He knew that trust is the foundation of a strong relationship. His nana had told him that once.

Knock knock kno-knock knock. As they waited for Nana, Luke forced a smile, reassuring himself that everything would be fine. *Oh no.* A thought suddenly dropped into Luke's mind like a great big ice cube in a large cup of Sprite, making splashes and unsettling it with its frigid crackling. *What if Lester's here again? What if Lester's here STILL?! Oh, God!*

But the door creaked open and there was Nana, sweet dear Nana, standing alone in her dusty pink cardigan and her indoor sandals. Her face lit up when she saw her grandson. "Luke," she said warmly. "Come in, dear. Hello, Sylvia. How are you?"

"Hi, Nana," Luke and Sylvia said in unison.

"How is your day going?" Sylvia asked through a plastic smile. She was all sunshine and sugar today. She was on a mission.

"Oh, just fine, just fine." Nana eased herself into her chair and turned to Luke. "I was afraid you would never come back after the other day." She smiled teasingly.

"Whaaat?" Luke said. "Nah, I just had to go to the bathroom. It was no biggie." *She has a bathroom in her suite, dummy. Nice excuse.* "And I was late," he added. *Late for what?* "For swimming lessons." *What are you talking about?*

Nana nodded, still smiling. "Of course."

She bought it. Luke felt a wave of relief followed by a pang of regret. *I just lied to Nana!* He had never done that before, not that he could remember. He felt awful about it, especially considering her deteriorating mental condition. Would this lie be the final confusion that would push Nana's frail psyche to its breaking point?

The three of them sat and talked as they had so many times before, but this time it was different. It was sullied by ulterior motives. Luke felt slimy. After a lull in the conversation, Sylvia saw her opportunity. "Nana, how has your health been?"

"Oh, well, you know, I'm getting old, Sylvia. I still have this nausea on the elevator and my wrist gets a pain when I write. It's gotten so bad I had to stop playing Bingo."

"Do you need us to get any other medication for you?" Sylvia asked eagerly.

"No, not just now. But thank you, dear."

"Well, do the pills seem to be working?" Sylvia asked.

Nana shook her head, "No, I don't think so. And besides, they make me so sleepy."

"Maybe you should ask the doctor for a different prescription," she suggested.

"Well, maybe you're right," Nana said.

"I'll call and make you an appointment right now," Sylvia told her, standing up for the phone.

"The number is on the fridge, dear."

By now Luke was distracted by Sylvia's ploy. On the one hand, he admired her cunning, industrious nature. On the other hand, he couldn't help but feel she was exploiting Nana. But back on the first hand, this was the woman who was going to help him pay his rent. Surely Nana wouldn't be upset about that.

"Luke, maybe you can help me with these last pieces."

Huh? Luke looked up. Nana was gesturing toward an almost-finished jigsaw puzzle of a steep white cliffside next to the sea.

"My wrists are acting up again, and you know how bad my eyes are getting. I spent all morning working away at it. I'm so close to the end now, I just need a little help."

"Sure, Nana. No problem." Luke started scanning the stray fragments of sky, rock, and sea scattered on Nana's coffee table, quickly becoming absorbed in his new puzzle.

"Alright, he'll come by tomorrow at ten o'clock, Nana. We'll come and bring the prescription down to the pharmacy for you afterward."

"Oh, you don't have to do that again. I can go down myself."

"It's no problem, Nana. We were going to come visit you anyway…"

"But you're visiting me no–"

" –because we can't stay long today," Sylvia continued, looking at Luke. In fact, we should get going, shouldn't we?"

Luke nodded. "Uh, yeah I guess we should. See you tomorrow, Nana." He placed a piece in the cliff before standing up and giving Nana a hug.

"Oh, alright, well thanks for stopping by. You two are such darlings. I'm so lucky to have you both."

"See you tomorrow, Nana," Sylvia smiled as she closed the door behind her and Luke. As they set off down the hall, Luke stared at the red carpet.

"I just feel kinda dirty about this," Luke said to Sylvia as he stared out the window of her mom's Pontiac.

Sylvia was humming along to a pop song on the radio. "Stop worrying," she told him. "Hey, remember what Bob Marley said."

"Stand up for your right?"

"What? No. Look, Luke. Do you want to stay a loser all your life?"

Luke turned his head around. "What do you mean?"

"Forget it."

Luke frowned and slid his hands under his thighs.

"Let's just go back to your place and snuggle and eat Pizza Pops."

"I'm all out," Luke said, pouting. He pulled out his phone. Maybe it was finally time to change his ringtone. All the small things were starting to annoy him.

Sylvia looked at him with a slight disdain and shook her head a little. Her voice was sharp and stern. "You better get yourself out of this funk of yours, Luke. We got a big day tomorrow."

~~~

Luke did get himself out of that funk of his. The next morning, as he stared into the empty box of Pizza Pops cemented to the bottom of his fridge freezer, the only thoughts in his head were of money and success. Sylvia was going to pick him up and the two of them were going to drive to Willow Lodge in time for Nana's appointment. Then they would be on the road to fortune — just him and his girl, making money, cornering the fake party drug market, moving up in the world.

Luke's phone buzzed and began playing the theme song to Transformers. He answered the phone.

"Luke?"

"What's up, baby?"

"My mom's car won't start!"

"What? Shoot!"

"I don't know how to fix it. We're gonna be late for the doctor."

Luke thought for a moment, scanning his brain for any traces of information about cars.

"Does it turn on?"

"No, Luke! That's the problem!"

Luke winced, feeling stupid. "I mean, does it turn... over?"

"What does that mean?"

"Um."

Sylvia sighed heavily.

"Maybe it's the battery?" Luke suggested. Luke, who had not driven a car since he was sixteen years old, was impressed with himself for remembering about the battery. He
~~~

had always considered it deceptive that cars, which run on gasoline, actually use electricity too. *Robots in disguise,* he thought.

"We'll have to take the bus. I'll meet you there ASAP."

"Okay, baby. Love you."

"Love you too. Bye."

Luke walked to the bus stop and waited until the bus arrived, feeling a little worried that he was already too late. What if Nana got her prescription filled before they got there? He doubted it, but there was always the possibility. The bus pulled up. It wasn't Hans. This was an earlier bus than he was used to. As he stepped on, he nodded to the strange bus driver, who faintly scowled at him. Then he took a seat at the back.

All the way to the Lodge, Luke daydreamed about him and Sylvia in a new bachelor apartment, wallowing in a pile of crisp twenty dollar bills. The cash was knee-deep, and he fell back into it and began swimming a backstroke and squirting money from his mouth like a whale spouting water. He became so enraptured in this fantasy that he almost missed his stop. Back on the sidewalk, he took up a brisk pace, only once getting distracted by a zig-zagging line of ants, and arrived at the Lodge. There he found Sylvia waiting for him, arms crossed, evidently uncomfortable to be near all the seniors lumbering about the front entrance.

"It's five-to," she said. "Let's get up there."

And so they did, after a quick hello from Luke to Tracy at the reception desk. They arrived at Nana's apartment just after Dr. Liard, who had left the door open a crack and was asking Nana about her drowsiness.

"And how sleepy does it make you?" he asked.

"Oh," Nana replied. "Well, quite sleepy. But I suppose not so sleepy that I need to sleep right away. Just so sleepy that I start to think about sleeping and that if I was on the sofa watching the TV, for instance, I might doze off."

"And do you spend a lot of time on the sofa?"

"Oh, only when I feel sleepy, really."

"And how often do you feel sleepy?"

"Well, only when I take my pills. And before I go to sleep at night." And so on.

Sylvia knocked twice in rapid succession before opening the door further to let her and Luke enter the room.

"Oh, hi Lukie! Hi, Sylvia."

"Hi Nana. Is this the doctor?"

"Peter Liard." The doctor reached out his hand toward Luke, who took it.

"Oh. I'm Luke," he responded. "Sorry, I thought you might be the doctor." Then, turning to Nana and covering his mouth with his hand quite conspicuously, he mouthed, "Who's this guy?"

"This is the doctor," Nana mouthed back with a wry smile.

"What?" Luke said out loud. "Well, the doctor should be here any minute, so I'm sorry, Peter, but would you mind–"

"Luke, he *is* the doctor," Sylvia cut in.

"What?" Luke snapped to Peter Liard and performed a complete top-to-bottom visual scan.

"I'm the doctor," the doctor said.

"What?"

"I'm your grandma's doctor."

"I thought you said your name was Peter."

There was a pause during which Luke's stomach made a faint but definitely audible gurgling noise.

"My name *is* Peter."

Sylvia, dumbfounded, spoke up: "Luke, what does that have to do with…"

"What? Oh yeah." Luke felt foolish. His cheeks turned crimson. "Well, he's not even wearing a steposcope."

"A what? A stethoscope?"

"Yeah… I have to go to the bathroom." And with that Luke walked briskly down the hall to the bathroom and closed the door. He didn't really need to go, but he sat on the toilet anyway until the doctor finished with Nana and left.

When he reentered the living room, Sylvia shot him a nasty glance, from which he averted his eyes.

"Well, how'd it go?" he asked with a contrived confidence.

"Well, he's having me go onto a new medication."

"Perfect!" Luke exclaimed. Sylvia shot him another look. "I mean, hopefully this one will be better, Nana."

"Yes, I hope so."

"Well, we better go get this filled for you," Sylvia suggested, turning toward the door.

"Oh, but you only just got here!" Nana beckoned her to sit on the couch.

"We'll come right back and visit for a while."

"Oh, alright. Well, why don't I just come down with you? I could use the exercise anyway."

Luke and Sylvia collectively panicked. The plan was in jeopardy. Luke tried to defuse the situation: "You don't need exercise, Nana. You look great!"

"Thanks, Lukie. But the doctor just said–"

"Don't listen to him," Luke said. "You're already very healthy. Well, I mean, listen to him about the drugs — I mean, pills — just not about… I mean."

Sylvia shook her head slightly in disappointment. "We probably have to go somewhere else anyway," she said, picking up the prescription lying on the coffee table and pretending to inspect it. "Ahh, yep. There's no way they'll have this stuff here at the lodge. I'll go to the pharmacy at Shoppers. Luke can stay and visit, though. Right, Luke?"

"Sure thing, baby!"

"Oh, alright," Nana said.

So Sylvia left the lodge and took the bus back to her mom's house, the whole way holding the prescription securely in her left hand. After making sure no one was home, she logged onto her mom's computer and meticulously copied every detail of the little slip of paper onto a new document until she had created a near-identical prescription. She printed it and carefully cut it to size. There was only one thing missing: the doctor's signature. Taking one of her mom's special gel pens from the desk drawer, she caught a glance of her mom's Virgin Mary mousepad — those serene blue eyes looked for an instant like Nana's and Sylvia momentarily felt the sting of their judgement. But she shook off this feeling and continued with her task. There was nothing to feel bad about. Even if what she was doing *was* wrong, Jesus had already died for all her sins. She raised the pen above the line on the paper and held the real prescription next to her copy, studying the doctor's signature with a furrowed brow. Then, when she felt confident, when she knew exactly which motions she would need to make, she brought the tip of the pen to the paper, marking the blank line with a bold "P," a slanted "L," then a frenzied flourish before lifting her pen and surveying her work. Yes, it was perfect.

Sylvia hopped on the next bus and rode across town toward the Lodge feeling deliciously devious, imaging herself as some kind of super spy. She entered the lodge and felt almost immune to the draining, envious gazes of the decrepit residents — almost immune. At the pharmacy she waited a good six feet behind a hunchbacked old woman wearing Crocs and a purple fleece vest. With her hand in the pocket of her hoody, clutching the real prescription which Dr. Liard had written, Sylvia watched the old woman struggle to pick up all her meds, along with several chocolate bars she had bought, from the counter, while Patti tried to help her by placing them into a plastic bag.

"No, no. I don't need that," the woman was saying. "On TV they're saying the bags are bad for the sharks."

"The sharks?"

"Yes, they get their snouts stuck in the loops. My grandson is in university to be a marine biologist and..."

Blah, blah, blah, Sylvia thought. *Hurry up, you old crone.* As the old woman finally staggered off, Sylvia made a split-second decision and, letting go of the prescription, she reached into her back pocket and pulled out the fake.

"Hello," she crooned sweetly. "I need to fill this for my Nana Esther."

"Oh, Esther. I love Esther," Patti said.

I know, Sylvia thought, annoyed that Patti did not seem to remember her from the other day. Panic mounted as Sylvia handed the piece of paper to Patti. She tried her best to look calm and natural. Patti glanced at the paper and then placed it in a tray on the counter behind her.

"It'll be a few minutes," she said.

"No problem." Sylvia sat in a chair by the wall and watched Patti out of the corner of her eye. Once, she picked up the paper and looked at it and Sylvia's heart jolted. But a second later she placed it back in the tray and disappeared into another room for a while. Then finally she emerged and approached the front counter with the medication.

"Here you go, hon. Tell Esther I said hi."

"Will do," Sylvia said, snatching the little white bag before scurrying down the hall, pulling the orange bottle from the bag and looking inside. *They're perfect,* she thought. They looked just like the pills she sold to the guy at the party. They looked just like party drugs, or at least they did to Sylvia, who had never touched a drug in her life.

It had worked. On the one hand, she wasn't surprised. On the other hand, she couldn't believe it had been so easy. Sylvia brought Nana her medication, sat down on the couch next to Luke and made small talk. Riding the peak of her thrilling success, she found Nana somehow more tolerable than usual. All the while Luke glanced nervously at his girlfriend, wondering whether she had successfully copied the prescription, whether the duplicate was at that very moment folded in her pocket. After their visit, Sylvia and Luke said their goodbyes and set off down the hall.

"Did you do it?" Luke whispered at a speaking volume. Sylvia just smirked. "You got it?" Luke looked down at the carpet as they walked toward the elevator.

On the sidewalk, out of earshot of the seniors, Luke and Sylvia discussed their next move.

"Okay, now we go to a different pharmacy and get the real prescription filled," Sylvia said determinedly.

"The real prescription?"

"Yeah. I used the fake one on Patti. She couldn't tell the difference."

"You lied to Patti?" Luke was upset.

"Just a little white lie, Luke. It's all a part of the plan."

"But you said we were only gonna lie to bad people."

Sylvia frowned. "What is your obsession with other women?"

"What? It's not like that," Luke pleaded. "I only love you, baby. Forever and ever!" He reached for her hand and she pulled it away and turned aside.

"How can you say you love me when you don't even trust me to take care of us?"

"I *do* trust you, baby! I'm sorry." He truly was. Sylvia slowly turned back to face him and took his hand.

"Okay, but from now on you need to trust me *completely*. Can you do that, Lukie?"

"Of course I can, Syl! You're my one and only."

At the pharmacy in Superstore, Luke stood awkwardly behind Sylvia as she spoke to the man behind the counter, who was explaining to her that they did not have Nana's insurance information on file.

"So I can't pick up her medication?" she asked, flustered.

"Well, you can, but the cost won't be covered," the man gently explained. Sylvia asked what the cost would be without insurance and the man rang it up on his computer. "Ninety-seven thirty," the man told her.

"What?! We can't afford that!"

"I'm sorry about that. Does your grandma *have* health insurance?"

Sylvia looked at Luke, who shrugged.

"Maybe you should give her a call. I'm sure they'll have all her information wherever she normally gets her prescriptions filled."

"Okay," Sylvia sighed. "Thanks, I guess."

"I don't get it," Luke said as they walked away, past the shelves of toothpaste and deodorant. "I used to come here all the time with my mom when she got her meds, and it was always free."

"They must have her insurance plan information on file, or whatever. I should have known better."

"Then we can just go back to the Lodge," Luke suggested.

Sylvia shook her head. "Get two identical prescriptions filled one right after the other? It would be too suspicious. Patti can't be *that* dumb."

Luke and Sylvia were in a bit of a pickle. This was an obstacle they had not been prepared for.

~~~

As they walked back to the bus stop, Luke's thoughts once again turned to money. It always came down to cold hard cash, it seemed. Now, instead of swimming in bills, he was watching his imaginary cash swirl down the drain. He was always broke. Always had been. But it had never been such a big issue until now. *Mo money, mo problems*, he thought. He had never really understood that quote, but for some reason it crossed his mind often.
~~~

"Okay," Sylvia interrupted his train of thought, "we can make this work."

Luke looked at her expectantly. Sylvia had always been good at having good ideas.

"If we had a hundred bucks, we could get the pills. And we already know we can easily make a hundred bucks by selling just a few pills at a party — and in this town it should be easy enough to find a party whenever we need one. We know where to get the pills, and we know how to sell them once we have them, so all we need to do is get just *a few* pills to sell at the next party, and then we can go fill the prescription to get more."

Luke stopped walking. "Oh yeah, you're right, baby!" He began to turn back the way they came.

"Where are you going?"

"Back to the… I thought…"

"Not back there. They only do it in the batches that the doctor tells them to. The hundred dollar batches. We need just a small batch first. Just a few pills."

Luke stared blankly.

"We can't buy a small batch, but tomorrow we can buy as many as we want. Then we can give back whatever we borrowed."

"Borrowed? Tomorrow? Who's gonna let us borrow pills?"

"I know someone who has plenty of them, and it wouldn't be a problem at all to lend us a few just for the night."

"Who?"

"Someone who just got a fresh batch with enough to last all month."

"Who, Syl?"

"Nana, silly!"

"No way."

"Come on, Luke! What's the problem?"

"I'm not stealing from Nana."

"Not stealing! We're just borrowing them and we'll give them back tomorrow. She won't even notice that they're gone."

"Well…" He considered it. Sylvia was right, of course. It wasn't stealing if you gave it back. And Nana did have a lot of pills. Maybe too many. Wasn't it dangerous to have that many in one place? What if she accidentally took too many? "I guess it's okay, as long as we give them back right away."

"Of course we will, Luke. And that means we get to have two extra visits with Nana."

"Yipee!"

~~~

By the time Luke and Sylvia rode the bus back to Sylvia's place to grab a few Ziploc bags, then back to Willow Lodge, then back to Sylvia's house again to make some Kraft Dinner, Luke was starving and exhausted. He slumped onto the couch and just stared at the photos on the wall.

"It's ready," said Sylvia from the kitchen.

Luke barely managed to drag himself off the couch and into the kitchen. The cheesy aroma invigorated just enough to arrive at the counter, where his bowl of macaroni waited for him. When he picked it up it felt almost too heavy to carry. For a second, he thought he should ask Sylvia to carry the bowl to the table for him, but then he thought better of it, and he mentally pep-talked himself just enough to manage the task himself. The thought of those delicious orange tubes of heavenly goodness was enough to get him through nearly any trial. A few spoonfuls later, his body was beginning to refuel and he felt a bit more like himself. He suddenly became aware of Sylvia's presence across the table from him. She had been unusually quiet. She was doing something on her phone, probably texting, Luke guessed from the way her fingers tapped at it. Sylvia wasn't one of those people who were always texting
~~~

their friends. She did have friends, Luke was fairly certain, but they weren't big into texting.

"Whatcha doin?" Luke asked.

"Trying to see if there's any parties tonight."

"Oh. Right." Luke had forgotten about that particular aspect of the plan. The idea of having to go out again was not one he relished. Maybe he could stay home and Sylvia could go to the party on her own. No, that wouldn't be good. He could never do that to her. Besides, he wasn't even home. He couldn't stay here at Sylvia's mom's house. She didn't even have any beer in the fridge.

"Well, how's that going?"

"A bit hard to say."

"You on findaparty.com?"

"Huh? Is that a thing?"

"I don't know."

Sylvia checked. "Nope."

"Did you spell it right?"

"Yeah."

"Huh. Weird." Now that he thought about it, Luke could have sworn that findaparty.com was a real website. He could even picture its homepage. It would ask permission to use your phone's location, then it would open up a map with a bunch of pins representing the parties happening in your area. There would be a drop-down menu where you could choose to search for parties happening just that night or for the whole week. There would be this purple logo that said 'findaparty.com' but the 'i' was a beer bottle, and if it remembered you were underage the beer bottle would turn into a balloon or something. It would be sweet. But apparently it wasn't real. He must have just made the whole thing up.

"Whatever. I'm just texting a bunch of people."

"Does anybody know anything?"

"Generally, no. And they don't know about any parties either."

Luke laughed. Sylvia's phone vibrated.

"OK, wait. Maybe I spoke too soon." She waited a few seconds as someone was typing.

"Yeah, sounds like maybe there is something. Not sure where yet." There were a few more rapid fire vibrations. "Oh yeah. Okay, a bunch of people just found out about one. It's at Shirley's place!? What the hell? I was just talking to her and she straight up denied it!"

Luke was sad. He and Sylvia had this joke that they always made together: whenever Shirley's name came up, one of them would say, 'Surely you jest.' It was one of their favorite jokes. He wanted so badly to say it now, but he thought it would have been rude to ignore Sylvia's indignation. Shirley had just lied to Sylvia, and Sylvia was pissed. He had to have her back. "That bitch!"

"Luke!"

Shit. He had gone too far.

"Don't call my friend a bitch! What the hell is wrong with you?"

He didn't know what was wrong with him. He never used that word. It was disrespectful to women in general. That wasn't his style at all. *I better cut back on the hip-hop,* he thought. It was a bad influence. *I gotta get back into the Blink-182.* "Sorry baby," he mumbled.

"Well, speak of the devil! Guess who just texted back?"

"Um. I don't know." How should he know? It could be anybody. And the devil wasn't much of a clue. What was that even supposed to mean?

"It's Shirley. She said she just decided to have a party after all."

"Surely you jest."

They both cracked up laughing.

<center>~~~</center>

Shirley's house was nicer than Luke had expected. He stood in the kitchen, surrounded by exuberant young adults. He bobbed his head to the beat of some indie pop tune as he looked around him. The kitchen sink had one of those fancy faucets that you could take off and hold in your hand, connected by a flexible hose that lived in a hole and disappeared under the counter. Luke had always imagined what it must be like to rinse your dishes off with one of those. "Cool, check it out," he said to no one in particular. Then he noticed the window above the sink, and through it, on a well-lit patio in the dim twilight, the hot tub. "Whoa! Awesome!" He looked around for Sylvia and located her across the impromptu dance floor, standing amidst a small group of rich-looking kids. He signalled toward the window with his thumb, and silently mouthed the words "hot tub," his eyebrows raised. She totally didn't see him. Instead she shook hands with one of the rich kids, a curly-haired blond guy in a windbreaker. Suddenly the guy was holding a small ziploc bag and motioning energetically to his buddies, and Sylvia was walking toward Luke.

"Syl, Syl, check it out. They have a hot tub! Did you bring your bathing suit?"

"You know I didn't, Luke! What, like I keep it in my purse?" It was possible. Sylvia had all kinds of things stored away in there. "Besides, you don't have yours either. And anyway, we're leaving."

"We are? We just got here." Luke hadn't even had a chance to think about who to approach to bum a beer off of. And no one appeared too eager to be offering any time soon. Everybody was engaged in conversation or dancing.

"Yeah, I sold the pills, so we can go. Unless you wanna stay for a bit. I guess we could."

"Wow, that was fast! Um, no. We should go I guess. Uh, just let me... wash my hands real quick." Luke turned toward the sink. "Haha, sweet!" Luke said. Hearing the spray of the detachable faucet, Sylvia attempted to roll her eyes.

11

Bread Flickies

Luke slept in, missing both breakfast and lunch, which actually worked out in his favour, because there was no food in the apartment. Well, almost no food. On the counter where he left them yesterday, sat half a loaf of white bread and an open jar of peanut butter. But Luke had been unable to find a knife, or a spoon, or any kind of utensil at all. Jason had started packing up to move. There was a pile of boxes stacked in the corner of the living room, and the apartment now had a sort of ghost town feel to it. It was likely that one of these boxes had food in it, but Luke just didn't feel right about going through Jason's stuff, now that it was all boxed up.

Luke grabbed two slices of bread and closed the bag back up with that little plastic clippy thing that bread bags have. He knew that the correct term for this clippy thing was actually "bread flicky." He knew that if you bent one of them down the middle and snapped it into two halves, the little half-hole fit around your fingertip. Then you could flick it off and it would sail gloriously across the room. It was way better than a paper airplane or even a finger-snapped bottle-cap. Luke couldn't resist a good bread flicky. He put down the two slices of bread on the counter, removed the bread flicky, and folded the bread bag back underneath the loaf to keep it closed. It was kind of crazy to think that the flicky could have just sat there pointlessly for days on end, just waiting for its freedom, it's moment of destiny, that few seconds of airborne greatness.

He took a slow breath and began his preparation, relishing the tiny 'snap' it released as it broke into two perfectly formed flickies. Placing one on his right index finger, he regarded the other half with a dubious intrepidity. Should he risk it? Should he attempt firing both at once? He had tried it many times before, and always with calamitous results. He had pretty much ruled out the one handed double barrelled approach. This was where a flicky would be loaded onto both the index finger and the middle finger at the same time. He had such great hopes for this method when he originally invented it, but it had proved impossible. There was no way to achieve adequate tension on the pre-launch phase, and the flickies inevitably punted lamely off at low velocity, landing only a few feet away.

The two fisted gunslinger, though, was another matter entirely. It had all the tried and true advantages of the standard single-handed method. Luke knew it had to work. He just needed to keep practicing. Maybe today would be the day that it would pay off. He had to try it. He loaded up the right finger, as usual. Now came the slightly trickier part, loading up the left hand while keeping the right finger loaded. It was not for the faint of heart, nor the feeble. It took a steady hand and mind, and Luke drew upon the power of his ninja breathing skills. He was in the zone. The energy of the ancients coursed through his veins. The bread flicky seemed to click into place upon his finger. Time slowed to a crawl and slowly spiralled around Luke, his bread-flicky-clad fingers consuming all his focus as the rest of the universe faded into a hazy background of swirling mist. The mist rose like thick smoke from a smouldering cigarette projecting proudly from the dry lips of an aged, wizened face. *It psychs you down,* croaked the old wizard. His voice seemed to echo around Luke as he raised his hands and positioned them in front of his chest, taking careful aim. Across the vast plain of battle, the drug-addled robot-elevator reared its grinning head and began powering up for an attack. The bread flickies began to glow with the secret square-root insignia.

The robot shot first — a beam of deadly ones and zeros aimed straight at Luke's head. But Luke countered, launching the bread flickies with perfect timing and precision. His projectiles sliced through the binary beam as if it were nothing, sending shards of digits scattering, and pasting the walls with a sickly electric glow. The flickies continued on and struck home, hitting the robot squarely in both eyes and knocking its head clean off its body. "Yes! Take that you stupid robot!" Luke screamed out loud, as he spun about performing drop kicks and air punches.

Exhausted from the fray, he grabbed the slices of bread and sat down on a box in the living room. The box, being empty, an unused leftover from Jason's packing, wasted no time in collapsing beneath Luke, depositing him quickly on his ass, atop a couple layers of flattened cardboard. The jarring blow reminded Luke of a lesson he had learned in the past — that cardboard boxes are not great furniture. This in turn reminded him that along with being furniture-less, he would soon be homeless unless he firmed up the plans for his new bachelor pad. He had to call Sandy right away. *Sandy?* That didn't seem right. What was her name? Summer? Santa? *No, no!* But it was okay, she would say her name when she answered the phone.

He grabbed his phone, which he noticed was almost out of battery, and glanced at his arm where he had written the number. It was gone! The ink had worn off of his skin, leaving nothing but a few faded scribbles. He called Jason instead. To Luke's relief, he answered right away. "Hey Jason."

"Hey, Luke. What's up, man?"

"Hey, good. I mean, uh. You know that bachelor girl? I mean the lady from the building thing?"

"You mean Cindy? Yeah, did you get that all sorted out?"

"Well, not quite yet. I need to phone her back, do you have her number again?"

Jason gave Luke Cindy's digits. "Oh by the way," he continued, "you might as well keep your mattress. I'm not gonna need it."

Luke had forgotten about the fact that his mattress actually belonged to Jason. He had even less furniture than he had given himself credit for. "Oh! Cool man, thanks a lot!" At least he had one furniture item now. Or two, if you counted the crushed cardboard box he was still sitting on. "Oh! What about the blankets? Can I keep those too?"

"The blankets? On your bed? Those aren't mine, man. Didn't your mom give those to you?"

Maybe she did. Luke honestly had no idea. "Oh yeah, you're right!"

Luke saved Cindy's number and name into his phone, then dialed her up.

"Hollyhaven Properties, Cindy speaking, how may I help you?"

"Hi Cindy!" Luke beamed to himself, figuring Cindy would be pretty impressed that he remembered her name.

"Hi Luke, how are you?" she asked.

"Pretty good. So anyway, I'll take it!"

"Oh good. Which one?"

"The Bachelor, of course. I'm still single after all!" As soon as he said it he was filled with guilt. What a terrible thing to say. He wasn't, like, *single* single. He was totally taken, and happily so. He wasn't trying to give the wrong impression. *Shit!* "I mean, not single like that. I have a girlfriend, you know. Her name's Sylvia. She's the greatest girl in the whole wide world, too. You'll love her, don't worry."

"Sure, 106." There were scratching sounds as Cindy wrote something down. "Now as far as availability... When were you thinking?"

What the? Is she hitting on me? Even after he had tried to explain himself and his situation? What more could he say to make it clear?

"Luke?"

"I... uh..." he stammered.

"It's actually vacant currently, so I suppose I could let you move in any time, really."

"Oh!" *Thank god!* "Yeah I knew that's what you meant! Yeah totally, I could move in anytime! Sure!"

"Okay great…"

"Yeah, cool! Bye." Even as he hung up the phone, he was already looking around the room to see if there were any other empty boxes. He needed to start packing right away.

Finding only one box, he took it to his bedroom and started throwing stuff into it. It was full before he knew it, and there was still junk all over the room. He walked around the apartment again, double checking for more boxes. He managed to find a few big black garbage bags, and the one crushed box which he had sat on. He figured he could repair it. But with only two boxes, he might have to try a new strategy. He dumped out the box he already packed onto the bed, then sorted its contents. The clothes he threw into a garbage bag, and the other stuff he tossed into the box — he knew that pointy things like pencils and comic books would just rip the bag open. A minute later he dumped out the box a second time, after realizing that some of the stuff he had put in there was just garbage. He sorted through the pile again, separating out empty beer cans and potato chip bags into a separate garbage bag for actual garbage. He found a couple of his old Game Boy cartridges, which stirred up fond memories, and though it made him sad to throw them away, he could see no point in keeping them. He hadn't seen the Game Boy itself in years. A pile of old X-Men comic books, which were pretty ripped up, could probably go too. There were also a lot of pencils for some reason. Luke decided he probably didn't need that many pencils. Then he decided he probably didn't need *any* pencils. But this knowledge proved to be a dilemma. He didn't want to waste precious box space with stuff he didn't need, but he couldn't throw the pencils into the garbage because they would almost certainly rip the bag. He was starting to feel stressed out. He didn't have time for this kind of conundrum. If only Sylvia were here. She would know what to do. He decided he better call her.

"Hey Syl!"

"Hi Luke."

"Whatcha doing?"

"I'm working on this prescription thing. On my mom's computer."

"Oh cool! How's it looking?"

"Well, really good actually. You know how we got the doctor to give Nana a new prescription because my mom's medication didn't look like party pills?"

"Uh..."

"Well, I realized something. We can simplify the whole process by just changing the drug name on the copy of the prescription. I can just Google it and find any kind of drug we want. I can't believe I didn't think of it before!"

"Really? That's amazing!" Sylvia truly was an amazing woman.

"I know, right? It's like the whole internet is our pharmacy!"

"So like, we could get some different pills. Like something more expensive, or like, better or whatever."

"Yeah. But of course we still have to pay for it first."

"Oh yeah, right." Money problems again. Luke fell silent.

"So what are you up to?" Sylvia asked, somewhat distractedly, and mainly out of what little disinterested social etiquette she possessed. She assumed Luke was up to nothing in particular and she wanted to get back to her prescription project.

"Oh. I'm moving."

"Oh good, so you got the place then. When do you get possession?"

"Huh?" Luke suddenly pictured his head rotating a hundred and eighty degrees like some kind of poltergeist.

"When do you move?"

"What?"

"When are you moving?"

"I just told you. I *am* moving."

"Yes, but when?"

"Like now."

"Right now?"

"Yeah. That's what I said."

"You're moving right now? Why didn't you tell me? I could have come over to help!"

"Yeah but I just decided. I just found out, I mean…"

"What the hell are you talking about? When did you find out you got the place?"

"Just a minute ago."

"And now you're moving right this minute?"

"Yeah."

"Wow. Okay. Well, do you want me to come help you?"

"Nah, it's okay. I'm almost done. Well, not quite, but like, there's not that much stuff. But I need your help with something."

"Yeah, so should I come over?" Sometimes Luke made no sense whatsoever.

"No, it's just a quick question. I'm just…"

"You just need my help to answer a question while you're moving?"

"Yeah."

"Okay, what's the question?"

"Well, you see, I have these pencils. And I don't want them, but like, they will rip the bag if I put them in the garbage."

Oh god. "How full is your garbage?"

"What? No, there's lots of room." *How big does she think these pencils are?*

"Okay, so like, the garbage isn't bulging or heavy or whatever?"

"No, it's pretty much empty."

Sylvia sighed. "Well, just put the pencils in and take the bag down the hall to the chute. As long as it's not too full it'll be fine."

"You think so?"

"I'm sure it'll be fine, Luke."

Luke was not a hundred percent convinced, but he figured Sylvia had a point about the bag not being full. On the other hand, the pencils had points too, and some of them were quite sharp. But all the same Luke decided to take Sylvia's advice. "Okay, thanks Syl! You're a real life-saver!"

"Well, can I come over anyway? I want to help and I want to see your new place."

. . .

"Luke?" Sylvia glanced at the phone. He had already hung up.

Luke was busily tying a loose knot in the top of the garbage bag, the pencils now safely inside. Sylvia was right after all. With this much slack in the plastic there was no sign of any protruding pencil points. "No points for you," Luke said to himself. "Ten points for me."

He headed for the door and stepped out into the hallway. Then on a whim he decided to set the stopwatch on his phone and see how fast he could make it to the trash chute and back. It was way down at the opposite end of the building, so he thought it would be a pretty good challenge. Could he do it in twenty seconds? Or maybe ten? That would be some kind of record for sure. He touched the START button and took off running as fast as he could. A few meters down the hall he jumped over an imaginary obstacle, which almost made him wipe out. But he recovered and regained top speed. He reached the chute and slammed the bag inside, spinning on his heels for the return leg and the glorious crossing of the finish line. As he pounded down the hallway, a door opened behind him, and a middle-aged woman peered out with her beady judgemental eyes. But Luke kept *his* eyes on the prize. He ran right past his door, and hit the STOP button, while slowing down and gasping for air. Twenty-seven seconds. Not bad! Still, he was sure he could do better. He had just decided to catch his breath and try again, when he noticed the woman still leaning out into the hallway, staring at him. He had more packing to do anyway. He opened his apartment door and began to step inside, but then paused for a second. "Twenty-seven seconds!" he yelled down the hall, just in case she thought she could do better. *She hasn't got a chance*, he thought to himself.

Luke took a break, washed his hands, and went looking for a snack. It was a fruitless hunt, of course, and he had to settle for a drink of water straight from the tap to his mouth. He went to the bathroom sink to do this. He hated drinking from the kitchen sink. There was something weird about the taste. But the bathroom water always hit the spot. In his experience, bathroom sinks always gave better water than kitchen sinks. He had told this theory to many people over the years, but no one had ever either believed him or cared enough to dispute his claim.

Back in the bedroom, Luke continued sorting and packing. Thankfully he didn't find any more pencils. This was a big relief since he only had so many garbage bags, and he still needed to pack the rest of his clothes and blankets. He did find more beer cans, and chip bags, and torn comic books, and eventually, near the end of his packing, he came across an old shoebox in the bottom of his closet, underneath a mound of junk. In the box was an elastic band-wrapped deck of Magic: The Gathering cards, a silver dollar that his great uncle had given him long ago, and his old Game Boy Advance.

"Oh, for crying out loud!" Luke yelled at the Game Boy. He picked it up and tried to turn it on, but the battery was dead. He rummaged through the box for game cartridges, but found only one — CRYPTOID III — the worst game of all time. *Dammit!* He cursed the makers of CRYPTOID III, and he cursed himself for throwing away all his good games. They were down the chute now, thirteen and a half seconds away. Gone forever. In frustration, he prostrated himself on his back and stared up at the ceiling. *Why, why, why?*

After about thirty seconds he realized he didn't actually care about his lost games. He reprimanded himself for losing his cool over mere material possessions. This stuff had been sitting in his closet for god-knows-how-long, and he had never missed it until now. He rolled onto his side, propped himself up on his elbow, and went through the rest of the shoebox's contents. A glow in the dark shoelace, a PAC-MAN pencil sharpener, some old AAA batteries, which were all leaky and corroded with white crystals, and a signed John Cena postcard, now caked with battery acid. There was also a pill bottle, still half full of little white pills. He read the label, which was seriously faded and yellowed. He could just barely make out his name, and "ADDERALL XR." These he shoved in his pocket. He wanted to surprise Sylvia the next time he saw her.

Luke finished shoving the rest of his stuff into the two boxes and a few more garbage bags, all of which he then carried down to the first floor, to his new apartment. It took him four trips, including the last trip where he dragged his mattress down the stairs. He set the mattress down beside the door and called Cindy.

"You've reached Hollyhaven Properties. Please leave us a message and we will be sure to return your call as soon as possible."

"Um, hi Cindy. It's Luke. Can you call me back please? Right away, if you can. Uh, I'm at the new bachelor place, and I was hoping you could let me in. I've moved all my stuff down here. Uh. I hope you can come soon… Okay, bye."

12

Taste the Rainbow

"So you spent all night in the hallway?!" Sylvia was incredulous. She dropped her spoon in her bowl and leaned back in her chair.

"Well, not all night. I also went for a walk outside. I really had to pee."

"But you slept in the hallway?"

"Yeah. It wasn't that bad. It's pretty quiet in the building at night."

Sylvia just shook her head. "Why didn't you call me?"

"I don't know, it was getting late." Luke scraped the bottom of his bowl for the last of the sugary remains of his cereal. Plus I couldn't have stayed at your place anyway. You know how your mom is."

"Well, yeah but… And you already gave back your old key but they didn't give you the new one? What's the matter with these people?"

"Well, no, but it's not like that."

"What?"

"They would never do that. Cindy's nice."

"Oh, I bet she is!" Sylvia could just picture her: some blonde hussy with a pink business skirt and a 69 IQ, draping herself all over unsuspecting young bachelors.

"We just didn't do the key thing yet. I'm gonna try to phone her again after I talk to you."

"What do you mean you didn't do the key thing?"

"You know, the trading of the keys."

"The trading of the keys? Wait, so you didn't give them back the key to your old apartment?"

"Not yet. Like I said, I'm still trying to get ahold of her."

"So you still have the old key?"

"Sure, but what good does that do? This is a totally different lock! I already tried it and it didn't fit at all."

"But you could have slept in your old apartment!"

"Well, yeah, I guess. But there's no bed up there."

"Oh my god, Luke!" Sometimes Sylvia just didn't understand Luke's thought process. This was actually not one of those times. She had grown used to this kind of decision-making in their four years together and was familiar with Luke's curious logic. Sometimes she thought she understood this logic better than Luke did himself. But nonetheless this time, as many other times, Sylvia became exasperated by Luke's particular brand of reason.

"So anyway, how much money did we make last night again?"

"Luke, that wasn't last night, it was the night before," Sylvia said. "We made a hundred bucks."

"Sick! That's enough for the new batch, right? Plus some left over for cheeseburgers!"

They were sitting at Sylvia's mom's kitchen table, their 12pm Corn Pops breakfast now over.

"Forget cheeseburgers. Soon we'll be eating sirloin steak!" Sylvia smiled coolly and pulled out a bottle of little white pills from her hoodie pocket.

"Woah, when did you get those?"

"Yesterday. Did you think I was just sitting around all day?"

"I guess not." Luke had been so distracted by his move yesterday that he had forgotten all about the fake prescription. The day seemed like a blur.

"There's eighty four tablets in here. At twenty a pop that's a thousand, six hundred and eighty dollars."

Luke's eyes widened.

"Plus," Sylvia said, a little hesitantly, "I took some of the dimenhydrinate."

"The what?"

"Nana's old medication. I figured she wouldn't need it anymore cuz it was making her drowsy."

Luke considered this and then slowly nodded.

"That's over two grand worth of product, Luke!" she said excitedly.

"Holy shit," Luke said with awe.

"It might take us a while to move it all, but when we do, we'll be rich."

"Sylvia, you're the very best! You're my queen, baby!" He leaned across the table and kissed her forehead. "Oh, I almost forgot!" Luke struggled to jam his hand into his jeans pocket and pull out the bottle of adderall he had found in his closet. "Look what I found when I was moving."

Sylvia snatched the bottle from his hand and examined the label. "Adderall? This stuff's actually worth money! We wouldn't even have to fake it!"

"So it's good?"

"Yes, Luke. It's good." She kissed him on the cheek and he beamed from ear to ear. "And I know just where to sell it."

~~~

Sylvia and Luke stepped out of Sylvia's mom's Grand Am and onto the gravelly asphalt of a big parking lot. The sun was shining, the birds were chirping their little songs back and forth to each other. There was a cloud in the sky that to Luke looked exactly like a T-Rex riding a skateboard. It was a lovely day to sell prescription drugs to college kids.

"Finals are coming up," Sylvia told Luke. "Which means college students are stressed out about studying. Which means they need something to help them focus. That's where we come in. We're their guardian angels, Luke." Sylvia thought of the picture her mom had hung up in the bathroom of the archangel Gabriel, with his fierce blue eyes, his long spear and his flowing locks of brown hair.
~~~

"So we're helping them?"

"Exactly. We're the good guys."

They entered the main building and instantly felt lost. Sylvia had been here only once before and Luke had never before set foot in a post-secondary institution. They stood in a long, wide hall with high ceilings and big bulletin boards covered in posters on the walls. Students milled about and passed by them in all directions — not just students, but potential clients. Luke felt strangely out-of-place. He felt like he didn't belong. He whispered this to Sylvia, and she told him to stop worrying and stay focused.

"Where should we go?" he asked.

Sylvia scanned the hall. "This way," she said, heading down the hall toward a large open area. "We'll find some place where there's people, but not too many people. We have to be discreet."

"Yeah, discreet," Luke repeated.

"We don't talk to anyone who looks like a narc."

Luke nodded. He had vague images in his head of what a narc looked like, which invariably included glasses and collared shirts.

"Ah, perfect. Let's go in here," Sylvia directed, opening the door to the library.

They slowly patrolled the library, weaving in and out of the stacks, peering over books to disguise their reconnaissance, until Sylvia settled on a target.

"See that guy sitting at the table? In the blue hoodie?"

"Yeah," Luke answered. "Do you think he's a narc?"

"No, he's cool. But I can tell he's struggling with his studying. He looks like he's ready to fall asleep."

Luke squinted his eyes but he couldn't make out much of the guy's expression. He had his hood over his face and he looked kinda blurry from across the room.

"Let's go," she said, tugging on Luke's sleeve. He followed behind her sheepishly. He was trying his best to be discreet — like a drug dealer. But not like a drug dealer, because what they were doing was actually a good thing and not really so much a bad thing like a criminal would do. He was really more like a doctor, giving a helpful prescription to a patient. Doctors had to be discreet too. Doctor-patient confidentiality and all that. Luke knew all about this from TV. Him and Sylvia, maverick physicians, roaming the college and helping the leaders of tomorrow pass their exams.

"Hey buddy," Sylvia whispered. Luke, not noticing they had arrived at the table where their first patient was sitting, bumped into Sylvia, who shot him a look. *Discreet,* Luke reminded himself. The guy had earbuds in and didn't notice them.

"Hey," she tried again. His gaze remained fixed on his textbook. "Hey, guy." This time she said it a little louder — a little louder, in fact, than she intended. She looked around to see if anyone was looking at her. Luckily there weren't many people around. Still the guy in the blue hoodie kept his head down. Sylvia crouched down and Luke followed suit.

"He's sleeping," Sylvia remarked. "See? He needs our help, Luke." Sylvia stood up and nudged his shoulder, a little too roughly. The guy in the blue hoodie stirred and looked up at Sylvia, then at Luke.

"Sorry," he muttered. "What's going on?"

"Don't be sorry. We–"

"We're here to help," Luke cut in.

"What? Oh." He pulled out his earbuds. "What?"

Sylvia shushed Luke and continued speaking. "You look like you could use some help focusing. You interested?"

"What?" he said again. He looked incredibly disoriented from his unplanned nap, like he had just fallen out of a tumble dryer.

"We have something I think you could really use."

He just stared at them, looking quite confused.

"You know what I'm talking about," Sylvia whispered.

"Is this a sex thing?"

"No, it's drugs!" Luke sputtered.

"Shh! It's not drugs, it's just something to help you study. You wanna do well on your exams, right?"

"Yeah," he answered, rubbing his eyes.

"Then you need these." Sylvia pulled out a Ziploc bag containing four little white pills.

"Oh." The boy looked suddenly nervous. "No, thanks. I don't really–"

"What's the harm? They'll take all the stress away. I promise."

The boy hesitated for a moment. "Well, what are they? Are they dangerous?"

"Not at all. It would be more dangerous not to take them, really. It's your future at stake here."

"They'll help me study?"

"You bet," Sylvia said. "With these guys you can study all night no problem. Won't even need to sleep."

"Really?"

"Really."

The boy was clearly considering the pills. He glanced around the room nervously and then looked Luke and Sylvia up and down. "How much does it cost?"

Sylvia paused as a cold panic set in. She had forgotten to determine a price. She didn't even know how much these pills were worth. But she knew that this boy didn't either. "Fifteen dollars a pill," she stated, trying to sound like she knew what she was talking about. "And that's a good deal."

"Okay, I'll take one," the boy said.

Sylvia had a thought. "There's no point buying just one," she said. "It'll hardly do anything. You gotta take 'em two at a time." The boy looked hesitant again, but Sylvia was quick on her feet. "Tell you what, I'll give you a deal. Two for twenty-five."

The boy pulled out his wallet and inspected its contents before looking back at Sylvia. "This is really going to help?"

"You have my guarantee," she told him, looking quite serious.

He looked back to his wallet. "Alright," he almost whispered. "Here." He pulled out a twenty and a five and handed them to Sylvia after another quick glance around to make sure no one was watching. Then Sylvia handed him the bag.

"Thanks," he said meekly. Sylvia nodded and tugged on Luke's sleeve and they disappeared back into the stacks.

Luke was impressed. "You're like a pro salesman," he whispered.

Sylvia smiled. "Come on, we got lots more product to sell."

But their next few encounters were less successful, to say the least. One student simply ignored them, two politely declined, and one scoffed at their price.

"Fifteen bucks per pill? That's way too much! I can get them for five from my cousin." This kid looked scrappy and malnourished. He was most likely a computer science major, Sylvia thought.

"I'll give you six for sixty," Sylvia offered.

"Read a math book."

"I've got some E, too."

"Get fucked," the scrappy kid said.

Three hours and a few more sales later they decided to call it a day. They hadn't sold as much Adderall as they had hoped, but they had convinced an adventurous first-year to buy a couple of the old dimenhydrinate for a slightly reduced price. Sylvia briefly worried that, not being drunk like her usual clientele, this girl would realize the pills were not, in fact, ecstasy. But she brushed these worries aside. After all, this girl seemed young, dumb, and harmless. That, she decided, was her ideal type of client. Luke and Sylvia headed back to the parking lot as a large cloud moved in front of the sun, casting a dull shadow on the world.

"How much did we make?" Luke asked.

Sylvia counted the money for the fifth time that day. "A hundred and ten," Sylvia said, stuffing the cash into her purse and zipping it closed.

"Aw, yeah!" Luke exclaimed, raising and clenching his fists in excitement.

"It's not bad, but we can do better."

Luke nodded.

"We'll have to put it all toward the deposit on your new place," Sylvia said.

"The what?"

"Your security deposit. You have to pay half a month's rent before you can… What the hell is this?!"

They had reached the Grand Am only to find a yellow parking ticket stuck under Sylvia's windshield wiper. She grabbed it and examined it. "Thirty bucks? What the fuck!?"

"What's wrong, Syl?"

"Well there goes one of our sales. Why the hell do you have to pay for parking at a college?!" Sylvia had a good point.

After going back inside to pay the fine, Sylvia and Luke drove back to Luke's apartment building, where Luke decided to check on his new bachelor pad. He and Sylvia turned down the hall and headed toward apartment 106. But something about the hall was different. "My stuff's gone!"

"Oh no," Sylvia moaned.

"Holly must have moved it into the apartment for me."

"No, Luke. Someone probably threw it away! What did you leave it sitting there for?" Sylvia seemed irritated.

"I told you, Syl," Luke said calmly. "The door was locked. I couldn't get in yet."

"Of course you couldn't get in, it's not your apartment!"

Why was Sylvia yelling at him? What had he done wrong? "Yeah it is! Cindy said!"

"Have you signed any papers?"

"What? What's that supposed to mean?" Even if it was just a joke, Luke was offended at the insinuation that he would run off and get hitched to another woman.

"God, Luke, you're so stupid sometimes!"

At that, Luke felt as though he had been pierced through the heart with a poisoned lance. "Syl…"

Sylvia sighed, regretting her choice of words. "Sorry. I'm just upset about the ticket." She looked at the floor. "And I'm stressed about you getting the place."

"Don't worry, babe. I got the place. I just have to call Cindy again and get the key, that's all."

Sylvia sighed again. "Okay, why don't you call her now?"

So Luke called Cindy, who seemed surprised by Luke's line of questioning. She seemed to be answering all his questions with questions of her own.

"So, you do want the place?" she asked. "When can you meet to sign the lease?" she asked. "That was *your* stuff in the hallway?" And they arranged to meet in the building office and sort out the details right after Luke retrieved his belongings from the dumpster where the maintenance guy had tossed it.

Luckily, Luke's boxes had remained closed and intact, although they now had some yogurt on them. Luke and Sylvia piled everything back in the hallway outside apartment 106 and then headed to the office, where Cindy had prepared the tenancy agreement and an information packet for Luke. She was a thin blonde in her late thirties, quite attractive for her age despite a slight underbite. Sylvia glared at her whenever she looked down at her papers or toward her computer screen.

"We do require a six month lease for new rentals. After that it's month to month. Rent is due on the first of the month, as I'm sure you know. We usually require a credit check, but as you've been living here so long, we can forego that. Does that all sound good?"

"Uh, yeah." Luke filled out his information on a form and signed it, not completely understanding what he was agreeing to. He felt a bit overwhelmed.

"Now we just need a deposit and you'll be good to go."

Luke swallowed audibly. "How much is the deposit?"

"It'll be four hundred dollars."

"Oh," Luke said. He didn't have $400. He hadn't worked for… How long had it been, anyway? He hadn't even heard from Scott about any upcoming jobs. Why hadn't he called? Had Scott forgotten about him? *Maybe I should call him*, Luke thought. *Maybe he can give me an advance. But I need the money right now. What do I do? Shit shit shit Cindy is staring at me. Does she have a crush on me? Sylvia is gonna be pissed! Maybe I can stay with Sylvia. No, her mom's Catholic. Maybe I can stay with my parents. No, they're moving to stupid Peachland. Maybe I can move to Peachland with them.* Peachland didn't sound so bad now. Luke imagined a meadow full of giant peaches — *like in that book!* Maybe he could hollow out one of the giant peaches and live inside it with the Grasshopper and the Centipede. *But what about Sylvia? How could he live without her?*

"On debit," a wary voice said.

Maybe she would come with him. They could start a new life together, rent-free and easy. But Nana was here. Someone had to stay and look after her. *Maybe I could move into Nana's place at Willow Lodge!* There Luke would never even have to worry about making meals. They had people there to do that. He and Nana could eat cookies and do puzzles all day and Luke could make sure Lester stayed out of Nana's pants.

"Do you need the receipt?" Cindy asked.

"No," Sylvia said coldly.

Luke snapped back into reality. He saw Sylvia putting her debit card back into her purse. What was going on? Cindy handed Luke a set of keys and Sylvia led him out of the office.

"Did you just– "

"Well, someone had to."

"But where did you get the money?"

"My savings account," she answered dully.

Luke could not and did not stop thanking Sylvia the whole time they moved Luke's belongings from the hallway into his new apartment, which, in all fairness, only took about thirty seconds.

"Okay, okay, just stop saying thank you!"

"Okay! Anything for you, baby," Luke responded enthusiastically.

"You gotta focus, Luke. Rent is due in five days. We need to start hustling." *Rent?* Luke had forgotten that the deposit Sylvia paid was not, in fact, his rent. *Shit,* he thought.

"Okay. No problemo. Let's just go back to the college tomorrow. And maybe we can find another party to go to too. Plus I'm gonna call Scott and see if he's got any more jobs."

"Who?" Sylvia had already pulled out her phone to suss out where the parties would be this weekend.

"Scott, my boss."

"Oh, right. The janitor thing."

"I'll call him right now."

Luke listened to the drawn-out robotic beeping of his cell phone as he waited for Scott to answer. Interrupting what must have been close to the final beep, Luke heard Scott's voice: "Hello?"

"Hi, Scott. It's Luke."

"Oh, Luke! Hi, how's it going?"

"Pretty good," Luke answered. "I just got a nice new bachelor pad."

"Oh, good for you."

There was a moment of silence.

"Uh," Luke said, just as Scott was saying something that sounded like, "So…"

"Sorry, go ahead," they both said in unison.

"No, that's okay," Scott said.

There was another moment of silence as Sylvia looked away from her phone to give Luke the side-eye.

"Oh, well," Luke started, "I was wondering if there were any jobs coming up."

Scott sneezed very loudly on the other end of the phone. "Sorry, excuse me."

"That's okay," Luke said.

"Uh, yeah actually, I was meaning to call. Things have, uh… slowed down a bit. But, uh, there's a job on Monday I could use you for."

"Okay," Luke said.

"I'll call you then. Probably pick you up around seven. Sound good?"

"Sounds great!" Luke said before hanging up.

"Syl, I'm doing another job on Monday!"

"That's great, Luke," she said. But Luke thought she didn't really sound like she meant it.

~~~

Luke and Sylvia returned to the college the next day, and made sure to pay for parking. This time they were met with more success. Sylvia started giving her phone number to select clients who she considered likely to be repeat customers. By the end of the day they had sold all the Adderall and a few more of the dimenhydrinate and were up a cool couple hundred. And for the second week in a row, Luke had forgotten all about dinner at his parents' house.

On Friday there was a big house party and Sylvia was all set to make another score. Luke was there too, of course, but Sylvia had decided that she had better do most of the talking.
~~~

Luke's role, as it had been described to him, was more that of a security officer and lookout, with a bit of reconnaissance sprinkled in. He would keep an eye out for potential clients and potential threats. Not that they had any enemies. But as the money started rolling in, so did Sylvia's paranoia. They had discussed potential dangers to their operation in the car on the way here:

"We gotta look out for other dealers," Sylvia told Luke, who nodded zealously.

"We gotta respect turf," he agreed.

"Right. And if the cops come-"

"Cops?" Luke spat. "Why cops?"

"Hey, hey! It's okay!" Sylvia reassured him, putting her hand on his shoulder. "There won't be any cops. But if there are…"

"But you just said there won't be any! I don't wanna get in trouble with the law, Syl! These drugs are legal, right?"

"Of course, Luke. This is all perfectly legal. They're just prescription medications. *But,*" she emphasized, "it might make us look bad if any cops start asking us questions, you know? Remember, our customers *think* the drugs are illegal. That's why they're buying them."

"Right," Luke said. This all made sense to him.

The hip-hop music thumped as Sylvia prowled the kitchen. She was trying to present the air of someone who had illicit party drugs available for purchase. She did this by holding her lips slightly pursed and her eyes slightly narrowed and making eye contact with anyone who looked like a potential user. But after getting the feel of the party, she determined it was too soon to start pushing. Everyone here was still too sober. So she hung back and leaned against the counter between a stack of Solo cups and a 2-litre of Fresca.

Luke was in the living room, intently watching the street through the window from a dilapidated La-Z-Boy and snacking on a bag of Hawkins Cheezies. No sign of trouble yet, but he had better not let his guard down. Every few minutes he scanned the room for potential narcs. No, this crowd seemed down to clown. Luke thought about this expression and decided it was really quite a funny and charming turn of phrase. *Down to clown, clown around. Get ready to clown around.* That was familiar. He heard a melody in his head. *Get ready, get ready, get ready to clown around.* Then he remembered. It was the theme song from "The Big Comfy Couch," that old kids' show. That show used to give him terrible nightmares. Even now he shuddered as he thought of it. Then he imagined that everyone around him was a clown. His skin started to crawl and his muscles tensed up. Then a powerful laser beam shot through the room and a group of clowns, who had been dancing to a song by Flo Rida, were disintegrated. The robots had arrived. They were after the pills. *The robot pills. Beep boop, give us the pills. No, watch the window,* Luke told himself, snapping back into reality. This music was too loud. His cheezies were basically all gone. All that remained in the translucent orange bag were a few little cheezie nuggets atop a layer of real-cheese flavour dust. Maybe someone here would spot him a beer.

Sylvia crouched down and put her hand on his arm. "See anything suspicious?"

"Not yet," Luke answered. "But there might be some robots in disguise." He smirked.

"Okay, well just remember not to get distracted. We're here on a mission, okay? Stay focused. Don't go chasing cats again."

"I won't babe. Hey, maybe I should have taken some of that Adderall."

Sylvia giggled.

Wait, Luke thought. *Maybe I* should *have taken some of that Adderall.* He couldn't remember why he had stopped taking it in the first place. He also couldn't remember the last time he had been to see his doctor.

"Okay, I'm going to go check out the porch. Let me know if you see anything." Sylvia stood up and disappeared into the crowd.

What did she say? Luke wondered. But then his thigh started vibrating. At first it seemed to be vibrating to the music and Luke wondered if this was some kind of emergent physiological abnormality. But no, it was just his phone. His dad was calling. *Oh yeah,* Luke thought, *I forgot to call Dad back yesterday — or was that the day before?* For all Luke knew it could have been last week. He had been so caught up in the drug game he didn't even know what day it was.

"Hi Dad," Luke said into his phone.

"Hi, buddy. How's it going?"

"Pretty good. How 'bout you?"

"I can't hear you. Can you turn the music down?"

"No, it's not mine."

"Are you at a party?"

"Yeah. I'm working." *D'oh! Quiet, dummy!* Thankfully his dad hadn't heard him. "Hang on, I'll go in the bathroom." Luke stood up, stuffed his mostly-empty cheezie bag into his pocket and walked down the hall to the bathroom. Once inside, he closed the door and unconsciously started undoing his belt, before remembering he was on the phone with his dad. He did his belt back up and sat on the toilet. "Okay, can you hear me now?"

"Yeah, that's better," his dad said. "We haven't heard from you in a couple weeks. You missed toad in the hole on Wednesday."

Damn, Luke thought. He loved toad in the hole. It was, in his opinion, one of the most underappreciated foods. "Sorry, dad. I totally forgot. Things have been crazy lately. Oh, hey, guess what? I got a new bachelor apartment." Luke awaited his father's impressed, approving response.

"You got your own place?" It sounded a little more dismayed than impressed, but Luke wasn't too picky.

"Yup! All to myself. Jason's moving to Vancouver."

His dad was silent for a moment. "Are you okay for money, Luke?"

"Yeah, I'm okay."

"You're sure you can afford it?"

Now Luke was a little perturbed. Although maybe not quite perturbed — annoyed? Miffed? No, more than any of those he was hurt. Hurt that his own dad didn't seem to believe in him. "Of course I can," Luke stammered, frustration evident in his voice. "I have a job, don't I?"

"You're still working for the cleaning company?"

"Yeah," Luke hesitated. "Eliminator Sanitation. I'm making good money."

"That's great, Luke. Are they giving you lots of hours?"

"Yeah. Lots." Luke knew he had just lied. But he couldn't tell his dad about the pill business — Sylvia had made that very clear. And he couldn't have his dad think he was a broke loser. But even if lying was the only option, Luke couldn't help feeling bad about it.

"Well, do you want to come over sometime this weekend?" It seemed like a good idea to change the subject. "There's only a couple weeks left before we move and Mom and I want to see you. We could use some help packing too."

"A couple weeks?! Okay, can I come over tomorrow?"

"Sure, Luke."

"Can Sylvia come too?"

"Oh," his dad said. "Uh, yeah, I guess so."

"Okay, cool. See ya tomorrow, dad."

"Bye, son. Have fun."

"You too." Luke sat up, washed his hands and went to resume his post in the living room. But his chair was now occupied.

"Oh, hello there," Luke said to the small furry occupant of the La-Z-Boy. "I'm not supposed to get distracted by pets. Run along now, little guy." The animal perked its ears. Luke remembered Sylvia's words: *don't go chasing cats again*. But this wasn't a cat. This was a cute little dog with golden-brown fur and frumpy jowls. And he was not about to chase it. It was, after all, sitting in his lookout chair. Luke gingerly picked up the dog and sat down, placing it in his lap once he was settled in. He scratched it behind the ears. The dog was old and lethargic and she didn't seem to care much that Luke had manhandled her. "You can be my lookout partner," Luke said. The old dog gave a low grunt as Luke resumed staring out the window.

Soon enough Sylvia determined that it was time to start pushing. She had run into an old friend on the back porch — well, not so much a friend really as an acquaintance. Or something like that. The whole time they were talking Sylvia couldn't remember if she liked her or not. But she was pretty drunk, so Sylvia sold her and a friend of hers some Dramamine, promising they would be able to stay up and party all night. Then she went back to the kitchen and quickly spotted her next client: a bleary-eyed red-headed kid in rave pants. Sylvia hadn't seen anyone wear rave pants in, like, ten years. It was another easy dimenhydrinate sell. Sure, this kid would probably have known it was a dud sober, but he was clearly hammered, and besides, Sylvia had already convinced herself of the power of the placebo effect. She had read about it on Cracked.com. Kids didn't know the difference between a real high and the illusory results of their own expectations.

After that, things were a little slow. No one was biting. *These people are squares,* Sylvia thought. *This party sucks.* She made her way to the living room to check on Luke and to see if anyone there was more inclined to party. Seeing the dog in Luke's lap, Sylvia's eyes narrowed. "Who's this?" she asked him.

"Oh, hey Syl. This is my lookout partner. Her name is Daisy."

"What did I tell you about getting distracted?"

"I'm not!" Luke whined defensively. "Well, I mean my dad called and I went to the bathroom and–"

"Luke! You were supposed to stay here!"

"I did! Mostly…" Luke didn't think it was fair that he was being scolded. He had been gone for only a few minutes. What if he had had to pee for real? What was he supposed to do, hold it? Actually, now that he thought of it, he really did have to pee.

"Can you take over for a sec? I gotta take a leak. I didn't see anyone threatening come in."

"Hey. Assholes!" A reedy voice protruded from the throng of partiers. Sylvia and Luke turned to see a guy in a CCM hoodie and a red backwards snapback glaring at them.

"Is he talking to us?" Luke whispered. *Who the hell is this shithead?* Sylvia thought. Luke froze in his chair as the guy approached. Daisy roused herself with a grumble and jumped to the floor, disappearing down the hallway. There was something familiar about this dude, but no name came to Sylvia's mind. Had she seen him somewhere before? Why did he look so pissed at her? And then the full recognition slapped her in the face like a fresh-caught Coho salmon.

"I want my money back, bitch."

Sylvia tried to play it cool. "What's the problem?"

"You're the fuckin' problem, bitch. You owe me."

Luke's mind was racing. *Oh my god,* he thought. *Is Sylvia a–*

"Owe you for what?" Sylvia was counting on this shithead's stupidity. She was using all her effort not to escalate the situation by raising her voice or in any way revealing her guilt. Luke was using all his effort not to pee his pants.

"For the fake molly you sold me." Sylvia's calm demeanour did not seem to be rubbing off on Red Wings Hat.

"Ohhhh," Luke said. Sylvia shot him a look. Luke finally understood, and was relieved to throw his prostitute theory out the window. On the other hand, they might be in real trouble here. Between the loud music and the crowd, no one else at the party seemed to notice what was going on. *If only the cops were here…*

"Speak up, bitch. Come on before I make you talk."

"I didn't sell you fake molly." Sylvia's voice wavered.

"Bitch, fuck you. That shit didn't do shit." Red Wings' fists were clenched at his sides. Luke tried to think of something to say, some way to help Sylvia. He felt useless. *People who take ecstasy aren't supposed to be angry,* he thought. But this guy was definitely angry, and so was Luke. His rage grew every time this dick called his girlfriend a bitch. Meanwhile, Sylvia was forming a plan. Everything would be fine. She could get them out of this. She was smarter than this shithead. She had the advantage.

"I never sold you molly," she said confidently.

Red Wings was nonplussed. "Bitch, I know. That's why I'm here."

"I mean, I never told you those pills were ecstasy."

Red Wings was silent as he considered this. Of course, he didn't remember all the details of the conversation. It was over a week ago that he had taken those pills, and he had not exactly been sober at the time.

"I never lied to you," Sylvia said. "You wanted to buy the pills, so I sold them to you. It was a fair deal."

"Fuck you." Red Wings was not satisfied. It didn't feel like a fair deal to him. "Give me fifty bucks right now. Don't make me make you."

Sylvia laughed nervously at his clumsy turn of phrase. "Actually, it would only be twenty-five bucks," she said. "Read a book, dick-brains." *Oops,* she thought. It became immediately apparent that she should not have said this.

"Okay, I'm fuckin' done talking." Red Wings' face was bright red with rage. He reached into his jeans and pulled out a pocket-knife. Without thinking, Luke reached into his pocket as well and grabbed whatever his hand found.

"Luke, run!" Sylvia shouted. Red Face fumbled with his pocket-knife, flipping out first a nail file, then a tiny pair of scissors. Sylvia turned and bolted down the hallway as Luke looked down at the little orange bag he had pulled out of his pocket. Almost automatically, and, as it seemed to Luke, in slow motion, he reached his other hand in the bag and spread his fingers. Removing his hand he pointed the gaping mouth of the bag toward his foe and quickly extended his arm before jerking it back, leaping from his chair and high-tailing it after Sylvia.

Orange Face screamed in agony from the cheezie dust in his eyes and nose. He dropped his knife and rubbed his eyes as he ran blindly down the hall. By now, nearly everyone at the party was watching. Sylvia had been sure to let everyone present know that she was being threatened at knife-point. She screamed all the way down the hall and across the back porch: "Help!... He's got a knife!... It's the guy in the red hat, he's trying to kill me!" She did her best to play the part of the maiden in distress, garnering sympathy and drunken moral outrage from her fellow party-goers until they resembled a lynch mob. Luke, who was also screaming, albeit less coherently, made it outside and, through the darkness, spotted Sylvia hopping the back fence. He weaved through the commotion as a spattering of muscled men fought to get inside to find the wrong-doer. Guys were grabbing each other left and right, making threats, demanding explanations: "You like threatening girls, huh?... it's not me, it's that guy!... she said a red hat... here he is!... I called the cops..." and so on and so on. Luke managed to escape the scene and get to the fence. He turned around and surveyed the pandemonium looking for Orange Face, demonstrating a steadfast commitment to his role as security officer and lookout. Seeing that he was not in the yard, he jumped the fence and landed with a splash in an inflatable swimming pool. Completely drenched, he emerged and climbed out onto the grass of a strange backyard. A light turned on in the stranger's house and Luke bolted for a clump of bushes in the garden.

"Luke!" A voice whispered from beside him, from within the bush. Luke was frightened. *God?* he thought. He had heard of this happening before. "It's me."

"Oh, Sylvia!" he whispered. "I'm freaked!"

"Everything's fine," she assured him. "The worst is over. We just need to get to my car."

A patio door opened and a deep voice boomed, "Shut the hell up over there!" Luke and Sylvia heard steps in the grass. They kept deadly still. The man spoke again, quiet and gruff. "I know somebody's back here." He took a few steps toward the bushes. Luke held his breath, his eyes wide with terror as he listened to the shuffling of the grass beneath the stranger's feet. The man snorted and spit before turning around to face the house. "I'm gonna give you five seconds to get the hell out of my yard," he said, walking toward the door. Luke and Sylvia bolted from the bushes and ran around the house to the street, where they hopped in Sylvia's car, locked the doors and roared away down the street.

Luke's heart was pounding. He really needed some robot pills. He tried to breathe deeply, but couldn't remember his technique. He knew he had to count. But what was the number? He kept hearing the voice of God stepping out through that sliding glass door. The soaking wet, orange-faced, angry voice of God, giving him five seconds. It was like a second chance at life. Maybe that's just what he needed.

"Are you okay?" Sylvia asked, glancing at him a bit too long as she raced through the night in her mom's Grand Am. She came dangerously close to sideswiping a parked car. For his part, Luke could not even manage to yell, "look out!" But Sylvia noticed at the last second and swerved wildly back into her lane.

"Shit!" she declared.

Luke gripped the edge of his seat, as Sylvia gradually coasted to a more reasonable speed. This was too many close calls for one night. Perhaps it was an omen.

"Syl," Luke started.

She glanced at him again, but more briefly this time, and purposefully kept her arms straight on the steering wheel.

"Syl?" he repeated.

"Luke, what? Spit it out."

"It's… All the lies!"

"Huh?"

"They've come back to haunt us."

Sylvia knew he was right, at least in a way, although he was being a bit overly dramatic about it. Still, that dude back there wasn't exactly a happy customer, and that was not good for business. And in a way they kind of *had* lied to him. Sort of. Or at least she could admit that their current business model did have a certain level of deception baked into it.

"You never could tell a lie, could you Lukie?"

He almost said, "not really," but stopped himself. That too would be a lie. He could tell them. He *had* told them. Too many of them.

Sylvia could read his confused internal indecision accurately enough. "Okay, babe. We won't lie anymore, I promise. We'll figure out a different way to make this work."

"You mean it, Syl?"

"Yes, Luke. I never want to make you go against your principles. We're good people, Luke. We don't do bad stuff."

"But what about the pills, Syl?"

"No, it's okay, we can fix it. We can make it so we don't have to lie about them. Ever."

"We can?"

"Yes." Somehow. Sylvia had an idea growing in the back of her mind. She couldn't see it clearly yet, but yes, she was sure it was the solution.

"How?" Luke sounded hopeful. He trusted her.

"Well..." As she drove down Lonston, a light rain began to splatter her windshield, refracting the colorful lights of the business district into strange-looking blobs. She turned on the wipers and slowed the car, preparing to pull into the Wendy's parking lot.

"Oh!" Exclaimed Luke, "JBCs?!"

"JBCs for everyone!"

"God bless us every one!" Luke sang gleefully.

A few minutes later they had their burgers in hand, and had settled into their usual table by the window. "Luke, remember that prescription that I made on my mom's computer?"

"Um, yeah. I think so. The spaghetti one, right?"

Technically no. The prescription in question was not the one that Luke had spilled spaghetti on — Luke was having a hard time keeping up with this convoluted series of events — but that wasn't important. "Yeah," she said. "And remember how what's-her-face couldn't tell the difference?"

"Patti," Luke corrected her.

Sylvia winced at her rival's name, and let out a loud sigh of exasperation.

"Oh. Sorry. Yeah, she couldn't tell at all. You did such a great job, baby."

"Thanks... But yeah, so here's what I'm thinking. We go on my mom's computer, right? And we make a bunch of those um... *fake prescriptions*." The last part was whispered, and only after a furtive glance around the restaurant. "But for drugs that are actually in demand. That way, we can get the real, um, *stuff*. The kind that our clients want. Then we don't have to lie to them, right?"

"Oooh." Luke thought for a moment. "Syl, that's brilliant!"

Sylvia smirked as she lifted her burger. "That's why they pay me the big bucks."

13

Lucky Charms

"Good morning, sleepyhead." Sylvia sat on the edge of the bed, and shook Luke gently.

"Wah?" His bleary eyes blinked once, then twice, before focusing on her face.

"I tried to make you breakfast, but it turns out you have no cereal. Also, no milk. Or spoons. Or bowls."

"Oh. Yeah." Luke yawned and rubbed his eyes. Sylvia found Luke especially adorable when he was sleepy like this. She had decided to stay over, despite a long accusing text from her mother, which she didn't finish reading. After their late night of close calls and scheming, Luke and Sylvia had snuggled until the wee hours of the morning, and Sylvia was now starting to think that maybe this bachelor pad situation would work out alright after all.

"Come on," Sylvia said. "Let's go shopping."

The shelves in Superstore were well stocked as always. Luke imagined the stock boys pushing pallet jacks down the aisles all night long, deftly wielding razor sharp box cutters and scooping up armfuls of bright and cheerful cereal boxes which they would then align on the shelves with perfect precision. They looked a lot like leprechauns, the stock boys did, and as they carried their boxes of Lucky Charms, he could scarcely differentiate between the leprechauns on the boxes and the ones carrying them. "They're always after me Lucky Charms," he chimed.

Sylvia laughed in agreement. They always were. And the charms were lucky indeed. Now she just needed to figure out exactly which charms were the luckiest. That is, which pharmaceutical drugs would be most in demand. Now that they were going to embrace truth in advertising, it would be important to have a product line that would satisfy their clientele. They needed the right name brands, as it were. She had learned all about this working at the liquor store. The premium brands could fetch a higher price, just because they were more familiar to the consumer, and because they had cool names like "Belvedere" and "Polar Ice." It didn't matter which products were better. After all, "better" was totally subjective. No, all that mattered was which products the customers *believed* were better.

"Hey Luke, what are the coolest drugs?" She wanted to see if the ones he had heard of were the same ones as the ones she had heard of. Neither of them were particularly knowledgeable about the subject.

Luke looked up from the Frosted Flakes box he'd been reading. "Um. I guess weed. Weed and coke?"

"Yeah, but I mean like pills."

"Oh, right. Of course. Um… maybe ecstasy? Or speed? Those are pills right?"

"Sure. Yeah." At least she thought so. She was pretty sure you couldn't buy ecstasy and speed at a pharmacy; she made a mental note to do some proper research as soon as she got home.

"Are we gonna sell the cool ones?"

"Of course," Sylvia answered. "Nothing but the best for our customers, right?"

"Yeah, a hundred percent." Luke put down the Frosted Flakes and put two more boxes of Lucky Charms into the shopping cart. "Nothing but the best." He began pushing the cart out of the cereal aisle and toward the dairy cooler. "What about robot pills?"

"Are those good?"

"Oh yeah, baby!"

"Alright, I guess. What's their real name though?"

"What do you mean?"

"Well they're not really called robot pills. You just made that up."

"Did I?" Luke was taken aback.

"Yeah. They were Nana's, right? We need to find out what their scientific name is."

"Were they from Nana? Oh! Do we need to get her some more then?" They should do that today, Luke thought. They hadn't seen Nana in — how long had it been, anyway? "Hey, we better go visit her."

Crap. The last thing Sylvia wanted to do was hang around Willow Lodge. They had important business to attend to. She needed to get onto her mom's computer stat. There was a lot of research to be done, not to mention Photoshopping the prescriptions.

As he pushed the shopping cart around a giant cube made of President's Choice Corn Flakes boxes, Luke felt his leg buzzing. He fished his phone out of his pocket.

"Hey, Dad."

"Luke. What time do you think you'll be here?"

"Huh?"

"You said you'd come help us today. With the packing and whatnot."

"Yeah, totally. We are."

Sylvia's brows lowered as she sensed herself being dragged into something.

"Good, good. We have a lot of stuff to go through, and a truck is coming from the Salvation Army this afternoon."

"Oh yeah? You buying something?"

"No Luke, we're giving stuff away. We have to clear out the garage."

"You're giving it to the Salvation Army?"

"Yes, they're sending a truck to pick it up."

"Oh, wow." Luke had always thought that stores were just for buying stuff. He didn't know you could give stuff to stores too. "Like what kind of stuff?"

"Hmm? You know. The garage. It's practically full of old junk we never use. Some of it's yours, though. That's why we need you to come over. We thought you might want to keep some of your things.”

“Oh. Uh. Are there any spoons?”

“Spoons?”

“Yeah, or any kind of dishes, I guess. I need some for my new bachelor pad. I was just about to buy some at Superstore.”

This part of Luke’s conversation peaked Sylvia’s interest. Technically, *she* was just about to buy some at Superstore, and frankly, she would have preferred not to. Luke’s new bachelor pad had already cost her too much.

“I’m not sure. Let me check with your mother…”

Luke could hear the muffled sounds of his parents shouting back and forth across the house about old dishes. He crossed his fingers. Sylvia crossed hers as well.

“Your mother says she’s sure she can come up with something,” Luke’s father eventually replied.

“Okay, sweet. We’ll come pretty soon, Dad.”

“Alright, son.”

Sylvia’s face bore the mixed feelings of someone who had better things to do on a Saturday, but who had at least found an opportunity to save a couple bucks.

“We have to go to my parents to get some spoons,” Luke told her.

“I heard,” replied Sylvia. “And bowls too?”

“Umm. I think so. They didn’t say exactly.”

“Well, I guess we’ll see.”

“I guess we will,” agreed Luke. Who knew what they might find in that old garage? He might end up eating cereal out of an old hubcap, or a tin formerly used to hold an assortment of random nuts, bolts and screws. As long as he had a spoon, he’d be just fine.

At the checkout Sylvia was still thinking about branding as she eyed a display of chocolate bars, bubble gum, and breath mints. She didn’t even notice that the pretty cashier giggled at Luke's three boxes of Lucky Charms and smiled at him as she took his money. She only noticed the names of candies, and the colours of their packaging. Hubba Bubba made bubble gum sexy, and Payday bars would obviously make you rich. She was less sure about the appeal of Baby Ruth. Was this a reference to an actual baby named Ruth? Babies were cute, supposedly, but that didn't mean people wanted to eat them. It seemed like a bit of a longshot from a marketing perspective. She picked up a Baby Ruth, and asked Luke, "Would you ever want to eat a baby?"

"Huh? Oh. Sure. I guess so." Luke took the chocolate bar and placed it on the checkout conveyor belt, then fished out some change from his pocket. It was nice to have a little bit of spending money for once, and if his gal wanted him to buy her a candy bar he couldn't complain about that. As they walked to the car Luke handed the Baby Ruth to Sylvia.

"It's okay. You have it," she told him.

Luke was surprised. "You don't want it?"

"I don't really feel like it right now."

"Oh. Because of the nuts?"

"Meh."

"Or maybe the caramel… Or that other stuff. What's it called?"

"Nougat."

Luke smirked. "Sure beats old gut!"

Sylvia groaned. "That's bad."

"Hey, it just came to me, what can I say? A joke's a joke." Luke spent most of the drive toward his parents' house trying to think of another joke to tell Sylvia. She was right, that last one was bad. Luke knew he could do better. He made a mental note to do some proper joke research as soon as they got home.

Sylvia pulled into the driveway, only to be waved off by Luke's father, who gestured for her to park on the road. Luke's father nodded somewhat approvingly to himself at the quality of her parallel parking job. This may have been the closest he had ever come to paying Sylvia a compliment.

"Hello, son."

"Hi, Dad."

Luke walked into the garage, ducking unnecessarily as he passed beneath the overhead door. His father had been organizing things, moving them into piles. There was stuff everywhere. A pile of boxes with 'LUKE' written on their sides in jiffy marker, sat waiting for him, along with his old bike and his skateboard. Luke grabbed the board excitedly and jogged out onto the driveway, where he successfully pulled off a caveman mount and began rolling down the asphalt toward the road. The slope of the driveway caused Luke to accelerate and he felt a surge of low-grade panic. He would have to act fast. It was time for an epic maneuver — the ollie.

Luke had never, at least to this day, managed to successfully perform an ollie. Today was the day that would change. He could feel it in his bones. He was going to do it, and it was going to be magnificent. He crouched down low, tensing up his legs in preparation. He closed his eyes and summoned all of his ninja skills to sense the exact moment... NOW! He hammered down quickly with his back foot, simultaneously sliding his front foot forward and up, which would allow the board to break off the shackles of gravity and rise into the air. That was the theory, anyway.

Sylvia watched Luke roll slowly toward the road. She watched him crouch on the skateboard. This was not a good sign. He looked like a paraplegic frog as he spasmodically propelled himself off the board and into the air — that is, about two inches off the board, which itself jolted slightly in a brief and pathetic "pop-a-wheelie" motion just before Luke fell back onto it. His right foot landed on the ground completely behind the skateboard and his left foot landed on the board's tail leveraging the nose upward into a truly majestic wheelie as the board proceeded to shoot completely out from under Luke and toward the road. As Luke fell on his ass, his board shot straight underneath a passing taxi, whose rear wheel met it in T-bone fashion, snapping it in half.

"And that's why you wear a helmet," observed Luke's father, which made little sense, unless he was privy to some kind of strange ass-helmet that no one else knew about.

Luke moaned as he lay on his side, rubbing his tailbone. Sylvia helped him up. "Oh my god, Luke. Are you okay?"

"Oh man. I think I broke my Cossacks."

"Your coccyx, Lukie."

Luke didn't seem to have witnessed the ill-fated demise of his board, and Sylvia wasn't sure how he would take the news. Perhaps it was best to distract him. "Except now instead of a cock-six," she said, "you're gonna have two cock-threes."

"Huh? Oh yeah, right." He almost laughed. Still rubbing his ass, he thought about it for a second. "Or at least a cock-five and a cock-one."

"Sure! Or maybe even a cock-four and a cock-two!"

"Cockatoo, cockatoo!" Luke crowed, flapping his wings. They both broke into laughter then, until Luke noticed the absence of his skateboard. "Hey, where's my board?" he asked, looking all around, before spotting half of it lying in the middle of the road. "Aiyhhhgh!" he shrieked at the sight of it, and instinctively started toward it. But Sylvia held him back, throwing her arms around his shoulders. "No! Leave it. There's nothing we can do."

Luke slumped into her, dejected and mournful. "You're right. Dammit! I can't look." He turned and trudged back to the garage just in time to see his father pull a helmet from a big plastic tub of sporting equipment.

"Found it!" grinned his father.

Luke moped around the garage for another hour with his father repeatedly asking him questions: "Do you still want this?" or "What about this guy here?" or "Are you sure you don't need any tools?" Luke consistently responded with "no," even though he sort of wished he could keep some of these things, like his old bike or his dad's weight set. But he knew he had no place to put them. His new apartment wasn't the most spacious, and it wasn't as if it had a garage. Luke's growing despondency reached its peak when he opened one of the 'LUKE' boxes to discover his old VHS collection. These were useless now. He could never afford to buy a VCR. He simply closed the box without a word, and moved on to the next box of junk, each one just as useless as the last.

Sylvia played with her phone intermittently but she finally got so bored that she decided to go into the house to ask Luke's mother about those spoons she had heard about.

"Uh, hi," she said awkwardly, entering the kitchen.

"Oh, hi dear. Tired of the men folk are we?"

"Yeah. I guess."

"I've been telling him for years to get rid of all that junk. Luke doesn't need any of it anymore, and it's not as though we would use it. Especially not in Peachland. You know, he's talking about buying a boat now. At least we'll be close to the lake down there so maybe that makes some kind of sense, I suppose, but I can't see sitting out there getting sunburnt and sea-sick all day, can you?"

Sylvia shook her head.

"But you really can't tell men a thing, can you?"

"Right," Sylvia mumbled.

"It's still early, and I wasn't going to start on dinner yet, but you look so hungry."

I do? Sylvia thought, looking down at her body.

"Why don't we get going on preparations? You can help me whip up the batter, and then I'll fetch you those dishes while it bakes."

This prospect didn't sound particularly appealing to Sylvia, but she had to admit that she was starting to feel a little hungry, now that Mrs. Clark had mentioned it. Sylvia once again had a recurring conversation with herself. It was an internal dialogue that arose whenever she thought of Mrs. Clark, which admittedly was not very often, and the topic unerringly swirled around two rather awkward facts.

Firstly, it occurred to Sylvia once again that she had no idea what Luke's mother's first name was. Nor his father's, for that matter. They were two supposed humans who seemed to have no names. She had never heard either of them refer to the other by name, and Luke of course just called them dad and mom. Despite this fact, Sylvia could only seem to perceive them as "Luke's father" and "Luke's mother," terms which were almost useless for an occasion such as now, which thankfully, occurred only rarely. And "Mr. and Mrs. Clark" was out of the question. The titles and last names seemed so old-fashioned. Using them made her feel like a child.

The second point typically followed the first, and was decidedly more disturbing. It concerned the distinct possibility that she and Luke might some day get married, and that Sylvia might actually and literally become "Mrs. Clark." This thought made her head swim, and even now she felt she needed to sit down. She promised herself that when she and Luke got married, she wouldn't become just another "Mrs. Clark."

"Would you get the flour from the pantry?" Mrs. Clark asked.

"Sure." Sylvia opened the closet door to reveal shelf upon shelf of canned goods, boxes of pasta, and sundry domestic food staples.

"It's the large tupperware bin on the bottom shelf. The one on the left."

As she hoisted the bin from the shelf, Sylvia realized that it would take a whole moving truck just to move Mrs. Clark's kitchen. She desperately hoped that they were planning on hiring professional movers. When it came down to it, there were really just two types of people in the world: the ones that hired movers and the ones that did it themselves — or rather, the ones that expected all their family and friends to help them.

Sylvia suddenly realized, with no small measure of trepidation, that she did not know for certain which type of people Luke's parents were. She really didn't know these people at all. This could end up going horribly wrong. She could envision them calling on Luke to come help them move. And of course, Luke would ask her if she wanted to come too. If she *wanted*. As if. There was no way in hell she was going to let herself get stuck helping Luke's parents move. Already she could feel herself being sucked into the trap. Here she was, already carrying a five-ton bin of flour, for crying out loud. Her feet instinctively stopped moving and she set the bin down on the floor, even though she was only four feet from the counter which had been her intended destination.

"I gotta go check on Luke," she mumbled, turning and walking briskly back out to the garage. Finding Luke there sitting on a pile of tires, listening to his dad rambling on about something that sounded dreadfully boring, she moved close to him, got his attention, and mouthed the words, "can we go now?"

"Now?" Luke blurted. "We're just in the middle of loading, and besides, we're having toad in the hole for supper!"

It was then that Sylvia noticed the large Salvation Army truck in the driveway, and the burly man leaning against it, smoking a cigarette. Luke was holding a desk lamp in one hand and a tennis racket in the other while his dad tried to hand him a bike pump.

Sylvia rolled her eyes. "Oh ehm gee, Luke. What the fu... What the *hell* is toad in the hole?" She generally tried not to swear too much in front of Luke's parents, or her mom, or Nana. It was not worth the trouble. Luke's dad didn't seem to notice.

"You know. We had it before, I'm sure. It has sausages, and like... dough? or whatever, and they're sticking their little heads out, looking around."

"Gross."

"No, no. It's super good, trust me. Oh, and you put gravy on it!"

Even Sylvia had to admit that anything with gravy on it couldn't be all bad.

"It's actually Yorkshire Pudding, baked in a pan, with sausages added," explained Luke's dad as he passed her carrying a large cardboard box, which he hoisted into the truck. There was still lots to load and Sylvia felt like Mr. Clark was about to ask her to help out. "I have to use the bathroom," she said, quickly dismissing herself.

~~~

Luke knocked on the bathroom door. "Syl? You still in there?" The handle turned and Sylvia finally emerged from the bathroom.

"Are you okay? What happened?"

"Facebook."

"Oh. Well, come on, supper's ready."

"Well, this smells delicious, doesn't it?" Luke's dad commented to no one in particular, judging by his lack of eye contact. He was already reaching for the serving spoon, even as he lowered himself into his chair with an exaggerated grunt.

Despite an initial perturbation at the appearance of the strange dish, Sylvia was pleasantly surprised by dinner. The toad in the hole was actually not bad, and there was a salad with sliced carrots and juicy baby tomatoes. Even though Sylvia rarely ate salad on purpose, she did like it if it had a decent dressing. And the baby tomatoes were so fresh they made her briefly reconsider the infantile branding decisions of the Ferrerra Candy Company.

Luke and his parents talked a little about Nana's health, and when Luke let on that he was slightly concerned about her mind, his dad dismissed him, saying no more than, "she's fine, Luke." Sylvia learned that Nana's medical bills were equally of
~~~

no concern, and that she was "doing alright" financially, due to her late husband's small chain of hardware stores.

"Say, that reminds me," Luke's dad now turned toward Sylvia, directing the conversation her way. "Luke tells me you recently started a new business?"

"Uh. He does? He did? I did?" What she wanted to say was something like, *What the hell, Luke!?* She considered kicking him under the table. But she could muster no response.

"So, what is it?"

"Oh, it's nothing really. Just small-time stuff."

"Well, give us an idea at least. Sales? Service industry?"

What's that supposed to mean? How slutty does he think I am? God! "Uh... sales... bespoke artisanal upcycling... primarily focusing on study aids. You know, trendy stuff. For the college crowd."

"I see."

As if.

"And you still work at the liquor store as well?"

"Oh, yes..." Mr. Clark seemed satisfied with her answers so far. *Thank God!* "Oh, yes, I meant to tell you, we have a very nice eighteen year old Lagavulin in stock right now." She remembered that Luke's dad, like many other pale suburban dads, fancied himself something of a scotch connoisseur. Sylvia thought this information ought to divert his line of questioning for good.

"Oh, very nice," Mr. Clark said as he slowly chewed his dinner. "Yes, I can picture myself enjoying a fine eighteen year old well into the evening."

Gross! Sylvia thought.

~~~

Eventually, the evening dragged on long enough that Sylvia could make an excuse to leave without seeming rude.
~~~

Sylvia reminded Luke to grab the large cardboard box by the front door — the one marked 'DISHES FOR LUKE' — and they said their awkward goodbyes.

"Well, we survived, I guess," said Sylvia, buckling her seatbelt.

"Yeah, that was fun," Luke agreed, staring out the car window at a funny-looking sparrow.

"But tomorrow I really need to get to work on the plan."

"The plan? For world domination?"

"Exactly."

Luke was quiet for a minute.

"What?" Sylvia asked, sounding a little annoyed.

"Well, I thought we better go see Nana tomorrow."

"Yeah... I just don't think I can." More silence. "You could go without me?"

"I guess…" Luke sighed.

"Oh, that reminds me. I was thinking, you know how you sold those pills to Horse-face?"

"Oh, yeah. The robot pills?"

"Yeah. He gave you twenty dollars for the bottle, right?"

"Yeah."

"Well, I was thinking you should try to buy them back from him. If they're good like you said we can get a lot more for them at a party."

Luke nodded. "Right, I guess so."

"So if you offer him twenty dollars for whatever is left, he basically got whatever he used for free, right? He'd be stupid to turn down a deal like that. Make sure you explain that to him."

"Okay."

"But don't actually say he's stupid."

"Sure."

A minute passed.

"Syl?"

"Yeah?"

"Can I have twenty dollars?"

Sylvia sighed and smiled. "It's always something with you, isn't it?"

"Haha, yeah."

Sylvia dug some cash out of her purse while she steered through the darkened streets. She handed Luke the money, then told him about her new theory, about how there are two types of people.

"Yup," said Luke. "Movers and shakers." He giggled. "And candlestick-makers."

Sylvia shook her head. "You're a goofball."

"Maybe," said Luke. "But at least I don't like moving by myself. I only do it 'cause I have to."

14

The Buy-Back

In the morning, Luke was happy to remember that he was now the proud owner of a spoon. At least, theoretically. He hadn't actually seen any of the dishes yet. Upon opening the box, he was confronted with a nest of crumpled newspapers. Digging into it, he found that the nest did indeed contain spoons. Shiny silver spoons, in fact, and forks and knives to boot. And underneath those, a pile of porcelain plates and soup bowls. He recognized the dishes as having occupied the glass cabinet in his parents' dining room for many years. He couldn't recall ever having used them before. "Wow! Brand new!"

It was a great way to start the day, eating Lucky Charms with a brand new bowl and a silver spoon. What more could a guy ask for?

<div align="center">~~~</div>

As Luke stepped onto the number 15, Hans greeted him warmly. "What's up, Luke?" he asked.

"Not too much, Hans. How's the old 15 treating you?"

"I can't complain. Life is good. Headed downtown?"

"Just visiting Nana."

"You're a good grandson," Hans told him, pulling the lever to close the door.

Luke smiled and headed toward the back of the bus. As he sat down, Luke's phone buzzed. It was Sylvia calling.

"Did you get the pills yet?"

"Not yet. I'm on the bus now."

"Okay. Call me when you get them."

"I will… Like right away?"

"Yes."

"Okay."

"Don't forget."

"I won't."

"You have the money?"

Luke panicked for a second, then heard the crinkle as he patted his pocket. "Yes, I have it."

"Okay, bye."

Luke said hi to a couple residents and staff members as he made his way to Nana's apartment, but he didn't see any trace of Horse-face.

He and Nana were as happy as ever to see each other, of course, and Luke was even happier to get a cookie from Nana than Nana was to give him one.

Luke went to the bathroom to make sure Nana's pill supplies were holding up. Then, back in the living room, he broached the topic of his day's quest. "So, Nana, do you know where Horse-face lives?"

"Oh, dear. It's *Horace*."

"Right. Horace. Do you know where he lives?"

"Right here in this building, Lukie! Isn't that something! All of our friends are right at hand! Lester too!"

Shit. He had almost forgotten about Lester. And now here Nana was, mentioning him and ruining a perfectly good day. And *"Right at hand*!?" Why did she have to say it like that!?

Never mind that, he scolded himself. *You've just gotta stick to the plan. Focus, man! Think of the robot pills. Think like a robot! Don't be distracted, it's world domination we're talking about here!*

"Bleep boop," muttered Luke.

"What's that, Lukie?"

"Nothing."

Eventually, after another cookie or two, Luke managed to find out from Nana that Horse-face lived "on the third floor, I think," but that if he needed to talk to him, he could ask the front desk to call him. It had been nerve-wracking, trying to get

Nana to spill the beans without blowing his cover. *I dunno how James Bond can stand all the pressure*, Luke mused.

Luke accidentally used the secret knock on Horace's door. *Shit! Nobody's supposed to know!*

Horace opened the door momentarily and said, "Shave and a haircut!"

"No thanks," said Luke. "Actually, I need to talk to you about our earlier, um, transaction…"

"Hmm?"

"The robot pills," Luke whispered behind his hand.

"Ah." Recognition twinkled in the old man's eyes. "You know what? They didn't seem to work too well after all."

"Oh. Really?" Luke was genuinely surprised.

"You got any different ones? How 'bout a trade?"

"Um, yeah! I mean, I don't have anything on me, but I could give you your money back for those. And I'll let you know when I have some other pills."

"I suppose that would be…" Horace trailed off as a group of elderly women suddenly appeared around the corner of the hallway. It was spooky how they seemed to materialize out of nowhere, like some coven of ancient spectral harpies. "Shhh!" Horace whispered to Luke, "It's the Bridge Hens! Don't say a word!"

"Hello-ooo Horaaace," gushed Laverne, the leader of the gang.

"Hello whore-ass yourself!" replied Horace in an affectation which somehow managed to sound completely innocent.

"How have you been keeping?"

"As well as one might reasonably expect, I suppose. And I see both you and your lovely friends are keeping up your girlish figures." Perhaps that observation was a bit of a stretch, but the ladies were obviously taking steps to keep active and fit, as was evidenced by the sweatbands they wore on their wrists and foreheads.

"Of course! Our bodies are temples! Isn't that right, girls?"

The ladies all nodded and muttered agreement, and Horace seemed to agree as well as he took in the glory that now surrounded him. Several of the women ran their hands along Horace's shoulders or chest as they passed by.

"Goodbye Horace. Don't forget, there's always room for one more at our bridge table!"

Horace stared at their sagging asses as they continued walking. Luke joined him in staring momentarily before realizing how gross that was — gross to look at them and gross to see them. He shook his head and tried to think of something else. Anything else. "What the heck is a bridge table?" he asked, imagining a long wooden table with suspension wires stretching up to the ceiling.

"Huh?" Horace was still gazing down the hallway. "Oh. Bridge. The card game, you know?"

"Oh. I'm not very good at card games. I played Canasta once."

"Indeed you did. As I recall you were in the rec room a couple of Wednesdays ago."

"Yeah."

"Lester tried to feed you his horseshit rules, did he?"

"What?"

"His rules. For canasta. They're horseshit."

It seemed ironic to Luke that a guy called Horse-face was standing here calling Lester out for horseshit. What were the chances? He was right, though. Obviously, Lester was a liar and a cheat who was up to no good. Luke realized that it might be a very good idea indeed to have Horace as an ally.

"Progressive my ass!"

"What?"

"Progressive, he calls it. Ascending and descending. Threes, Fours, Fives! It's ludicrous! Totally wrecks the whole game!"

Luke had no idea what Horace was on about, but it clearly had something to do with Canasta. "You play?"

"Played. Emphasis on the E.D."

Luke stifled a giggle at that. Erectile Dysfunction was no joke, even at Horace's age, and Luke wouldn't wish it upon his worst enemy. Well, maybe his worst. Maybe he did wish that Lester's old member would shrivel up and fall off like a withered leaf in October.

"Nope. I'm a Pinochle man now," Horace continued. "One game with Lester and I hung up my Canasta shoes for good."

Oh right, shoes. Luke had forgotten that Canasta somehow involved feet.

"It's too bad, though. I used to be quite good, you know. But those stupid rules of his... No thank you. I'll stick with my three cards. It's the proper way, see? Three cards, three cleans, three dirties. It all makes sense. It's perfectly logical and consistent. Three, dammit! It's good enough for the holy trinity and it's good enough for me! He can take his 'progressive' and shove it up his ass, I say. I only play good old 'conservative' canasta. If it ain't fix, don't broke it!"

"Yeah, sure. For sure." Luke pretended to agree. He was hopelessly lost now and needed to get the conversation back on track, so he pulled the twenty from his pocket. "Anyway, this is for those robot pills."

Horace regarded the twenty dollar bill. "Sure, sure," he said, then disappeared into his apartment. He re-emerged a minute later holding three pill bottles. "How much would you give me for these ones?"

"Um. Well. I was only supposed to buy the robot pills..."

"Ah. I see how it is. Hey, no problem. Why don't you take these two back to your, um... business partner." Horse-face's horsey teeth shone as he flashed a sly smile. "You kids figure out what you want to do, then make me an offer. I'm sure we can work something out, so for now just take these samples, and you can owe me.”

“Uh. Alright, I guess.”

Horace was fingering the pack of smokes in his shirt pocket. “I’m heading to the roof. You want one?”

Luke shook his head. “I’m good.”

“Are ya?” Horace chuckled. “Well, catch you next time then. You know where to find me.”

“On the roof?”

“Sure kid, sure.” Horace shuffled off, leaving Luke standing there with a handful of pills, wondering what he was getting himself into.

15

Umbrellas

Luke's jacket pocket rattled like a maraca as he jumped off the bus a block down from Sylvia's place. He played a rhythm as he walked, and soon began singing quietly to himself. "Na-na, na-na, na-na na-na, naa na. Na-na, na-na, na-na na-na, naa na." How had he never noticed this before? Blink 182 was singing about his Nana! *Of course! Surprises let me know she cares!* He continued the song all the way to Sylvia's, then had to purge it from his head so he could think of the rhythm of the secret knock.

He rattled the pill bottles at Sylvia as she opened the door. "Check it out! Castanets!"

"What's all this?"

"I got samples!"

Sylvia grabbed Luke by the jacket arm, and pulled him into the house. "Tell the whole neighborhood, why don't you!"

"Sorry."

"Let me see them. Where did you get these from?"

"From Horse-face. He said I could pay him later."

"Luke, what the fuck!? You were supposed to just get the ones you sold him, not clean out his whole medicine cabinet!"

"Yeah, but-"

"So now he thinks we owe him money?! How much did you promise him?"

"It's not like that, Syl. He said for us to tell him how much they're worth. These are samples, he said."

"Samples? He said that?"

"I think…"

"So like, he wants to be our supplier?"

"Umm, I don't know."

"Does he know about us?"

"Well, I think it's pretty obvious," Luke said. "I mean we're always together."

"No, I mean about our... business."

"Oh, I don't know. Kinda seems like it."

Sylvia thought over the prospect of working with Horse-face. It was probably a terrible idea. But then again... It could actually reduce their risk. Maybe they wouldn't have to rely completely on the pharmacy. If, that is, his shit was any good. She sat down at her mom's computer and peered intently at the labels on the bottles.

"Are you mad, Syl?"

"Just let me... I don't know yet. Give me like ten minutes, okay?"

"Okay." That wasn't too much to ask, Luke supposed, although he didn't like the idea of having to wait just to find out whether she was mad at him. By that time, he might not even remember what she was mad at him for. Luke really disliked it when people were mad at him, especially when he couldn't remember what they were mad at him for.

It didn't take long for Sylvia to track down info on the pills, and as much as she hated the idea of being in bed with Horace, she had to admit that his product might be too good to pass up. One of the bottles was OxyContin, a painkiller that was apparently pretty in vogue on the party scene. But according to the internet, the kids called it "oxy," or "the OC." *Oh God, what a douchey name. I am not calling it that,* she promised herself. The other bottle contained Seconal, also known as "Red Birds," which seemed to be a holdover barbiturate from a bygone age. They were now quite rare.

As for the "robot pills," they turned out to be a bit of a dud. The technical name for them was dimenhydrinate, but the drug was commonly known as Gravol. Sylvia was bummed to learn that what they had been pushing was the same stuff you give kids to keep them from throwing up on road trips. Not all hope was lost, however. Sylvia read that you could get high off them if you took enough. It would be stupid to sell stuff that you needed to take whole bottles of, though. Clearly they still needed to get ahold of some higher quality merchandise.

"We need better stuff, Luke."

"Is that stuff no good?"

"Some of it's okay. Horace said he could get more of this?"

"I think so."

"Okay, well let's keep that in mind, I guess. But we really need more high demand products. Adderall, Ritalin, maybe Codeine?"

"What about LSD?"

"Yeah, right."

"What?"

"That's not exactly... That's totally different, Luke. We're talking about prescription stuff."

"Can't you make a prescription for LSD?"

"Phft! Sure." Sylvia raised her eyebrows and rolled her eyes in two different directions.

"What? Why not?"

"Are you serious? Luke, LSD is not a medication. It's a designer party drug. Same with cocaine or shrooms."

"Oh. Well how am I supposed to know?"

"Some drug dealer you are!"

"So we can't get cocaine, either?"

"No! Not unless we travel back to 1910."

"Well, how the hell do you design a shroom anyway?" Luke pouted for a moment. "Well, what about Valium?"

"Valium? Umm, yeah, I think we can get that."

"Better get some Valium for sure." Luke felt a bit of smugness mix with his embarrassment. It wasn't like he didn't know anything.

Sylvia spent the next hour making prescriptions for Valium and Adderall, while Luke suggested fake patient names for her to use.

"What about Dan Touine? Like from Star Wars?"

"I've got a bad feeling about that one," she responded coolly. Luke laughed, but Sylvia remained laser-focused on the screen.

"What about Harry Johnson?" Luke was cracking up.

"Luke…"

"Dusty Balzac?"

"Luke, I'm not going to use those! I already have it figured–" She turned from the screen. "I mean, they're really funny, baby, but they're not going to work, okay? Maybe you should go write them down on a piece of paper and we can laugh about them later."

"Okay!"

"I'm just gonna put the finishing touches on these and then I'll meet you in the living room."

"Sounds like a plan, Stan… Duptapee HAHAHA!" Sylvia flashed a lazy smile and set back to work. But as Luke turned to leave the room, he got a phone call from his mom, which was kind of weird because Luke's mom didn't call him very often. When he answered she seemed to be in an uncharacteristically mothering mood, which was also weird.

"Luke honey, I'm just worried about you. How are you gonna manage when we're not around?"

"What?! Mom, why didn't you say anything? Is it cancer!?"

"Oh, silly. I mean when we move. It's just starting to feel real to me now, you know?"

Luke wondered why his mother was acting so strange and affectionate. He had no way of knowing that during her packing and cleaning activities, his mother had found an uncorked half bottle of Chablis hiding in the back of the fridge. It seemed risky to pack any liquids without a good solid screw-on cap, and she had never been the type of person to waste perfectly good wine.

"Mom, I'll be fine."

"I know, honey. I know. I just worry about you and her."

"What? Who, Sylvia?"

Sylvia's eyes were suddenly locked onto Luke like laser beams — laser beams that locked on — and her ears seemed to swivel and twitch like those of an attentive cat.

"Well you know how she is."

"No I don't! What are you talking about?"

"Oh, nothing. It's just that she can just be a little aloof at times."

Luke didn't really know what that meant, but it didn't sound like a compliment.

"And a little… domineering? Well, you just have to be careful with girls like her…"

"Girls like her?" *Domineering?* Luke was shocked. He and Sylvia had never been into that lifestyle. "Mom, I dunno-"

"Hey, what the hell!" Sylvia interjected angrily, and Luke took the phone away from his face. She lowered her voice to a harsh hushed tone. "Did she seriously just call you up to bitch about me?!"

"Hey don't call my mother a-"

"Oh, so now you're taking her side?!"

"Hey, come on. What did I do?" Luke momentarily brought the phone back to his face. "I gotta go, Mom."

"Yeah. Maybe you better go," Sylvia agreed.

What? Luke couldn't believe it. Was Sylvia actually kicking him out? Damn! What the hell was going on? His mom calls up just once and all hell breaks loose. It made no sense to Luke at all. "Unbelievable," he muttered under his breath, then made for the door.

~~~

It was a long walk home. Luke didn't feel like waiting for the bus. He didn't want to be around people right now. He
~~~

trudged along the sidewalk. It started to rain — not extremely hard, but hard enough. Like life. Everybody gets soaked by the time they get home. Luke sank into a reflective mood. Sometimes everything just kinda sucks, he philosophized. Maybe that's why people turn to drugs. Maybe it's just a way to forget about the suck for a little while. To keep the rain off. Like an umbrella. He really could use an umbrella right now.

He kept trudging on through the rain. What else could he do? He trudged past the happy park, but this time there were no happy children playing or walking their happy dogs. There were no happy couples sitting on happy park benches. The lawns and the trees were bedraggled and sad. The shadowy spruce grove was dark and misty. Two high school kids huddled under a black umbrella and smoked a joint. Were they sad or happy? Luke wasn't sure. You never could tell with teenagers.

<p style="text-align:center">~~~</p>

"Syl?"

"Yes."

"Are you still mad?"

"No."

"Are you sure?"

"... Yes."

"What are you doing tonight?"

"I don't know."

"Do you wanna come over?"

"I don't know. Don't you have to work tonight?"

"Oh yeah. I forgot."

"Let's do something tomorrow, okay?"

"Okay."

"... Do you wanna go to the Lodge?"

"Really? Yeah, of course!" That was a new one, Sylvia suggesting that.

"We need to talk to Horace." And frankly, she wasn't sure she could trust Luke with the necessary negotiations. She had to establish some parameters and expectations with this Horace guy if they were going to be doing business together.

"Yeah, okay. And visit Nana too, right?"

"Of course."

"Okay see you tomorrow."

"Yeah."

Luke went to work and, like a diligent robot, cleaned the insides of the corporate mega-robot that was Denecorp Systems. He still felt off. He had not entirely sorted out his feelings. In any case, they gave him an uncanny energy which made him clean faster than he had ever cleaned before. He scuttled around making beeping noises like R2-D2 and sweeping with unprecedented gusto. Scott must have been working fast too, because they got the whole place clean in record time — only two hours. Luke was pretty happy about that, until he remembered he was paid by the hour. It would be a pretty small cheque. *Bummer.*

16

The Cough

They found Horace on the roof after there was no answer at his door. The way he smiled widely as he held his cigarette in his mouth suggested that he was genuinely happy to see Luke. And he was even happier to see Sylvia.

"Aren't you looking splendid," he crooned.

She did look quite splendid, standing there against the blue sky in her leather boots and her jean jacket, radiant with the afternoon sunshine. All eyes rested for a moment on her, as if she were the only thing worth looking at on the whole roof, which she most certainly was. The roof, the entire structure beneath it, and all the people inside it, and maybe the rest of the world too, may just as well have been merely a platform for the splendid splendour that was Sylvia on this fine afternoon. At least, according to Luke and Horace. But Sylvia's eyes looked out over the city, looked down on all the world like a due inheritance.

Horace took a long drag on his cigarette. He held out the pack toward Sylvia.

"Why not?" she said, to Luke's surprise. He almost objected, but she shot him a quick glance.

"Why not indeed," said Horace, offering his lighter, and flashing Luke a quick wink. They stood savouring their cigarettes and staring resolutely into the horizon. Horace finished his smoke and flicked his butt off the roof. "So?"

Sylvia was in no hurry. She took a few more drags, then ground her butt under her boot. "So." She took a few steps toward the edge, her back facing Horace. "Firstly, we should thank you for providing these samples. Obviously you know we're trustworthy, and we think you are too. Now, about the products in particular. These aren't exactly what we're looking for. But we think we can do something with them. I'm thinking twenty a bottle."

"I like the sound of thirty."

"How about I meet you halfway?" Horace scratched his scruffy chin. "And we would be interested in future business as well," Sylvia added. Now he rubbed the back of his neck. "Well. You drive a hard bargain, miss. But I suppose that'll work for me."

Sylvia gave Horace the cash and they shook hands. Horace shook hands with Luke too, just to make him feel like he was part of it. But they both knew he was just a mule.

~~~

A few minutes later, Luke knocked on another door. But there was no familiar call from Nana to come in, and no other sounds either. He tried again and was met with the same results. Finally, trying the door handle, he found it unlocked, and cautiously opened the door. "Nana?" Still nothing. And she didn't appear to be home. "That's weird," Luke told Sylvia. "She's not here."

"Uh… Luke?" Sylvia pointed at Nana, who was sound asleep on her recliner, under a grey blanket.

"Whoa!" whispered Luke. "I didn't see her there! She's so stealthy sometimes. Like a cat!"

A dead cat maybe, Sylvia thought.

"She must be tired. We'll sit with her and wait."

"Wait? While she sleeps for god knows how long? Come on Luke, let's just go."

"No, no, come on. We came all this way to see her!"

No, we came all this way to have a business meeting.

"Let's just wait for like a half hour and see if she wakes up."
~~~

She pretended to consider the idea. So far, staying silent was working well. If he kept going, Sylvia thought, Luke might just bargain himself right into leaving.

"Okay fine, let's just have a cookie or two. That'll only take a minute. And if she wakes up we can stay for a little while and visit, and if she doesn't we can go, okay?"

Bingo.

Luke got the cookies from the cupboard and sat on the couch, on the end nearest Nana, as was his custom.

Sylvia didn't feel like a cookie so she played on her phone, which gave Luke the same idea. He read his favorite funny meme feeds as he munched on cookie after cookie. Sylvia was just about to tell Luke that time was up, when suddenly he broke the silence with a violent guffaw, spitting cookie crumbs, and somehow also inhaling a few, which triggered a loud and long coughing fit.

Nana stirred and snorted, but went back to snoring softly, as a knock came on the door. Luke was trying to recover by gulping down a can of soda, so Sylvia approached the door.

"Hi," she said to the man at the door.

"Oh hello, uh, I'm Doctor Parnell. Is everything alright? I heard a commotion.

"Oh, yes Doctor. Thank you for checking. She seems to be fine now, but our Nana seems to have developed quite a cough."

"Huh?" Luke questioned from the couch, "But Syl…" He stopped himself. *She must have some kind of a plan. Some kind of a* sneaky *plan.*

"I wonder, Doctor — Parnell, was it? Since you're here…"

Parnell. Why do I know that name? thought Luke.

"Nana ran out of her medicine this morning, but this cough, I think it might be getting worse. Is there anything you can do?" She ushered Doctor Parnell into the apartment and tried to maneuver him toward the counter where there was plenty of room for writing prescriptions. Doctor Parnell instead approached the old woman, listening carefully and observing the rise and fall of her breathing. He peered at her face.

"Luke, can you go get Nana's empty pill bottles from the bathroom?"

Luke, looking a little confused, trundled down the short hallway.

"The *empty* ones, remember."

"Uh huh." The medicine cabinet had plenty of pill bottles, but none of them were empty. "Uh, Syl?!" he called.

"Need help, Luke?"

"Yeah."

Moments later, Sylvia joined him in the bathroom and shut the door behind her. "Come on, hurry. I think she's waking up!" Sylvia started grabbing pill bottles and quickly reading their labels. "Um, I dunno!" She ripped the lid off one and quickly dumped the contents into the pocket of her jean jacket. She was about to open the door, when Luke grabbed her by the arm.

"Wait! Sylvia! Did he say Parnell?"

"Yeah," she answered slowly, stretching the word out. This was not the negative reaction she had expected from Luke in this situation.

"I know that name! He's the bass player from Soundgarden!"

"You mean the singer. You're thinking of Chris Cornell."

"Oh right. Right. But somebody's Parnell."

"There's the guy from SNL. Oh Yeah! That's right! And he was a doctor too! On 30 Rock! They called him Spu-che-min, but they spelled it like spaceman. It's funny 'cause I always assumed it would be spelled Specimen, you know?"

"Why?"

"You know, like a stool specimen."

"Like a little chair?"

"No, a stool — never mind. Like a urine specimen!"

"Oh, I get it! Dr. Specimen! Yeah that's hilarious."

"Okay, come on." She reached for the door handle.

"Wait!"

"What now?"

"Remember before? We were here that one time, and there was a different doctor, wasn't there? Remember? Or was that guy a fake?! Or is this guy a fake?"

"There's more than one doctor, you know."

"Well, yeah but..."

Meanwhile, in the living room, Nana had woken up, and had been startled to see a man's face inches from her own. She had almost slapped him. But now they had made amends and resumed a more traditional doctor-patient style of relationship, with him asking her questions, and nodding knowingly at her answers. He scribbled something on a pad and ripped off the top page to hand it to Nana.

"Oh, Doctor, Lukie runs my errands for me, don't you dear? Could you pass it to him please?" Luke arrived just in time to receive the slip of paper, which Sylvia promptly took from him and began to examine.

Hydrocodone. Never heard of that one. "Um, Doctor Parnell? Here's that other medicine I was telling you about." Sylvia handed him the empty bottle.

The doctor looked at it and wrote another prescription which he also passed to Luke, and which Luke immediately passed to Sylvia.

Aricept. Another one to research. And now she had a pocket full of them. The doctor talked with Nana a bit longer, and Sylvia saw an opportunity. "Well, we better give you two some privacy. Come on Luke. Doctor-patient confidentiality, right? It's the law."

"Oh!" Luke certainly didn't want to break the law. On his way out he called, "Goodbye Nana! Goodbye Doctor Specimen!"

In the elevator down to the lobby, Luke chuckled. "Man, these doctors just hand out these prescriptions like candy," he said. But then he realized that they had just done it again — they had told another lie. He drooped his head and ran his hands through his messy hair.

"Okay," Sylvia chimed. "Now we'll get these filled and then later I'll go and fill the fake ones in my purse. There's a party tomorrow night and we're going to make a killing. Then on Monday we can go back to the college and–"

"Syl…" he began.

"What?"

Luke took a breath and started to voice his concerns as the elevator door opened. "You said we weren't–" But then there was Lester. Wicked Old Lester, standing there with his hands on his hips, a leatherbound Bible clutched against his right side. Luke snapped to attention, suddenly far too conscious of his posture.

"Well, well, look what the cat dragged in! Hullo, son. Hullo, little darling."

"She's not little," Luke exclaimed, stepping out of the elevator toward Lester.

"Luke!" Sylvia snapped.

"No, I didn't mean it like that! Aghh." *Stupid Lester.* There was that sly toothy grin of his again.

"Here visiting Esther?"

"Yeah, so?" Luke mumbled, now looking at the carpet.

"I was thinking of paying your dear grandmother a visit myself. I just came from Bible study. We're going through the major prophets."

Luke and Sylvia both saluted. It was a bit of an inside joke with them, whenever they heard the word major, or general.

Lester continued, oblivious to their gag. "You know, you kids could learn a thing or two from that Jeremiah." He puffed up his chest and held his Bible out in front of him. "'The prophets prophesy falsely, and the priests rule by their own power; and my people love to have it so. But what will you do in the end?'"

"Huh?" Luke said. *Shut up, you wrinkly old freak,* he thought.

"Why don't you join us for chapter six next week, Luke? I'll introduce you to the fellas. It would be a chance for us to get to know each other better. I'd invite the both of you, of course, but it's just a men's group. You understand."

"We can manage our profits on our own, thanks," Sylvia said.

"Suit yourself," chimed Lester. "Well, I'll see you kids in the funny papers." He chuckled as he stepped onto the elevator. *I'll see you in hell!* Luke thought with contempt. As they turned to leave, Lester called out again. "Oh, one more thing." He held his finger on the button to hold the door. "A little birdie told me you've been hanging around with Horse-face up on the roof." Luke swallowed nervously, but Sylvia stayed cool. "You kids watch yourselves around that one. A real wolf in horses' clothing."

"Yeah, well, at least he doesn't play cards with his feet," mumbled Luke.

"We can take care of ourselves, thanks." Sylvia stared him dead in the eye as she spoke. Luke thought she sounded like an action hero, like Trinity from *The Matrix*.

Lester examined them for a moment. "Of course," he said. "Well, you two take care, eh? As our Paulo says, 'Vaya con Dios.'" His lips formed a thin smile and he slowly nodded as the elevator doors closed.

"I hate that creep," Luke muttered as they crossed the lobby. "Horses don't even wear clothes!"

After filling Nana's new prescriptions, Luke and Sylvia rode the bus to Luke's place. As they sat at the back of the bus, while Luke took in the sights of the city through the filthy window, Sylvia was bothered by a remark Patti had made at the pharmacy. She had commented that Nana seemed to be going through a lot of medication. Sylvia had covered by telling her about how Nana had been feeling unwell, had even described her terrible cough in great detail. But what disturbed her most of all was not Patti's comment or the possibility of her suspicion; it was that only now did Sylvia fully remember that it was Luke who had been coughing, not Nana. Yes, she had known this from the start. Of course she had, at least on some level. But somewhere along the line she had convinced herself that the stories she had told were the truth. But this aside, Patti was a liability. What if she ran into Nana at the lodge and asked her about her cough? No, everything would be fine. Nana was going senile anyway, and everybody knew it. And no one had any reason to suspect any wrongdoing from her and Luke, the kind young couple who always visited their Nana, who always cared for her and brought her her medicine. Yes, everyone at the lodge knew they were good people. Or at least that's what they believed. And wasn't that what really counted?

Through the flecks of dirt on the glass Luke spotted a man with a scraggly beard lying on a bench. *Lying* — the word rang out in his head and echoed again and again. Now Luke remembered why he had been upset on the elevator — before the run-in with Lester, that is. What was it that Lester had said? *Prophets lie false and the peace rules with almighty powers; and people love to have it.* Luke sighed. People love to have it alright. *So what will you do in the end?* He felt the weight of this question's great importance. What would he do? He had to talk to Sylvia about this. Or to *someone*. Would Sylvia even listen to him anymore? She had already told him they would stop lying, but now it seemed that had been a lie too.

17

Red Bird

Luke met Sylvia at the Wendy's by the mall — this felt wrong somehow. The inside was almost exactly the same as the one on Lonston, but Luke didn't recognize any of the employees. In fact, they all seemed strange to him, like aliens from another planet disguised as fast food workers. *Or like robots,* Luke thought. *Where are my robot pills?* He really could have used something to take the edge off. Sylvia had been running errands that morning. Apparently she had been shopping as well. She was wearing big sunglasses and a shiny leather jacket when she walked through the door.

"Woah, Syl, you look like Arnie!"

She sat down across from him. "Ready for the party tonight?"

"Yeah, I guess so. How much do you think we can make?"

"If we play our cards right, we could score a few hundred."

"Holy moly!" Luke exclaimed before Sylvia shushed him.

"Hey, Syl," Luke's expression turned morose. He hesitated a moment, staring at the salt shaker on the table before continuing. "There's something I want to talk to you about."

"Anything, Luke. What's up?"

"Well, it's just–"

Sylvia's phone buzzed. "I'll be back," she told him, getting up and heading to the bathroom.

Luke sighed before getting up, walking to the counter and ordering three Junior Bacon Cheeseburgers.

Sylvia seemed to have forgotten all about Luke's pressing concern by the time she returned from the bathroom.

"I need you to be lookout again tonight, okay? And I need you to make runs to and from the car with the money and the product. I don't want to carry too much on me at once."

"Okay," Luke mumbled. He desperately wanted to make some kind of Terminator joke, but couldn't think of anything remotely relevant.

"Thanks, Lukie." She smiled at him.

Lukie? "I got you a JBC," he told her.

"Oh, okay. I wanted chicken. Whatever. So, I got all the prescriptions filled this morning. All we have to do now is wait until tonight. And I've been thinking…"

"Yeah?"

"We should have some kind of safe word."

"What?! Shhh!"

"No, not like that! I mean, in case something goes wrong. We don't want a repeat of last time. We need a way to warn each other, but subtly — discreetly, remember?"

"Oh, I get it. Like in spy movies. 'The eagle has landed,' right?"

"Yeah, just like that."

Luke's order was called and he got up to grab his tray of food. He returned and placed down the tray. "The patties are on the table. Repeat, the patties are on the table." He chuckled at himself.

Sylvia scowled. "No, they're not."

"What? What's wrong, baby?"

"Why do you always have to bring her up?"

"Who?"

"Patti. Or Round Patty, for that matter."

"Hey, don't call her that. But that's not what I was saying anyway. It was a code. Like the eagle, remember?"

Sylvia's expression was firm. She was deciding whether or not to be angry. "Oh. Right. Well, anyway, we need something better than that." She unwrapped her burger. "It needs to be something that would be normal to say in a regular conversation, but that we won't say by accident."

They chewed this over as they chewed their burgers. Sylvia finished hers first and swallowed. "How about this? 'My aunt called. The dog is on the loose.'"

"Which aunt?" Luke asked, his mouth full of masticated beef.

"No, that's the safe word. Well, safe sentence, I guess."

"Oh, I get it. 'My aunt called. The dog is on the loose.' I like it!"

"So if things look like they're turning south, one of us will say that to the other, and we'll calmly and discreetly leave."

Luke nodded.

~~~

The party was in full swing when Luke and Sylvia pulled up in the Grand Am, the early summer sunset reflecting brilliant hues of orange and pink off the cracked windshield. Sylvia placed an assortment of pills in an empty Excel mint tin and locked the rest in the glove box, giving Luke the key. "When I slip you money, you drop it here and bring me more supply."

"Okay, baby." Luke was trying to cheer himself up. They were going to make a lot of money tonight. And besides, parties were supposed to be fun. But Luke didn't end up having any fun at all. He spent a lot of time walking from the backyard, where music blared and people mingled, to the car, where the relative silence bid him stay and sit for a while. But he had a job to do. So despite his inclinations to rest he returned each time to the backyard and looked for a vacant, isolated piece of patio furniture to sit on. There were too many people at this party and it was getting late. Luke was worried the cops might show up. He remembered the code and stayed alert, ready to use it at a moment's notice. Then another worrying thought entered his
~~~

mind: What if Red Wings showed up? Now *that* would be bad. *Unless...* Maybe Luke could turn Red Wings back to the light side of the force. He was obviously into the colour red — and birds. So, Luke thought, it stood to reason that he would really be into these new Red Bird pills they had scored from Horace. Surely such a tantalizing treat would lure him back into their good graces.

In the end, neither of these things happened, and Luke and Sylvia left the party around one in the morning, $300 richer. Their profits put Sylvia in a great mood and Luke considered using the opportunity to talk to her about the lying. Maybe she wouldn't get so defensive now. Then again, why would he want to bring her down when she seemed so happy? He decided to forget about it. There was no harm done, after all. Maybe those last couple lies had been necessary, and from here on out it was all honest work and rightful reward.

~~~

The next week brought a veritable financial windfall to Luke and Sylvia's operation. After a rocky start at the college — with neither Luke nor Sylvia realizing that the spring semester had ended, leaving only a small population of summer students — things had picked up when Luke had pointed out the bulletin board full of posters advertising the upcoming summer mixer. At this party Sylvia was even able to make a bulk deal with the club treasurer of the engineering club, a previous client. By the end of the week, Sylvia was almost out of product. It was time to restock.

Sylvia watched the clock on the POS computer at the liquor store. The minutes seemed to be flowing by like frozen molasses. Although she appreciated the employee discount, Sylvia was tired of her job. In fact, she suddenly decided, she hated her job. What was she still doing here anyway? Hadn't she proven that she could be her own boss? She had made more
~~~

money from selling pills in one week than she made here in three. Granted, she had to split that money with Luke. But she had big plans. Soon she would be out of her mom's house. Soon she and Luke would get married. Why not? They could even afford a nice wedding, just like her dad's second one, with champagne and ice-cream cake and a wicker arch covered in real flowers. And, of course, a beautiful white dress. It was all lining up. If she and Luke got married, her mom would get off her back — and Luke's nana and his conniving mother would be powerless to drive them apart. And they could live together and keep running the business, building it into a robust empire, until they had made enough money to settle down somewhere in Nova Scotia, far away from Willow Lodge, in a gorgeous mansion right on the ocean. Yes, that was what she wanted, and that was what she would have. But Luke would have to propose first. She frowned and traced her finger along a deep scratch on the wooden counter.

Charlie emerged from the back room across the store. "Hey Sylvia, would you mind stocking that new wine shipment?" She gestured toward a pile of boxes next to the till. Sylvia groaned. "There's already tons of wine stocked already."

"Right," Charlie said quizzically, "but this is new wine. It's a different kind."

"Oh, it all tastes the same anyway."

Charlie stood still and blinked at her. "Okay, but it still needs to get put on the shelf. And that *is* your job."

"Is it, Charlie? Is it?"

Charlie was mildly taken aback. "Yes, it is," he said calmly. "You've been doing it for years."

"Yeah, I have!" Sylvia shouted. Her nostrils flared and her brow stiffened. "And all you've ever done is boss me around and make fun of me."

"Make fun of you?" Charlie chuckled incredulously.

"You're doing it right now!" Sylvia threw her arms in the air, knocking over a display box of rolling papers.

"Just stock the wine, please." He turned his back and entered the back room again. "Time of the month," he muttered to himself, shrugging his shoulders.

"Well, I quit," Sylvia whined. But, unbeknownst to her, Charlie did not hear her.

In a fit of rage, Sylvia walked straight from the liquor store to the Superstore pharmacy. By the time she arrived, her anger had subsided a little. She took a deep breath as she approached the counter, behind which stood a tall friendly-looking man.

"Hi there," the pharmacist said warmly.

"Hello," Sylvia replied. "Just refilling these." She pulled two empty pill bottles from her purse and placed them on the counter.

"Sure thing," the man said. He took the bottles and examined the labels. "How's your day going so far?"

Sylvia sighed. "Not so bad. I got a new job today."

The pharmacist walked behind his counter. "You don't sound too thrilled about it."

Sylvia shrugged. "No, I am," she offered.

"Well, congratulations..." He glanced down again at one of the bottles. "...Dianne." He smiled at her.

"Huh?"

The pharmacist looked more closely at the bottle, then back at Sylvia. "It's Dianne, right?"

"Oh, my name?" Sylvia felt her face flush. "Yes, Dianne... I thought you said Iceman."

"Iceman?"

"Yeah," Sylvia sputtered. "Like from X-Men? He's the ice one."

"Oh. Right." The pharmacist looked down at his work, keeping Sylvia in his peripheral vision. Sylvia turned around, trying to casually look around the store. She felt a bead of sweat roll down her underarm.

"Oh, you know what?" The pharmacist's voice sent hot-and-cold icicles up her spine.

"Hmm?" she replied, only half turning around, pretending to examine a box of lip chap hanging from a rack.

"I should have asked you for your ID. Do you mind?"

"Oh," Sylvia said. "Sure, no problem." She pulled out her wallet and opened it up, pretending to search through it. She furrowed her brow. "What the heck?" Her performance was commendable, if not Oscar-worthy, as she dug manically through her purse. "I'm so sorry," she said, sounding as if she were asking a question. "I don't seem to have it. That's so bizarre."

"Oh no," the pharmacist said, with affected sympathy.

"Can I bring it in next time?"

The pharmacist paused, watching her. She glanced up and met his eyes, hoping her face wasn't bright red. She tried her best to sound helpless, to soften her features, to weaken him with her feminine gaze. "I really need my medication," she pleaded. He looked away. "Please have it next time," he said, before walking away.

When he returned a few minutes later, Sylvia had regained her composure somewhat. She took the pills, smiled at the pharmacist and turned away, resisting the urge to run as she felt his wary eyes on her back. That was too close.

18

The Catch

No more mistakes, Sylvia repeated to herself as she drove downtown to pick up Luke. *No more mistakes and no more close calls.* The sidewalks were busy, full of pedestrians waiting for the right moment to jay-walk, just itching, it seemed, to jump out in front of her car. Sylvia scowled. She hated driving downtown. She braked at a four-way stop and watched an old lady in a motorized cart cross in front of her like an asthmatic turtle on wheels. Just as she was reaching the other side, a young couple started crossing the opposite way. "Come on!" Sylvia moaned. Sylvia glared at them as if it would make them walk faster, which it didn't. The boy, a stupid-looking stringbean with light brown hair, glanced over at Sylvia and she promptly looked away and cursed him under her breath. Sylvia thought that the city was kind of like a zoo, full of stinky animals. Except instead of being locked up in cages, the animals were free to run around wherever they liked. Because of this, Sylvia thought that the city was even worse than a zoo.

Luke and Scott had had a great time cleaning a newly-leased office building. The job itself was pretty run-of-the-mill, but the two had been riffing for hours, and had reached a real groove. It all started when Scott had made a joke about the new Goof Off stain remover he had bought. "Well, if I start to Goof Off," Luke had responded, "you can always use some Goof Gone!"

"It's called Goo Gone, ya goof!" Scott said with a smile. But the goofs didn't end there, and soon Luke and Scott were veritably busting up. And so, when he said goodbye to his boss and stepped into Sylvia's car, Luke was in a very giddy mood. "Hey hey, honey bunch!" He leaned over and kissed Sylvia on the nose.

"What are you doing?" Sylvia spat.

"I'm just giving a sweet kiss to my sweet girl." *Now what did I do?* he thought helplessly.

Sylvia took a breath. "Sorry, babe. I'm just stressed. I didn't mean to snap at you. It's just, you have to be careful when you go for a girl's nose with no warning."

"You're right," Luke responded. "I'm sorry." Luke understood. You had to watch yourself these days.

Then Sylvia smirked and quickly kissed him on his nose.

"Hey, what the?! Why I oughta!" They laughed. "I love you," Luke said.

"I love you too," Sylvia said. They shared this moment together, staring into each other's eyes. If they had looked close enough, they could have seen their own reflections.

"Hey, I got you something," Sylvia said, reaching for her purse.

"Woah! Like a present?" It wasn't even Christmas, and Luke's Birthday was still months away. Sylvia pulled a small black pouch with a velcro flap out of her purse and handed it to Luke.

"Here. Open it." Luke held the pouch up to his ear and shook it. "It's not LEGO," he joked, giggling to himself.

"Luke…"

"Alright, alright." He tugged on the flap and pulled out a sleek pocket knife. "Woah, badass!" He flicked open the blade and examined it with awe. It had one of those cool rainbow blades.

"Do you like it?"

"Totally! Thanks, Syl!"

"I was thinking it would be a good idea to keep it on you when we're working. Just in case."

Luke felt a knot form in his stomach. "Oh."

"You won't ever have to use it — I promise. It's more like a safety precaution, okay?"

"Okay," Luke mumbled as he folded the knife and returned it to its pouch. Luke didn't feel giddy anymore. He felt a different way — sort of weird and slimy, like a banana slug.

"Ready for dinner with your parents tonight?"

Right! How had he forgotten? This was going to be the last time he would see his parents before they moved to Peachland. This only made him feel worse. "Oh yeah, I guess I just need to get changed."

Sylvia smiled patronizingly. "That's why we're headed to your place."

"Okay," Luke said. They sat silently through every red light on 10th, Sylvia exhaling sharply and muttering under her breath each time they were stopped. But once they left downtown Sylvia spoke. "Luke." Luke had heard this intonation of his name before. He recognized this pause between it and the matter at hand. He braced himself. Sylvia continued, "I've been thinking." *Oh no.* "We've been together for almost four years now. And it's time to start thinking about our future."

"Okay," Luke said cautiously. "What about it?"

"Well, what do you *think*, Luke? I'm not getting any younger. I want people to know we're serious. I want a commitment."

"What do you mean? You're still young, baby."

"Luke, are you happy with the way things are now?"

"Of course!"

Sylvia frowned and furrowed her brow. "Well, I'm not." Luke winced. "I need to know that this is serious, Luke. I need to know that I'm the only important woman in your life. I don't understand why you haven't..."

"Haven't what? Syl, you know you're my whole world! Just tell me what you want and I'll do it!"

Sylvia parked the car abruptly on the street outside the apartment building. She looked Luke in the eyes. "Propose to me!"

Luke was silent. "Like, for getting married?"

"Yes, Luke! For getting married! God, why are you like this?!"

"Like what?"

"Forget it." Sylvia turned to stare out the driver's side window. Luke heard her sniffling, watched her still shoulders hunched up and her beautiful hair that smelled like strawberries.

"We can get married," Luke offered meekly. "Of course we can."

Sylvia turned back to him cautiously, her eyes now wet with tears. "You mean it?"

Luke nodded. "Yeah. After we make a bit more money, of course."

"Okay," Sylvia said, smiling. She nuzzled her head into his chest. "I'm sorry I've been such a bitch lately."

"No," Luke assured her. "Don't say that." He held her against him and stroked her hair. She had said what she had wanted to. He had said what she had wanted him to. But Luke knew that there were other things that had not been said.

~~~

For the rest of the day Sylvia seemed to be back to her sweet cheerful self. Luke had somehow been able to convince her not to mention the marriage plans to his parents yet — after all, he hadn't even bought her a ring yet. So at the restaurant Luke, dressed in his best collared shirt, and Sylvia, in a stunning skirt and blouse combo, greeted Luke's parents with hugs and sat down at the table.

"It's going to be so strange not living in the same city as you anymore," Luke's mom said. "We'll miss you, Luke." Luke's dad nodded agreement.

"I'll miss you too," Luke told them.

Sylvia added saccharinely, "We both will."

Luke and his dad ordered the same beer, a final father-son ritual before they departed.
~~~

"But we won't be far. You can visit whenever you like."

"Thanks, Dad."

"Oh!" he said. "We have to tell you about the call your mother got last night."

"Oh, yes! It's so bizarre!" Luke's mom put down her glass of wine as her eyes widened.

"So we were just finishing up the packing in the kitchen and–"

"No, we were in the living room. We had just finished the last box."

"That's right. And then the phone rings–"

"My cell," Mrs. Clark interrupted. "We had packed up the landline."

"Yes, your mom's phone. And anyway– Well, why don't you just tell it, Dianne?"

"No, you tell it. I'm not good at telling stories."

"No," Luke's father insisted, a tinge of frustration evident in his voice. "You go ahead."

"Alright, fine, I'll tell it. So my cell rings. And I pick up the phone and they say it's the pharmacy. So, I ask what they're calling for — not in a rude way, I mean, just because I was confused. They never usually call, so–"

"Okay, you guys, I have your breadsticks for you." The waitress hovered over the table with the basket of breadsticks, looking for a spot to place it down. Luke had assembled a large triangle with his and Sylvia's cutlery, which took up a large portion of the table's surface. The waitress moved Mrs. Clark's glass of water out of the way and plopped the basket down. "Do we still need a few minutes to decide on the food?"

"Yes, please," Mr. Clark said.

Luke eyed the breadsticks like a starving buzzard. He hadn't had a breadstick in ages. And these ones were covered in herbs and parmesan cheese. He snatched one, loudly said, "GET IN MAH BELLY," doing his best Fat Bastard impression, and shoved it in his mouth.

"Luke!" Sylvia looked around the restaurant to see a few people looking curiously at her boyfriend.

"The story," Luke's dad prompted his wife, taking a breadstick.

"Oh right. So, anyway, I pick up the phone and it's the pharmacist, and I ask them what's the matter, and they say…" Luke's mom had read in a magazine once that a good way to make a story more engaging was to take dramatic pauses to heighten anticipation. Here Luke's mom inserted such a pause into her story for this effect, but also to take a bite of her breadstick. She continued, "They say that someone with my name had been there to fill a prescription — well, no, it was more than one prescription, they said. And that's why they were a little suspicious, because it wasn't me, and the person didn't have any ID. But anyways, it went out under our health plan. So they don't know what to think."

"Well, they think this girl was trying to cheat them by using a fake name," Mr. Clark added.

"Well, maybe. Or maybe it's a coincidence, they said. But in any case, I told them it wasn't me and that this other Dianne Clark, real or not, shouldn't be covered by our insurance."

"Right," Luke's dad said.

"But the scary thing is, if it was really some kind of scammer, how did they know I was a customer at the pharmacy?"

"Weird," Sylvia said. "Lucky guess, maybe. Who knows? Could be hackers, too. There's a lot of bad people on the internet."

"Isn't that the truth." Luke's dad took another breadstick and ripped it in half.

"Anyway, since we're moving I just told them I wouldn't be back there and that they can delete my information, or whatever it is they do."

"Smart," Sylvia said. She was holding it together pretty well so far. But she felt her face flushing again. "I'm just going to run to the washroom," she announced.

After this, there was no mention of pharmacies or deceits, and our party shared a satisfying and reasonably priced meal, courtesy of Luke's father's credit card company. And then came the good-byes. The Clarks were not skilled at parting, and no one was certain when the right time was to get up from the table and leave the restaurant. Sylvia, for her part, simply smiled and assured everyone that they would come down to visit very soon, satisfied that the Clarks had turned out to be the type of people who hire movers. But as soon as she and Luke walked out of the restaurant, arm in arm like a couple at the end of an old movie, worry set in. The Superstore pharmacy had quickly gone from last resort to non-option. She needed a new plan.

"Wanna go to the movies?" Luke asked suddenly.

Apparently the whole arm in arm scene had penetrated his psyche. "Ooh yes! Something romantic!" Sylvia agreed.

The movie was anything but romantic, with Luke spilling popcorn all over the place in the midst of nearly continuous blazes of gunfire. Sylvia lost the plot near the beginning, being too distracted by her worries. She sighed repeatedly in the dark for nearly two hours, not that Luke noticed.

~~~

"Hi Luke," Patti greeted him as he approached the pharmacy counter.

"Hi Patti"

"How's that cough?"

"What? Oh, um..." He coughed into his sleeve exaggeratedly. "Getting better I guess. Slowly."
~~~

Patti looked a bit confused, but pasted on an awkward smile as Luke handed her the paperwork. She took the forms into the back room, then reappeared about five seconds later.

"Whoa, that was quick," said Luke, before realizing she was not carrying any medicine.

"I almost forgot," explained Patti, "I'm supposed to deliver all the medications directly to the residents now. The bosses..." She looked around furtively as if her bosses might be lurking around any corner. "Well, we need to be more careful. Don't want any medications going missing or anything."

"Why would..." Now it was Luke's turn to look around. Maybe there really were bosses hiding behind the corner, just waiting for him to screw up so they could catch him in the act and spring their trap.

"Oh it's just... It's nothing really, just a couple of silly pieces of paper 'go missing' and it's suddenly a big deal."

"Oh. I see. Um. I hope you didn't get in trouble?"

"Not so much me personally, but they had to call in auditors and everything. It was really just a big waste of time if you ask me."

"Oh, well that's good. About you, I mean."

"Aww thanks hun."

Luke wasn't sure what to do next, so he simply stood there.

"Was there anything else?"

"Um. So like, you're going to bring the medicine to Nana yourself?"

"Yep, should be by later this afternoon."

"Like, to her room?"

"Yes, I'll bring it right up. Don't worry about it at all."

"Uh, okay, I guess."

Luke ended up visiting with Nana for hours while he waited for the pills to arrive with Patti. On the one hand, it was nice to have so much time to spend with Nana. But on the other hand, he did start to get bored after a while. Plus, he was kind of freaking out about how to salvage this situation. He texted Sylvia to ask her what he should do. After several exchanges, Sylvia was clearly becoming more and more frustrated. Finally, she texted back, "I'M COMING THERE."

Luke was able to relax a little, knowing that Sylvia was on her way. He now summoned enough mental clarity to really enjoy the plate of cookies that had sat almost unnoticed on the coffee table in front of him. By the time her knock sounded on the door, he was in good spirits, and he jogged over to open the door and give her a big hug.

"Okay, okay," Sylvia told him, as his hug persisted somewhat longer than required. She brushed him away, then brushed away the cookie crumbs that he had managed to transfer onto her shirt. "God!"

"Thank God you made it!" chimed Luke.

"Did she show up yet?" Sylvia whispered, quiet enough that Nana probably couldn't hear her.

Luke seemed surprised, and looked around the room.

"Patti, you idiot!"

"Oh! Not yet."

"Good. Just let me handle it, okay?"

"Yeah, of course. That's why I called you."

"Oh, Sylvia dear," interjected Nana, "would you like a cookie, sweetheart?"

"I'm good. Luke already gave me enough." She subconsciously brushed her striped T-shirt once more, just in case any rogue crumbs had gone undetected.

"Are you sure?"

"Oh yes, I couldn't possibly." She smiled sweetly at Nana. She was laying it on pretty thick now.

"Now, that reminds me," continued Nana. "Sylvia, you remember my friend Horace, don't you?"

Her friend? Um, okay. "Yes. Why?"

"Oh! Well, he was asking about you. I think he wanted to talk to you."

"Oh, I see…" She exchanged a look with Luke.

Just then there was another knock on the door. Since Sylvia was still standing relatively close to it, she opened the door to reveal Patti, holding a small white paper bag.

"Oh, hi. Thanks so much for bringing these up," Sylvia gushed, reaching for the bag.

Patti instinctively pulled back her arm. "Oh! Umm… Sorry, they… I'm only supposed to…" she glanced toward Nana, "Well, the bosses, you know, they were very insistent."

"Bosses," Sylvia shook her head sympathetically. "I know how that goes." Still, she stood in the doorway, blocking Patti's entrance.

Patti stood at an impasse for a moment, until Nana caught her eye and the two waved at each other awkwardly over Sylvia's shoulder.

"Hello Patti!" called Nana.

"Hi Esther, how are you?"

"Won't you come have a cookie with us? You know Sylvia don't you? And of course you remember Lukie?"

"Nana!" Luke objected to his pet name being used in public.

"Of course. Hello. Um, well I really can't stay. I have several other residents to deliver to…" she glanced at her watch.

"Oh that's too bad!" Nana frowned a little. "But I understand. They do keep you busy, don't they?"

"They do."

"Well then. Give the bag to Sylvia, dear."

"I'm really not allowed…"

"Come come, Sylvia will hand it right to me, won't you dear?"

"Of course." Sylvia concurred perhaps a bit too quickly.

"You can watch her hand it right to me, see?" Nana was now stretching out her arm, expectantly.

Patti looked Sylvia in the eyes, only to find Sylvia already looking in hers. Patti's arm began to move slowly forward, as if under Sylvia's volition. Patti felt as though she were powerless to stop it. What choice did she have? The bag drifted slowly forward right into Sylvia's firm grasp.

"Thank you Patti," she smiled. Then, turning sharply, she strutted, beaming, straight toward Nana, sat down primly onto the couch beside Nana and placed the bag into her still-outstretched hand.

"Thank you Sylvia, and thank you Patti." Nana exclaimed with misplaced exuberance, as she placed the bag onto the coffee table.

"You're welcome," replied Patti dryly.

Sylvia stared at Patti with her best cover-girl smile until the closing door all but erased her. "Now," she turned to speak to Nana, "why don't I put these away for you in your cabinet?"

"Oh thank you, that would be wonderful."

As Sylvia stood with the paper bag, Luke let out an enormous sigh, garnering a questioning look from Nana, and an evil eye from Sylvia. He tried to cover it by morphing it into a fake cough, which spiralled into a real cough and sent him stumbling toward the kitchen sink, where he stuck his head in to drink directly from the tap.

"Oh my. Lukie, are you alright?" Nana attempted to rush toward him to offer assistance. With his head still in the sink, Luke saw out of the corner of his eye a blurry Nana appear over the countertop. His unfocused perspective made her appear like a teetering turtle rushing at him with benefactorial intent. The idea of an ambulance turtle leapt into his mind with such clarity and speed that he burst into a laughing fit, which, given the current location of his face under a stream of cold water, did not alleviate his condition in the slightest. He was now sputtering and coughing worse than ever and he fell to the floor, into a semi-fetal position, and tried desperately to breathe.

Nana hovered uselessly, making strange exclamatory noises, just as one might expect from an ambulance turtle, and down the hallway, Sylvia's head popped out of the bathroom momentarily, more than once. Luke caught this in his peripheral vision, adding more fuel to his turtle hallucinations

By the time Luke had settled into a limp but steadily-breathing mass on the kitchen floor, he had given Sylvia enough time to not only stash the medication in her purse, but also to conduct a brief inventory of said medications, which she had amazingly managed to somehow memorize and recite back to Luke once they safely reached the hallway outside Nana's apartment.

~~~

The sun nearly blinded Sylvia as she stepped out onto the roof. She instinctively adjusted her sunglasses as she strode toward the faded silhouette of a man smoking a cigarette.

"Got a smoke for me?" she inquired.

Horace drew out a Craven A and handed it to her.

"I thought you were a Player's man."

Horace shrugged. "Love the one you're with."

Sylvia accepted the cigarette and the light Horace followed it with, then walked a slow circle, surveying her surroundings as she took a long drag. She inhaled the city sprawled below her. The sun was at her back now, ensconcing her in a dazzling halo, gleaming through her hair and faux fur collar.

Luke shielded his face with a forearm and squinted in astonishment. Horace grunted.

"So?" Sylvia directed at Horace. As if waiting for his cue, he gently knocked over an old upside-down coffee can with his shoe, revealing a crumpled paper bag. The two looked at Luke expectantly.

"Oh! Let me get that." Luke stooped and picked up the bag before handing it to Sylvia.

She examined the bag's contents, making indistinct yet somehow affirmative sounds. There was a wide variety of
~~~

medications inside. Some she recognized, some she didn't. A few were easily marketable — drugs she could move in a pinch. A couple bottles of benzodiazepine were the clear winners here.

"You've been busy, Horace."

"The smoke trade is always stable."

The two men could almost see the gears in her head turning — crunching numbers, analyzing. "I'll give you two hundred." It wasn't a question.

Horace considered for a moment. It was a bit of a low-ball. They both knew it. But finally he nodded, extending his hand. Sylvia tossed the bag to Luke and sealed the deal with Horace.

Luke stood five stories up, in the middle of town, jutting up across the skyline, holding a bag full of drugs. He could almost hear their private helicopter coming in for the pickup.

19

Munchausen By Proxy

Sylvia sat at her kitchen table with an Excel spreadsheet open on her laptop. She sorted the pill bottles while Luke looked on, eating a Space Pop. "Look. For anxiety, panic attacks, and insomnia, there's Benzos. Got Alzheimer's? Donepezil."

"Donna who?" Luke grinned.

"Quit goofing off, Luke! This is important. What if I have to send you to the college one day to make a sale? I can't do all the work, you know."

"I know," he mumbled sheepishly. Then he muttered to himself, "Donna Pezzel." *Sounds Italian for sure. That's-a one spicy meat-a-ball!* He wished he could say this out loud, but Sylvia clearly wasn't in the mood.

"For pain, we got Oxy. Pain plus a cough? Hydrocodone. Dizziness? Well that's just plain old dimenhydrinate — Gravol, remember?"

"Of course I do!" he snapped. But he didn't. He remembered gravel though. Once, when he was a kid, Luke fell off his bike and got his knee scraped up pretty bad. The gravel had stuck into the wound and his mother had poured rubbing alcohol on it, which hurt like he couldn't believe. *Right, gravel for pain.*

Sylvia's phone rang and she answered it. "Yeah... Yes... Yeah, for sure... Okay... Today? 2:00?" She looked at her watch, then at Luke, who stared blankly, not even trying to guess at what she was talking about.

"Yeah, yep, five each... Uh huh. I'll send my guy... Library, sure." She hung up, then turned to Luke. "I need you to take this to the college." Luke stared at her, taken aback. "You better hurry or you'll miss the bus."

"What?!" Luke objected. "But Scott's coming to pick me up for work!"

"Forget about that!" Sylvia had certainly forgotten about it. "You'll just have to tell him you can't make it. We're gonna make way more on this sale anyway."

"Yeah but... Can't *you* go to the college? Then I can still go to work and we can make even *more* money."

"No, I can't. Look, these supplies are running out. That dude I was just talking to? He said his buddy is gonna call later. We gotta track down more Donepezil right away. I'm going to the lodge."

"To the lodge? Without me? But, Nana–"

"It's not about Nana, Luke! I have to talk to Horace right away! This is serious."

"Well what if *I* go to the lodge–"

"Right! You go make the big deals with Horace! As if, Luke. What are you thinking?"

"I could–"

"Look, just take this, hurry up, he's gonna be in the library and he'll give you a hundred bucks, okay?"

I could make the big deals, Luke told himself, as he jogged toward the bus stop, *I would just need Sylvia to tell me how much stuff was worth, and what it's for, and... who to sell it to... and...*

<div align="center">~~~</div>

Horace and Sylvia stood on the roof. Two of Horace's cronies waited in the background, by the roof access door, their dark silhouettes looking like stern statues. Horace snorted and spat on the gravel rooftop. "Hmm. Who knew the "old timers disease" would be such an opportunity, eh?"

"Ironic in a way," Sylvia responded.

"Well. So here's the thing. It's not quite so easy getting these ones. They don't wanna give 'em up. You see, them what got it, these folks actually *want* to take their pills. They figure they need 'em. Who knows, maybe they even work. And it's not just the crazy pills. It's the painkillers too. They're not so easy to get ahold of."

"Still, there has to be a way. You're a smart man, Horace. I'm sure you can think of something."

They stood in silence for a few moments, contemplating the issue at hand. One of Horace's henchmen coughed. Sylvia looked up. "What if they didn't need the pills?"

"You got some sort of miracle cure?"

"No, I mean what if they didn't really have it at all?"

"Oh believe me, they have it alright. It's all this sittin' around they let them do in here. It's just like in prison." Horace rubbed his chin in thought. "Idle minds are the devil's playground."

"Sure, some have it. But what about your buddy here? He got it?" She gestured at the man who had coughed.

"Him? Naw, he's just naturally stupid."

"Okay, so you get him to pretend."

Horace stared at Sylvia and took a long drag on his cigarette.

"It's actually kind of perfect," Sylvia continued. "It's all in your head, right? There's nothing for the doctors to see, really. You tell them, 'I'm having trouble remembering.' What're they gonna say? 'You're full of shit?'"

"Hmm," Horace grunted. "Give me a minute." He shuffled over to his henchmen. The three of them spoke in hushed tones with plenty of animated gestures, the third guy glancing in Sylvia's direction several times. It didn't worry her. Horace would get his guys in line. He knew what he was doing. As did she. The movers and shakers had to move and shake. There were leaders and there were followers. And there was a thin line to walk between trust and manipulation. She understood that.

She turned toward the skyline. Smoke streamed from her nostrils to the east, toward the smokestacks of the mill and beyond to the distant mountains. Their streams merged into the river, which flowed on resolutely, as it would for a thousand years. An eagle drafted silently, high upon invisible currents.

Horace returned as she snubbed out her depleted butt on the roof balustrade. They shook hands and exited the roof wordlessly. A gust of wind tugged at the cigarette butt, causing it to shiver once, then twice, before sending it twirling to the ground far below.

~~~

Luke walked into the library with a strange sensation in his stomach. Even after being here a few times, he still felt out of place. In fact, due to a growing anxiety about the nature of his business at the college, and the fact that he was here for the first time without Sylvia, this feeling was stronger than ever. Still, the college inspired in Luke a certain awe, like some kind of holy ground. He felt that if he'd had a sword, and if he were to partly unsheath it, he would notice an eerie blue glow emanating from its blade. As he looked around, Luke began imagining each of the library's occupants as a type of avatar. The short red-head seated at the table nearest him was obviously a Mountain Dwarf — it was probably best to leave her alone. Similarly, a dark shadowy figure in the corner with his face masked by a large book was a clear read — Luke knew a Warlock when he saw one. The bartender paid Luke no mind as he stood in the doorway between the anti-theft sensors and scanned the room.

Here we go. Across the crowded tavern he spotted the adventurer. He was dressed for travelling, his backpack stuffed with all his essential inventory items — all except his potions. Luke approached the man, ignoring a group of giggling High Elves seated nearby.
~~~

"Ahem," Luke signalled the traveller.

The traveller ignored Luke.

"Ahem," he tried again.

The man looked up. "What do you want?"

"Ah. My good man," Luke replied, in a strange affectation that somehow fit his new shopkeeper persona. "I believe the question is, 'What do YOU want?'"

"Okay, what do YOU want?"

"No, I mean… You've got it backwa…" Luke trailed off, noticing movement in the corner of his eye.

"Dude!" A kid at the next table was calling him. "Wrong dude, man."

"Sorry?" Luke stammered, coming to his senses. He was in the library. He was talking to the wrong guy. "Sorry," he told the wrong guy, then made his way pseudo-casually over to the real guy, and began to pull out a chair.

"Don't sit down," said Real Guy.

"What? Why?"

"Let's just get this done quickly."

"You're the guy, right?"

"Yeah."

Good, good. Identity confirmed. "I'm…" *Wait, no, don't tell him your real name!* "I'm uh, Donna Pezil." *Shit! What am I saying? Who's gonna believe that?*

Luke took the bottle from his pocket and placed it on the table. Real Guy snatched it quickly and it disappeared into his inventory. Scowling, he slid five twenties toward Luke.

"Ah, five gold pieces. Thank you, adventurer."

"Whatever." Real Guy promptly opened his book and pretended to be engrossed in his studies.

20

Empire

"Okay, are you ready for this?" Sylvia handed Luke several pill bottles.

"Yeah! I got this!" Luke was confident. "Oh! Almost forgot." He rifled through the glovebox and pulled out a bottle of red pills. "I got a plan."

"Oh yeah? Well you go get 'em, tiger!" She came around the car and tossed Luke the keys. "I'll still need you to run back for supplies, though, hey?"

"Yeah, sure baby."

She gave Luke a kiss and a hug, and as she moved into him her furry leopard-print jacket tickled his forearm.

"Ho-Lee! Baby, you smell amazing! You smell like fuckin'… like fuckin'… like fuckin' Christmas, baby!"

"It's my new perfume," Sylvia beamed. "We're finally doing good, you know? Making actual money. I thought I'd treat myself to something special."

"Yeah baby!" Luke was practically bouncing up and down now. He grabbed her hand and they skipped toward the house as the sounds of partying emanated out through the warm evening air.

The party was booming, and getting bigger and louder by the minute as a steady stream of fashionably late and lately fashionable partiers trickled through the door. The house was soon bursting and the crowd leaked out into the backyard. Luke and Sylvia almost had to shout to hear one another. "Stay in the living room in case I need to find you," Sylvia told Luke. "I'll cover the back."

"Okay!" Luke responded, though he was not a hundred percent sure what Sylvia had said. Momentarily, a guy Luke vaguely recognized approached him. His blue and white striped shirt reminded Luke of a sailor's outfit. His mouth moved but it did not seem to make any sound.

"What?" Luke shouted.

"Whaddya got?" the sailor yelled louder.

Luke pulled two bottles from his pockets and held them up so the sailor could read the labels. The sailor pointed at one of the bottles, then raised four fingers. Luke realized that this silent communication was actually his ideal style of salesmanship. It was nice not having to think of what to say — or not to say, for that matter. There was a tidy flow to it — hands, fingers, pills, cash. Yes, this would be a good system. Money comes in, pills go out. *Like the tide,* Luke thought. He soon got into the rhythm of if. Customer after customer materialized in his vision, and he processed each transaction with great efficiency. It didn't take Luke long to empty one of the bottles. It didn't take him long to empty the next one either.

Soon his pockets were empty, save for one bottle of red pills. But these weren't for just anybody. No, he had one particular customer in mind for them, and he scanned the room now, searching for that telltale clue. Yes, there it was — the distinctive red cap. And as the crowd churned and spun, the unmistakable flying wheel of the Detroit Red Wings logo rotated into view. Luke approached the hat. His hands preceded him, extended forward like blades to separate the mass of roiling bodies until the hat floated just ahead. The body beneath it was dancing clumsily, holding a can of beer in one of its hands. Its face transformed into a pattern of confusion upon noticing Luke standing there, demanding its attention. This body was clearly not up to the nuances of non-verbal communication that Luke had now grown accustomed to. Luke raised his hand to give it the one signal that could not be missed: it indicated, "Come with me."

Luke exited through the front door, only bothering to check behind him once outside. But sure enough, there was Red

Wings closing the door, leaving the two of them standing on the cement doorstep.

"Wha's goin' on?" Red Wings slurred.

"I have something for you."

"What?"

Luke held up the bottle of red pills.

"Wait a sec. You're that guy… Where's your bitch?" He almost spat the last word.

"I don't know. It doesn't matter."

"Huh? Oh!" The guy's reeking breath assaulted Luke as he looked him in the face. "Oh, you dumped her ass? Well good on you, bro!"

Luke shook the pill bottle. "You like the Red Wings, right?"

"Yeah, man. Bertuz rules!" Red Wings shut his eyes, tilted his head skyward and gave a high-pitched whoop.

"Right, totally. Well, then you're gonna love these." Luke removed the cap, grabbed a single pill, and held it between his finger and thumb. "These are called Red Birds." Luke's prospective customer stared at the red pills and blinked his eyes slowly. Luke continued, "Red birds are where red wings come from, right?" Red Wings gave a giddy little laugh. The pill bobbed gracefully up and down like a bird flapping its wings as Luke held it between his fingers and moved it slowly through the air. "These babies will take you to the statusphere."

Red Wings grabbed the pill and shoved it in his mouth before downing the rest of his beer. "That's right, fly! Be free!" Luke encouraged him. Red Wings stared off into the distant clouds, enthralled by his newfound freedom. "A hundred for the rest," said Luke, sad to bring up such mundane necessities.

Red Wings' face took on a sour expression. "Naw man, I'm good."

"Come on dude, I got these ones in special just for you. Red Birds for the biggest Red Wings fan!"

"Really?" asked Red Wings guy.

"Yeah man, for real!"

"Well I dunno. Let me see… Hold this, will ya?" Red Wings guy handed Luke the beer can, and began to fumble with his wallet. The can was empty, and Luke let it drop to the ground. "Umm… All I got's ten bucks." He shoved a purple bill at Luke.

"Okay, I guess. Here." He shook four pills from the bottle and dumped them into Red Wings' hand.

"I'll hold the rest for you for next time." Luke left Red Wings examining his Red Birds and attempting to make one of them fly between his fingers as Luke had done.

Luke got the rest of the bottles from the car and returned to the living room. He slipped back into vending machine mode, as he now decided to call it, making sale after sale without a word. The customers appeared one after the other like clockwork — Purple Pants Guy, Denim Skirt Girl, Old Bald Wizard. A bunch of completely unmemorable, nameless, faceless robots. And then the most beautiful human woman in the world. She was waving and shouting frantically as if she didn't comprehend the complex operations of Luke's machine. "LUKE! LUKE!"

"Oh! Hi Syl!"

"What the hell's the matter with you?!"

"Nothing! I just…"

"I need you to go get the rest of the pills."

"Yeah, here, take them."

"No, you keep these, I need more from the car."

"These *are* from the car."

"Ugh. The OTHER ones. The REST of them!"

"Syl, this *is* the rest of them! I already went to the car."

How was this possible? It didn't add up. "So they're all gone? What did you do?!"

"I sold them, baby."

"You sold *all* of them?" *Oh geez, what is this? Liquidation World?* She cocked her head, more than a little skeptical.

"Yep. Even a few of these Red Birds."

"Lemme see the money."

Luke gave her the "come with me" signal, and then headed outside where he showed her that he had indeed sold all the pills at their correct prices and had the legal tender to show for it.

"Huh. Well, good job, baby," she said, a little vexed that Luke had outsold her.

~~~

Sylvia cringed imperceptibly as they entered Willow Lodge. As if the place wasn't bad enough on a normal day, there seemed to be some kind of special event brewing. The lobby crawled with the hunched and decrepit husks of former humanity, milling about and dragging themselves aimlessly around bunches of garish helium balloons. It smelled like an old sock covered in fresh bandaids.

Nana and Lester waved. Sylvia could not bring herself to return the idiotic gesture. Not far away she spotted Horace, talking to an equally gangly-looking woman who had to have been at least a thousand years old. The woman noticed her and approached at an alarming pace. How was such speed even possible in her condition?

"Oooh, hellooo," the woman crooned. "It's um, oh dear, it's Sylvia, isn't it?"

"How do you–"

"Oh it's terrible! I'm having such a bad time with names! Oh, and the headaches, and the coughing…" She looked around dramatically, smiling a little while producing a strange half-gurgle-half-bark.

"Um, do I know you?"
~~~

"It's Laverne, dear! It's alright. We'll talk later, I'm sure." She spun on her heel and retreated as quickly as she had appeared.

"Okay, then," said Sylvia. But she was alone. Luke had already made his way over to Nana, and appeared not to have noticed this whole scene.

Lester was blathering on about God-knows-what as Nana patted Luke's hand like some kind of puppy dog. A racket behind Sylvia startled her, and she whirled to see a pair of white-haired Q-tip-looking women hacking their lungs out and staring right at her. One of them winked at her, and the two scuttled away giggling.

"What the hell is going on around here?"

"What the HECK, you mean," replied Lester. "And what it is is the Watermelon Day Extravaganza! You got here just in time! The spittin' contest is about to start any minute now. You know, I've won it three years running."

"You don't say," Sylvia responded flatly.

A staff member pushing a small cart with a large plate of watermelon slices stopped in front of Sylvia.

"Go ahead, dear." Nana nudged Sylvia's arm gently.

"I'm good," she replied.

Luke, of course, took this nudge as his cue to reach for another slice, even though he was somehow already holding one in his other hand.

"Where did you — never mind."

Luke shrugged and took a large bite of watermelon.

"So, Nana," Sylvia began. "How is your cough doing? Still pretty bad, hey?"

"Cough? Oh, no. It's much better."

"Still, with this air quality. Seems like everyone's got a cough."

Nana nodded agreement. Luke shot Sylvia an evil eye as he swallowed the watermelon. "Nana doesn't have a cough. You're fine, Nana."

"Oh yes, I'm fine," Nana nodded.

Sylvia frowned at Luke.

"Excuse me, miss." Horace approached with a toothy grin.

"Back off, Horse-face," growled Lester.

"You back off, and mind your own business, you filthy swindler."

"I am minding my business—"

"Excuse *me*," interrupted Sylvia. "I'm not your business. And it's *my* business who I talk to. So back off."

Both men stopped abruptly.

"Shall we?" She crooked her elbow toward Horace, who joined arms with her, and the two walked away, leaving Lester, Nana, and Luke flabbergasted.

"My goodness," said Nana.

"I think that feller just stole yer girl," Lester told Luke.

"Naw, it's not like that," explained Luke. "They're just, um..." He couldn't really say they were talking business. "They're friends."

"Well, she sure knows how to pick 'em."

"Yeah."

Sylvia and Horace walked to the elevator without another word, followed at a subtle distance by Laverne, who ducked into the elevator with them as the doors were starting to close. Sylvia said nothing as the elevator ascended. She said nothing as the bell dinged upon their roof level arrival. She said nothing as Horace exited, walked down the short hallway, and held open the roof door for her. She even said nothing as this Laverne, for whatever reason, followed them right out onto the roof. Finally, she turned and addressed her two companions. "Somebody wanna tell me what the hell's going on here?"

Horace licked his lips. "My boys and me, we've been getting you what you need. But, uh... well, there's only so many folks 'round here you can trust, y'know? So I uh—"

"I want in," Laverne cut him off. She was blunt and forceful. Sylvia could appreciate that. Maybe she wasn't such a fool after all. She obviously knew what was going on. "My girls are just as capable as Horace's old boys. More so, in fact…"

"That's what all the coughing and winking was about."

"You got it. And what's more, I've got a whole new supply for you too, if we can cut a deal."

"How's that?"

"Same deal as with him, but I also have external sources."

"External?"

"Willow Lodge isn't the only game in town."

"I'm listening."

"I've got connections in every care home in town. Canada Post, thirty-five years. I was doing the North Judson route when you were still shitting your Pull-ups, pardon my French. I bet you'd like to see this little operation of yours grow, right? Well, you can expand alright. But you can't do it without me."

Sylvia considered Laverne's words. She was probably right. The supply was barely keeping up already, and if Luke turned out to be as good a salesman as he appeared to be at the last party, well, they were gonna need a lot of pills to push. And besides, knowing what she did, Laverne was now a liability. Sylvia might as well make an asset out of her.

"My girls and I will take care of everything," Laverne went on. She proceeded to outline details about her contacts at Shady Lane and Hill House, the two biggest drug havens in the local independent living scene. She even had plans for who was going to fake what symptoms, and who had already been building up a backlog of pills they just never bothered taking. Sylvia was exhausted just listening to her.

"Fine," Sylvia conceded. "But all the stuff goes through Horace. Let's keep things simple." Sylvia didn't want to have to interact with Laverne again. There was something about her

Sylvia found off-putting. Actually, several things. For one, she had this habit of scratching below her eye with her pinkie when she talked. Luckily there were no qualms about Sylvia's condition.

Horace tipped over the coffee can, and groaned as he stooped to pick up the bag before handing it off to Sylvia. "This from you?" she asked, turning to Laverne, who nodded with a self-satisfied smile. It was a decent mix. "Try to get more Oxy next time," Sylvia told her. There was another bottle of Red Birds, which she held up and inspected more closely. "Seconal," read the label. Her research had not identified any demand whatsoever for this particular drug, but somehow Luke had managed to sell five of them in one night. That fiancée of hers was still full of surprises, she had to admit it.

21
The Bridge Hens

"Come on Syl, JBCs! How can you go wrong?" Luke had a real hankering. He could almost taste that wavy applewood smoked bacon.

But Sylvia was hesitant. "Well…"

"And besides I haven't seen you for days," Luke whined over the phone.

"I know. But I'm just really busy."

"Too busy for snuggles?"

"Hmm."

"Why don't you pick me up from the Lodge, and we can go to Wendy's real quick, and then head over to my place?"

"Okay. I guess."

"Woohoo!"

After a one-word text from Sylvia to announce her arrival, Luke jogged through the lobby, toward the front door. He could see Sylvia's mom's car idling just outside. He was ecstatic to finally see his girlfriend again. Plus, there would be JBCs.

"Lukie!" A voice from behind.

"Nana?" He turned. No, it was Laverne. Luke would have been surprised to find himself talking to Laverne at all, had it not been for a favour she had asked him to do for her the day before. "Oh there you are. I was looking for you earlier," he told her.

"The girls and I were power-walking," said Laverne. This much was evidenced by the uniformity of their sweatbands. "Doris, hurry, take the girls out and distract that one."

The Bridge Hens swarmed out the front door and stood between the Lodge and Sylvia's mom's car, talking loudly in a feeble attempt to form some kind of elderly smokescreen. One of them even went around to Sylvia's side of the car and gestured for her to roll down the window. There was no way in hell Sylvia was falling for that. *What are these bitches up to?*

Laverne and Luke were talking — about what? What the hell would Luke possibly have to say to her? Unless it had something to do with the product flow. *Fuck!* Already, her process was breaking down. Laverne was supposed to go through Horace, who would come to her. How did Luke get into the mix? She began to fume. Between the gaggle of women trying their best to shield him from view, Sylvia saw Luke take what looked like a crumpled-up shopping bag from his jacket pocket and give it to Laverne. Sylvia was about to open the door and go investigate, but there were the Hens, clucking and pecking all around her car. *God!*

Luke was on his way over now, and the cloud of Hens suddenly dematerialized into the night, letting Luke pass through to join Sylvia in the car. She glared. Luke pretended not to notice. *Really? You want to play that game? Fine!* She drove off with a chirp of tires, and the two rode along in silence.

"What's the matter?" Luke asked, trying to sound innocent.

"Yeah, right!"

"What?"

"What? Really? What the fuck was that!?"

"What?"

"I saw you talking to that bitch. I saw you give her something! What was it?"

"Huh? Nothing!"

Sylvia didn't say another word. Her lack of response was probably the worst response Luke could have imagined. He knew it meant she was furious. He could almost smell it in the air now. She was some kind of wolf-beast. She would attack within seconds. Or worse, she wouldn't, and the longer she waited the worse it would be.

"Okay, okay, just let me explain…"

"This better be good."

"Look I was just… well, you know… Laverne has this pharmacy thing going on at this other place, right?"

"Yes I know, Luke. Who do you think brought her into this whole deal?"

"I know, I know. So anyway, she has these other ladies…"

"Yes, yes, get to the point, Luke!"

"Well, she asked me to help her out."

"What are you talking about? She's helping *us* out, not the other way around!"

"Well yeah, but she just…"

"Just what?"

"I just had to go pick up something for her, that's all."

"You had to pick up something for her?"

"Yeah, that's all! She said she had a transportation problem."

"What, the pills?"

"Um, I don't know. Maybe, I guess. She just asked me to do her a favour."

"At the other lodge place?"

"Yeah."

"And that seemed normal to you?"

"Well…"

"So let me get this straight. Laverne, who works for me, asked you to do her a favour, to go over to this place and pick up the drugs, that she is supposed to be selling to me, so that you can give them to her, so she can give them to Horace, so Horace can sell them to me? Is that pretty much right, Luke?"

Luke had no reply for that.

"What kind of idiotic system is that?! No! This is not allowed, Luke. You are not allowed to do any more favours for Laverne! Or for any of her Hens, in case they should ask!"

"Geez, okay, okay."

"You know I'm right!"

"Yeah, I guess."
"God!"

22
Fall

"You know what? Fuck those bitches!" Sylvia had thought about it the whole drive to Wendy's. Laverne and her hens thought they could weasel their way into her business — horn in on her action. They pretended to be so important, so necessary. As if Sylvia needed them in order to function. As if she needed anybody. She wouldn't let them treat her like this. She wouldn't stand for it. She was cutting them out.

"Huh?" Luke managed, around a half-chewed ball of cheeseburger.

"Those Bridge Hens. Fuck 'em. We don't need them. They want to make all their little power plays…"

"Yeah, we don't need 'em!" He was just happy that Sylvia's attention had shifted onto them instead of him. The drive had been filled with an awkward silence. "We can get our supply somewhere else, right? We can just…" *We can just what?* He really didn't know.

"Right." Sylvia thoughtfully nibbled a french fry. "We can just…"

"What if we…" No, he really had no idea.

"Yeah, what if we — What about that dude, what's his name? Jason's guy?"

"Jason? My old roommate?"

"Yeah, he had a guy."

"Huh?"

"His dealer. He had a dealer, right? He used to buy a lot of weed, right?"

"Yeah, I guess so."

"So maybe… No, that's no good. He's a dealer already, so even if he did…"

"Huh?"

"Never mind. Forget I said anything. We'll just have to keep thinking."

Luke swallowed a handful of fries. "We'll think of something, Syl. I know we will."

But they did not think of something. Not over dinner, not on the drive over to Luke's, not while they sat on the couch and watched *X-Men* on Sylvia's phone. In fact, they spent all night not thinking of something. Luke didn't sleep well at all. His dreams were entirely occupied by shadow clones of himself, all trying desperately to think of that elusive *something*. In the morning, as he poured Sylvia a bowl of Lucky Charms, he was still trying to think of that something. He stared at the cereal for inspiration. Purple horseshoes, green clovers, pink hearts, yellow moons. None of those things were it.

Sylvia abruptly put down her spoon. "Hey, maybe you *should* call that guy."

"Yeah," Luke agreed. "What guy?"

"Jason's guy."

"Oh, right. What's his name again?"

"I don't know, ask Jason."

"But Jason's gone!"

Sylvia looked at Luke. Sometimes he was so exasperating. "You have his number, don't you?"

"No, I don't even have his name!"

"Not him, you idiot. Jason! Call Jason, and ask him for the guy's name and number!"

"Oh." That was a good idea.

"God!"

"I'm sorry, Syl." He had noticed himself saying that a lot lately. Too much. He was a disappointment to her. He was a disappointment to even himself at times.   So often he would say or do the wrong thing. He continually found himself unable to think of the right thing. It was starting to really stress him out. But it wasn't his fault, really. There was just too much going on. There was too much to keep track of. He wished he could slow it all down. He needed time to breathe. Yes, that was it. He needed to breathe. His breathing always helped.

He took a deep, slow breath, emptying his mind of worry. Staring at his cereal bowl, he let his eyes lose focus. No longer did he see horseshoes, clovers, hearts and moons, but a glowing rainbow of light that seemed to hold some ancient wisdom. Beneath the rainbow a wise robot appeared. "The square root of zero one one one..." it told him, "yum yum yum." *Oh, of course. The Robot Pills!*

He stood and began rummaging through the kitchen drawers, rattling around their sparse contents. "Dammit! Where are they?"

"What are you looking for?"

"My pills. You know, my Robot Pills. Have you seen them?"

"Since when do you take pills?"

"Oh God, where are they? Maybe in the bathroom?" He ran into the bathroom, then realized he didn't even have a medicine cabinet. He opened the cupboard under the sink just for good measure, then slammed it closed again.

"Luke, calm down—"

"Calm down? That's easy for you to say." He tried to focus on breathing, which made him wheeze. If only he had a small paper bag — that's what they used in the movies. But no one in real life ever has a small paper bag lying around, do they? Where do you even get those? Maybe there's one in the drawer? He rummaged again through the drawers, even more frantically.

"Luke, we have the pills here, remember? We have all kinds of pills." She rifled through her purse.

"Here. Take this." She handed him a small blue tablet, then a glass of water, which he swallowed gratefully. "There. Feel better?"

Luke managed to take a slow breath. "Yeah. I think so. Thanks baby." Sylvia hugged him, and he really did start to feel better. He inspected the bottle of blue pills. "Don't we have any Robot Pills, though? I like those ones."

"Luke, these are better. The Robot Pills don't even do anything."

"Yes they do! Syl, you don't know!"

"Well we don't have any anyway."

"How do you know? Can you just check?"

"Fine." Sylvia emptied her purse onto the counter. There must have been a couple dozen pill bottles in there. She quickly scanned them by color, then looked more thoroughly at the white pills. "Well, what do you know? Here's your Robot Pills after all. But listen, you need the blue ones. They really are better. If you want to take a Robot Pill too, that's fine, but take the blue one first, okay? And if you feel like you need it, you can take the Robot Pill after. Got it? Blue first."

"Sure Syl. Blue then white, blue then white."

"Take these red ones too, since you seem to be the only one who can actually sell 'em. Okay, now can you please phone Jason? Then we gotta get going. I have a ton of shit to do today."

"Yeah. Okay. I will call him right now." Luke began scrolling through the call log on his phone. Sylvia, Sylvia, Nana, Nana, Sylvia, Nana, Sylvia, Sylvia, etc. This was no good. He would need to scroll forever to find Jason.

"What are you doing?" Sylvia grabbed his phone, and flipped over to the contacts list, then handed it back to him. "Look, it's right there."

"Oh, thanks." Yes, there was Jason's name. This was way better. His phone seemed to know everyone's name. There was Jason, then Hollyhaven Properties — "Oh my God! Cindy! I think I need to pay rent!"

"Yeah you better get on that. They'll kick you out if you don't pay."

"I know, I know." *Oh my God, oh my God!* He could not remember the last time he had paid rent. It might have been months ago. There might be cops already on their way over here to confiscate his stuff and throw him out on the street. What would the cops do when they saw all these pills? *Oh my God, they'll arrest us both!*

"Luke, snap out of it! Are you gonna call him or what?"

"Yeah. I just..." He looked at the phone again. The list continued: Mom & Dad, Nana, Scott... Fuck! Scott?! What ever happened to Scott? He hadn't heard from him in... Did that mean he was unemployed? *I can't be unemployed! How am I gonna pay the rent? Oh God, oh God!*

"Luke! Come on! Seriously!" She grabbed his phone and dialed up Jason. She started to hand the phone back to Luke as it rang, but then thought better of it. She decided she'd talk to him herself. The phone kept ringing. "Come on, pick up," Sylvia muttered. "Oh for fuck's sake! I don't have time for this!" She hung up and handed the phone back to Luke. "You have to promise me you will call him later, okay?"

"Okay, Syl."

"Promise me?"

"I promise."

"Now let's get going. You want me to drop you at the lodge?"

"Yes, please."

~~~

Nana did not answer her door. Luke tried the secret knock again. Then he tried pounding the door real loud. A woman appeared behind Luke from the door across the hall. "Can I help you?" she inquired.

"Oh. Um. I'm Luke. My Nana lives here and she isn't answering the door. We gotta get help."

"Are you sure she's in there?"

"Well. Uh. I don't know."

"It's craft time, isn't it?"
~~~

"Umm…"

"Let me check…" The lady disappeared into her apartment, leaving the door half open. Luke followed the outline of her door frame down to the carpet with its mess of wiggly interwoven lines. The old lady returned a few moments later. "Yes, the Evergreen Room. I bet you'll find her there."

"Really?" Luke had never heard of the Evergreen Room. Could it really be that Nana had some secret pastime that Luke knew nothing about? It seemed unlikely.

"You know where it is, don't you?"

Luke shook his head, so the lady gave him directions. Down on the second floor, at the other end of the hall. It felt like a wild goose chase, but he had to do something. He could run to the Evergreen Room in search of Nana, but she might not be there, and precious time was wasting. He needed to get help right away. The front desk! Tracy! Tracy would know what to do. She could call Dr. Liard or Dr. Specimen, or that Soundgarden guy. They would fix Nana up right as rain. Luke took off running down the hallway. He ran past the elevator and bolted into the stairway, where he ran down the stairs two steps at a time. By the time he reached the lobby he was out of breath.

"Tracy! Tracy! Help!"

"Oh my gosh, Luke, what is it?!" Tracy stood up so quickly that her chair went sailing backwards and crashed into a filing cabinet.

"It's Nana! She's not answering her door!"

"Alright. Okay, well maybe she's… Let's see here…" She looked at her watch and ran her finger along the weekly calendar that was tucked under the clear plastic cover of her desktop.

"You gotta call the doctor or something. But, um, not the cops, Okay?"

"Well Luke, I think I may have solved your mystery. See? It's craft time in the Evergreen Room."

"Yeah, but… does Nana do crafts?"

"Oh yeah, she always goes to craft time." How was this possible? "Why don't you go on up? It's on the second floor."

"At the other end of the hall?"

"You got it!"

Luke tried to walk casually back to the stairwell, but as soon as he was through the door, he broke into a run again. He ran up one flight, through a door marked "2," and all the way down to the other end of the hall. The Evergreen Room had a set of double doors. They were the kind of doors with a small window for looking through. Luke smashed his nose against the glass. He peered left and right. There were a lot of people in there, hunched over the tables, working feverishly with crayons and glue sticks. It looked exactly like kindergarten.

Suddenly, he saw her. Nana! She was safe. The kindergarten teacher would keep her safe. Luke careened around, leaning with his back against the wall, and allowed his body to slide down until he was sitting on the floor. "Oh thank you, thank you!" he whispered to some unknown supreme power, or perhaps to the kindergarten teacher, he really wasn't sure.

After a few minutes he picked himself up and entered the Evergreen Room somewhat timidly. The teacher caught his eye, smiled, and beckoned him in assuringly.

"Nana?"

"Oh hello Lukie, what a surprise! Take a seat, dear. Would you like to make something?"

"Um." Would he? "I don't know."

"They're leaves, dear, see? We are celebrating the coming change of season and preparing our decorations."

They did look like leaves. They were made of paper, but rather than simply cutting out the shape of a leaf from a sheet of paper, these leaves seemed to involve the gluing together of several layers of different coloured paper, and a lot of cutting and ripping, and shading with crayons. "Looks complicated. That's not how we made leaves when *I* was in kindergarten."

"Oh, Lukie. Always a kidder." She began to stand to leave, gathering her scraps into one hand and then holding it out to Luke. "Never mind, then. Come, let's go find you a cookie. Now put this in the trash for me would you, dear?"

"Oh. Uh. Isn't there a recycle bin?" Luke looked around.

"Don't be silly, dear. It's only paper."

Luke did as he was told, feeling vaguely worried about something, but looking forward to getting a cookie. When they reached her apartment, Nana held the door open for Luke, then made him a tray of cookies, which she left on the counter beside a shopping bag, which she now began to unload.

"I need your help with this. Take this to the medicine cabinet, won't you? And you can fill it up for me, alright Lukie?" She handed Luke her new seven day pill organizer. Luke thought it was quite fancy-looking. It was color-coded like a rainbow for each day, and had little spaces for Morning, Noon, Evening, and Bedtime. It was labelled in both English and French, so what it actually said was 'MORN/MATIN, NOON/MIDI, EVE/SOIR, BED/NUIT.'

"Bed, knew it," said Luke. "Funny." There were a lot of pill bottles in Nana's medicine cabinet. To say nothing of the tubes and vials of various ointments. *Gross.* Nevertheless, his hands were full so he shoved the bottles into his jacket pocket. "Eve sour, noon midi," he sang quietly to himself, nodding his head rhythmically as he walked back into the kitchenette. Jason used to make music with his computer, so Luke knew about MIDI. It was some kind of computer language, or maybe a headphone jack of some kind. Now he pictured Jason playing on his computer, making music, eating a sandwich for lunch as a naked woman from the Bible stood nearby holding a sour green apple. *Granny smith. Don't worry. She's wearing a leaf over her... well, you know.*

"Did you say something dear?"

"No, Nana. But actually," he suddenly remembered, "I do have to make a phone call. Just a sec." He dialed Jason, but again it just rang and rang. Would he ever be able to get ahold of Jason? And what about Scott? And Cindy! *Oh shit!* "He's still not there," he told Nana.

"Who's that, dear?"

"Just my old roommate. You remember Jason?"

"I don't think so."

She's getting forgetful. Like me. I need a Robot Pill. "Blue, then white. Blue, then white," Luke mumbled.

"What's that?"

"Nothing." Luke took his pills, then ate a cookie, then began the task at hand. Nana had a lot of pills. He needed to come up with a way for her to remember which ones to take when. *Blue, then white. Bed Nuit. Bed knew it. Morn mat in. Taste the rainbow. Yellow moons, green clovers.* He would dump all the pills out, then arrange them into piles. That way he could pick up a pile easily, and drop one at a time into each container. No. That wouldn't work. He would need to leave at least one pill in each bottle, so he could match up the pills in his hand with the label on the bottle to determine if it was for morning, or evening, or both, or… Wait a minute, some of them just said 'ONE PER DAY,' or 'TWO PER DAY WITH FOOD.' Oh God. This was complicated.

"Nana, can you help me with this?"

"I need to sit a spell. I can do it later, I suppose."

What was he doing? Nana had asked him for help. He couldn't just turn around and ask her for help helping her. No, he could figure it out on his own. *Okay, wait,* Luke thought. *Noon is lunch, so that's got food. Okay, we can make this work.* "It's okay I figured it out, Nana."

"I knew you could do it, Lukie."

He figured out a system and was almost finished with the task when he noticed that something didn't look right. He dumped all the pills out and started over again. Yes, this time he did it right, he was sure of it. He brought the organizer over to Nana. "I'm done. Does it look okay to you?"

Nana took the organizer, opened a few of the little chambers, and closed them again. "It looks wonderful, dear. These chambers are still a little bit hard to open, but they're better than those silly pill bottles. I'm sure I'll manage it. Thanks, Lukie."

"No problem, Nana! It's the least I can do."

~~~

Back at his apartment, Luke alternated between looking nervously out his window and looking nervously through the peephole in his door. A strange paranoia had set in about Cindy and his rent. He imagined big henchmen with buzzcuts and broad shoulders knocking on his door. He knew that Cindy probably didn't have henchmen, but then again, how could he be sure? All he really knew was that he did not have enough money to pay rent. He would have to ask Sylvia to lend him some more. This worried him. Sylvia already seemed more frustrated with him than usual. Lately he felt like he was walking on eggshells around her. That reminded him that he had better try calling Jason one more time. He pulled himself from the peephole and picked up his phone to dial Jason's number. Beeeeep. Beeeeeep. The phone was a robot too. Luke had never realized this before. It was robots all the way down. This thought reminded him of a scene from *The Matrix*. He pictured Keanu Reeves waking up in his slime bath surrounded by robot overlords. *You take the blue pill, the story ends. You take the red pill... Wait, how does that go?*

"Hey, Luke."

"What?!" *Morpheus?!*

"Luke? You called me." Jason sounded confused.

"Oh. Jason?"
~~~

"Yeah. What's up?"

"Oh, hey! Not too much, what about you?"

"Not much, just hangin' out."

"Oh, cool. Me too." There was silence for a few seconds.

"So… what's up?" Jason asked a little more pointedly.

"Uh, not much." Luke almost giggled a little. He had already asked him that. This was classic Jason. He was probably stoned right now.

"I mean, what are you calling for?" *Oh.* Suddenly there was a knock on the door. Luke panicked. It was the henchmen, he knew it! He considered climbing out the window.

"Uh, I gotta go!" Luke hung up the phone and stood still and wide-eyed in the middle of the bare living room. What was he going to do? The robots were right outside his apartment door. He remembered how in the movie they would use their cell phones to get pulled out of the matrix and into the real world just in time. He looked back at the phone in his hand. Why had he hung up?

"Luke! Open the door!" He heard a muffled voice through the door. It didn't sound like a robot. So they weren't robot henchmen. Wait, why did he think they were? Luke didn't understand what was happening. No, that was Sylvia's voice. "Come on, we have to go!" Luke snapped back into reality and walked across the carpet to the door. He turned the lock and opened it. "Why is your door locked?" Sylvia was not in a good mood.

"Because… nevermind." He didn't want to get into it.

"Are you ready to go? Did you call Jason?"

"Yeah, I did. Go where?"

"What did he say?" Sylvia grabbed his hand and pulled him out into the hallway.

"Wait, my shoes." Luke grabbed his sneakers from inside the door and slipped them on in the hallway.

"Did you get his guy's number?"

"Oh, right. No, not yet."

"Seriously?" Her voice was flat and harsh, like a cafeteria tray to the side of the head. "You talked to him, but you didn't get his guy's number?"

"No, because they were coming for me!"

"What? Who?"

"You!"

"Luke, I just don't understand how you can be so useless." The word cut Luke right to his core.

"I'm not useless," he said, his voice trembling a little. "Why do we need this guy's number anyway?"

"So we can expand our supply! We talked about this!"

"But why do we need to expand our supply?"

"So we can make more sales! Come on, let's go!" Sylvia started power walking down the hallway. Luke locked the apartment door and followed along behind her.

"But what for?"

"So we can make more money?"

"Why?"

Sylvia stopped. "Luke, sometimes I wonder if you even care about what we're doing. I'm working my ass off for you, you know that? I get you this apartment, I pay your rent, I set you free from that shitty job, and you don't even say thank you. But that's fine, I don't need a thank you. That's not why I do it. I do it because I love you and I want us to have a life together. A good life. And I just don't understand why you seem so bent on destroying that good life before it's even begun."

Luke didn't know what to say and Sylvia took his silence as contrite submission. She kept on walking, not looking back, not even waiting for Luke when he noticed his shoe was untied. He knelt on the carpet and tied his lace into a bow, trying to remember what Sylvia had said about his job. She had called it shitty, for one. But what was so shitty about it? His boss Scott had never called him useless. Scott had always made him feel good about himself. Luke got up and jogged to catch up to Sylvia, wondering where they were going. Probably, he thought, to another stupid party.

~~~

Sylvia and Luke pulled up to a house where another stupid party was happening. Luke was sick of this. It felt like they spent more time at parties than anywhere else. He sighed as he closed the passenger door and turned toward the dumpy house. The vinyl siding was falling off, there was cardboard duct taped to the inside of a broken window, the stairs were rotting away. And these were the kind of people who were going to make them rich? "Hmmph," Luke scoffed.

"What?" Sylvia asked.

"Whatever," Luke said.

They climbed the steps and Sylvia stopped at the door. "You got your knife on you?"

Luke's stomach twisted. "No. Why?"

"You should really carry it with you, just in case. I mean, I'm sure everything will be fine, but… Just be ready, you know?" Luke nodded. He had no idea where the knife Sylvia gave him had ended up. The last time he saw it was three or four parties ago when he had used it to open a particularly unyielding bag of jalapeño beef jerky. Luke couldn't imagine himself using the knife for any other purpose than to access difficult snacks.

Sylvia opened the door and the smell of cannabis hit them like a sickly sweet wall of skunk. Sylvia took a mental inventory of all the uppers she was carrying in her purse. She would bring balance, and they would pay her handsomely for it. Green was a wonderful colour. "I'll check in with you later," she told Luke, following the scent like a bloodhound through the kitchen and down the hall.

Luke didn't feel like selling pills. And besides, it was still early. He looked around the living room for somewhere to
~~~

sit, but all the couches were occupied. He decided to cross his arms and pout in the corner of the room. Next to him stood a dilapidated beige cat condo. He leaned over to look inside the little hole and see if anybody was home. Maybe, he thought, the cats were having their own party in there. That was the party he wanted to be at. There was no party inside, but there was a white cat staring at him. It meowed and Luke dropped his pouty expression to smile. "Hey, little guy," he crooned. "Not a partier, huh?" The cat inched closer to Luke's face. "I guess I'm not either." It inched forward again and stretched its neck out of the hole to brush the side of its head against Luke's nose. Luke felt incredibly lucky to have made a new friend in this inhospitable place. He felt that somehow already he and the cat had reached a rare level of connection. Luke then resumed leaning against the wall with his arms folded and the cat continued to lie with its head peeking out of his little house. And although neither of them spoke, it was understood by both that they were definitely hanging out. The two of them tuned into a conversation that was happening on the nearby couch.

"...and buddy comes up and just *decks* him." There was a clumsy gesticulation of an arm in a grey hoodie.

Another voice jumped in: "That's what I woulda done too."

"No you wouldna."

"I don't like liars, man."

"Do you like getting the shit kicked out of you?" A few people laughed loudly. The white cat meowed.

"Hey… Luke?" Luke heard his name but didn't realize that it was him who was being addressed. His eyes hovered over the heads of the couch-sitters. "Luke Clark?" He focused in on the speaker, a muscular guy with dark spiky hair and sunglasses hanging from the neck of his polo shirt. He knew he knew this guy, but he couldn't remember how.

"Oh, hey, uh…"

"Mike Gardino." He stood up and approached Luke's corner. "How's it going, man?"

"Oh, yeah, Mike, hey man." Now it was coming back to him. Mike Gardino had lived in the same neighborhood as Luke when they were kids. Luke remembered one time in grade four he and Mike had walked home together and found an unopened pack of Yu-Gi-Oh cards lying in the grass by the sidewalk. There was a Blue-Eyes White Dragon in that pack and Mike made Luke give it to him even though he barely even played Yu-Gi-Oh anymore and Luke still played basically every lunch.

"So, how's life? Haven't seen you in years, man."

"Yeah, no kidding," Luke said. "It's pretty good, I guess."

"Yeah? What are you doing these days?"

"I'm... a sales...pharmacist." *Shut up, shut up.*

"Decent, man."

"I'm engaged too." Luke didn't know why he had said that. He felt small next to this big man from the past.

"Congrats, dude! Hey, let's celebrate! You smoke?" Mike Gardino reached into his shirt pocket and pulled out a thick joint.

"Sure," Luke said. He had only smoked weed a couple of times before. He couldn't remember why it never stuck. It probably had something to do with money. Luke looked back at his new friend as he followed his old friend to the couch. An older guy passed a lighter to Mike Gardino and he lit the joint, sucking in hard before exhaling a cloud of smoke. Mike Gardino passed the joint to Luke, who took a modest puff. He held it back out for Mike, who gave an upward nod in the direction of a girl sitting on the end of the couch. Luke passed the joint to her, scanning the room for Sylvia. If she found out Luke was smoking weed on the job, she'd be pissed.

Luke had a fun time getting high with Mike Gardino and his friends. One of the guys on the couch, a skinny blond with a neck tattoo, even showed Luke how to do a French inhale. But when Luke tried it he just ended up violently coughing.

"First time?" Mike Gardino teased. Everybody laughed. But Luke shrugged it off. These people meant no harm. Then Luke saw the telltale red hat of Red Wings approaching. He momentarily panicked. Maybe he wasn't happy with the pills Luke had sold him. But when he arrived, Mike Gardino gave him a fist bump and passed him the joint. As it turned out, they were good pals. Luke and Red Wings exchanged greetings and Luke's panic subsided. He was enjoying himself now. His face felt pleasantly warm and his mouth felt strangely dry. He decided to tell one of his favourite jokes.

"There's a cowboy in a bar," Luke began, drawing the confused attention of the group. "And he finishes his drink and goes outside–"

"Is this a joke?" Mike Gardino asked.

"Yeah!" Luke said excitedly. "It's a good one."

"Don't interrupt him," the skinny guy said. "I wanna hear it. Keep going, man." He nodded encouragingly in Luke's direction.

"So he finishes his drink and goes outside and then… Oh yeah, and he's like all tough-looking too. That's important. And when he finishes his drink and goes outside he says… No, wait…" The girl on the couch giggled as she dropped the roach into an empty Twisted Tea can. Red Wings presented another joint and lit it. Luke continued, "Oh, no, so the cowboy goes outside and then he comes back in and he says, 'Listen up, I'm gonna finish my drink and then go outside, and if my horse ain't back where I left it I'm gonna have to do what I had to do back in Texas!'" The girl giggled again, this time at Luke's light Southern accent. "So he sits down and he finishes his drink. I mean, he gets another drink. A beer."

"Beer?" Mike handed Luke a Colt 45.

"Sure, thanks." Luke opened it and took a long, malty swig. It seemed to satisfy Luke's every desire. It refreshed his soul and sparkled on his dry tongue. "Uh, where was I?"

"Another beer?" Red Wings said.

"No thanks, I just started this one." Everyone laughed. Luke was glad they were all enjoying his joke. "Oh yeah, so the cowboy comes back inside and he orders another beer and says, 'If ah come back in here and mah horse is back where ah left it, ah'm gonna haveta do what ah done back in Texas! And ah really don't wanna have to do what ah done back in Texas.' Luke exaggerated his accent this time. He continued after another sip of his beer: "And the bar goes silent. And the cowboy drinks his beer, all tough. And then he finishes his beer and he walks outside. And then he comes in and says… No, wait. Did I tell that part already?" By this time everyone was on the verge of cracking up. The new joint was passed to Luke and he took a puff before passing it on to Mike Gardino, who smiled serenely, his eyes now as red as a Texas sunset.

"Okay, I know, I know. So he finishes his beer — his *second* beer — and he goes outside and sure enough there's his horse tied up where he left it. And this other guy is there too and he asks him, 'What was it you had to do in Texas?' and the cowboy says, 'Ah had to walk home.'" Everyone burst into raucous laughter. Luke felt like the king of the world. He sipped his beer and reveled in his newfound popularity.

Luke's joke set off a series of jokes and laughter. Mike told a good one about a priest and a canola farmer that Luke tried his best to remember for later. The laughs died down after a while and Red Wings pulled Luke aside to whisper in his ear. "Hey, you got any more of those Red Birds?"

"You bet," Luke told him.

"Can I get like ten?"

"You bet," Luke told him. He pulled the bottle from his pocket and gave Red Wings ten of the little red pills in a small baggy. Red Wings left the group shortly after, winking at Luke.

Luke continued talking and joking around with Mike and the gang for what felt like hours. Luke had completely lost his grip on time. Maybe he had better start selling pills soon. Maybe one of his new friends wanted to buy something. But Luke didn't feel right taking advantage of his new social connections that way. Luke also didn't feel right in general. He could feel every part of his shin bones. His stomach felt like a black hole. The more he focused on these sensations, the more uncomfortable they became.

Then he felt something furry against his leg. He looked down to see his friend the cat brushing up against him, its head cocked up to look him in the eyes. It clearly wanted Luke's attention. It crept through the crowd and out of view. Luke followed as if hypnotized. *You take the red pill, and I show you how deep the rabbit hole goes.* Luke followed the white cat down the hallway. He felt the carpet absorb his toes as he walked. He heard the buzzing of the lights overhead and a muffled whirring sound in spite of the chatter of the party guests. Why didn't he hear music? Wasn't there music playing? Or *did* he hear music? Yes, there it was, underneath it all, a thumping buh-bum, buh-bum. The cat stopped and rolled playfully on the floor outside a closed door. "What's up?" Luke asked. "Something in there?"

"Mrrooww" Luke watched the cat stretch into a pale crescent moon, its arms pointed toward the door. The whirring sound was louder now, the thumping quieter. Overtop of both, Luke could hear the sound of his own breath. He cautiously approached the door, then reached for the doorknob. He touched its cold metal and turned. The door seemed to open almost by itself, revealing first the yellow-white of a growing wedge of linoleum floor, then a sink and a mirrored cabinet, and then — "Oh my god." It was Red Wings, lying face down on the floor, his limbs splayed wildly, his right arm sticking up unnaturally, pinched between his head and the bathtub. Luke freaked out. He started yelling for help, his body paralysed. The cat darted away as a few people rushed into the hall to investigate.

"What happened?" someone asked. But Luke couldn't answer. He just kept repeating the words "red" and "wings." Now there was a sizable crowd pressing in around him and the lively chatter of the party had changed to a subdued murmur. Someone said the word, "OD'd." At that, Luke ran. Nothing existed except him and a way out.

He was halfway across the living room when something grabbed his arm. Warm bodies rushed past him but he couldn't move. He heard the words "9-1-1" and "ambulance." There was Sylvia's face. His breathing quickened. Where were his Robot Pills? Sylvia was talking to him. She looked angry. "Luke? Are you stoned?!" Luke nodded yes. No more lies. "Are you fucking kidding me?!" Luke shook his head no. No more. She pulled him toward the door but he tripped on something and she lost her grip. Luke struggled to get up off the floor, a horrible mass of legs rushing by him. By the time he reached the outside, Sylvia's Grand Am was revving down the street. Luke reached into his pocket and pulled out two baggies of pills. *Blue then white.* Somehow he was still holding his beer. He swallowed the pills and started walking home.

<p style="text-align:center">~~~</p>

That night as Luke slept, he was visited by Morpheus, who directed him to sit down in an enormous leather chair. Luke was terrified because Morpheus looked very angry. His eyebrows were bright red and his tongue was blue when he spoke, like he had just eaten a popsicle. "We just needed a little help. Did you help?" Morpheus demanded.

Luke stammered, but could not form a reply.

"So what will you do?" Then Morpheus turned into a brilliant snow-white panther and leapt into Luke's mouth. Luke was taller than the chair now, and he tried to pick it up, but he couldn't because it was too heavy. The chair's eyes began to glow as it grabbed him. It threw Luke against the wall and he fell to the floor. A battalion of robots now loomed over him, standing in formation. Their mouths gnashed at him, opening and closing horizontally like elevator doors. The whole room was washed in a harsh red light. Two of the robots sat down on Nana's couch. He was in her room. He got up off the floor and looked for Nana, avoiding the robots. He heard his voice echo strangely throughout the apartment, "Nana! Nana, where are you?" He crawled along the hallway, which was lined with dozens of electrical outlets. He desperately peered into each one. The hallway seemed to stretch on for miles. Now he could hear music playing in the distance. His head nearly touched the ceiling as he entered Nana's bedroom. The whole room glowed a blinding white and there were brown leaves on the bed. Luke felt angry at the leaves. He wanted to get away from them, so he walked across the hallway to the bathroom. Stepping through the bathroom door, he plunged into a black abyss, screaming as his stomach lifted into his chest.

Luke woke up, panting and covered in sweat. There was a dim pale light slanting in through the window. He reached for his phone. There was a missed call from his dad. He called him back, still disoriented from his dream.

"Luke?"

"Yeah?"

"It's Nana."

"What is?"

"She…"

"Huh?"

"She passed away…"

"…"

"Luke?"

23

Reality Bites

Luke watched the brilliant ripples flitting across the surface of Lake Okanagan as the bus to Peachland weaved down Highway 97. They were so ephemeral — appearing just long enough to be recognized as reflections of an unfathomably large sun, just long enough to disappear immediately into a deep dark blue, and then be replaced by another white glimmer. It all happened so fast that one could not be completely certain the flashes of light had actually been there at all. There was a lot that Luke was uncertain of, but there were other things he had come to know as absolute truth. He knew, for one, that things would never again be like they were. He knew that things didn't last, that something always changes.

There was a black double-layered garbage bag on the seat next to him, almost bursting with his belongings. He was doing it himself. Of course, in his case, hiring professional movers was more than a little superfluous. He didn't feel like laughing, but Luke had to admit that there was a humour in the way things had all worked out. He had been in love. *They* had been in love. He was almost sure of that. He had spent so long trying to figure out what he had done wrong. Now, at least, he was beginning to see.

Ahead of him were dozens of other passengers. He wondered if they even realized. Some wore headphones, bobbing their heads to invisible patterns, some just shut their eyes. In the seat in front of him a woman sat next to her teenage daughter. She was reading a magazine and shaking her head. Suddenly she spoke. Luke didn't know if she was speaking to her daughter or to herself. But in a way, he felt she was speaking directly to him. "When you got a bunch of supposedly healthy people popping pills just to get by, maybe that's the real sickness."

Luke wept.